WONDERS

OF THE

INVISIBLE

WORLD

CHRISTOPHER BARZAK

WONDERS

OF THE

INVISIBLE

WORLD

EMBER

Text copyright © 2015 by Christopher Barzak
Cover art by Lynn Buckley
Painting detail: Ralph Albert Blakelock, American, 1847–1919, *Moonlight Sonata* (detail), about 1889–92, Oil on canvas, 77.15 x 55.88 cm. (30-⅜ x 22 in.), Museum of Fine Arts, Boston, The Hayden Collection—Charles Henry Hayden Fund 45.201. Photograph © 2014 by Museum of Fine Arts, Boston.
All rights reserved.

Ember and the E colophon are registered trademarks of Penguin Random House LLC.

Visit us on the Web! randomhouseteens.com

Educators and librarians, for a variety of teaching tools, visit us at RHTeachersLibrarians.com

The Library of Congress has cataloged the hardcover edition of this work as follows:
Barzak, Christopher.
Wonders of the invisible world / Christopher Barzak.—First edition.
pages cm
Summary: Seventeen-year-old Aidan has been living like a ghost since his mother tried to stop a family curse by causing him to forget his psychic experiences. But when Jarrod, a childhood friend, returns, so do the memories, and Aidan is compelled to seek the truth and release them all from the story that has trapped them.
ISBN 978-0-385-39279-2 (trade) — ISBN 978-0-385-39280-8 (lib. bdg.) — ISBN 978-0-385-39281-5 (ebook)
[1. Psychic ability—Fiction. 2. Supernatural—Fiction. 3. Blessing and cursing—Fiction. 4. Death—Fiction. 5. Gays—Fiction. 6. Farm life—Ohio—Fiction. 7. Ohio—Fiction.] I. Title.
PZ7.1.B3735Won 2015
[Fic]—dc23
2014022809

ISBN 978-0-385-39282-2 (pbk.)

Printed in the United States of America
10 9 8 7 6 5 4 3 2 1
First Ember Edition 2016

For my family

Past, present, future

'Tis a thousand pitties,

that we should permit our Eyes

to be so Blood-shot with passions,

as to loose the sight of many wonderful Things,

wherein the Wisdom and Justice of God,

would be Glorify'd.

Some of those Things,

are the frequent Apparitions of Ghosts,

whereby many Old Murders among us,

come to be considered.

—COTTON MATHER,
THE WONDERS OF THE INVISIBLE WORLD

This is the story

I will tell Old Black Suit

when he comes for me.

This is the story I will tell

when he takes off his hat

to stay a while and listen.

chapter one

MY LIFE IN PAPER

Here's the thing: we're all as thin as paper. Like those paper people you used to find in old children's magazines, inhabiting a two-page spread with other paper people, all of them hanging out somewhere together—at the park, at church, at school, at the mall, in the family room—until some kid took a pair of scissors to the dotted lines surrounding them and cut them out of their paper world. That's us, that's anyone. That was me. A cut-out paper person removed from the world I once belonged to.

Until, one day, someone called my name.

"Hey, Aidan. Aidan Lockwood!"

And I looked up, startled, as if I'd just woken from a dream.

I was leaning over, grabbing my copy of *Hamlet* from the bottom of my locker so I'd have it with me after history and not have to come back for it, when I heard my name. Normally I can recognize people by voice alone—a loud laugh from Aaron Anderson as he moves through the hallway with other basketball players flanking him, or the sound of Natalie Miller as she sings an old blues song in the choir room—but this was a voice I didn't recognize. I could feel my brow furrow even as I pulled Shakespeare out of the locker and turned toward this voice, which, in a school as small as mine, should have been easy to place.

"Look at you!" the voice said, almost like a command. And after peering down at myself like I might have a stain on my clothes or some unknown wound gushing blood, I looked up and spotted the guy who'd said it.

He was my age, tall and lean, and he was carrying a couple of books under one muscle-knotted arm as he came toward me, pushing a wave of floppy brown hair away from his even darker brown eyes. When he stopped in front of me, he said, "You haven't changed a bit," like we were old friends meeting for the first time in a long time. I looked around, hoping someone else would recognize him, would see him and say, "Hey, *So-and-So*, where have you been?"

But no one did. It might as well have been just the two of us in that hallway, two strangers looking at each other, blinking.

2

Two paper people in a high school background.

I cocked my head, as if looking at him from a different angle might help me place him, but it was no good. Eventually I had to give up on the idea of identifying him and say, "I'm sorry?"

He shook his head, biting his bottom lip a little. Then, after releasing his lip from the pinch of his teeth, he said, "I can't believe it. You really don't remember me, do you?"

"Should I?" I asked. And it was a serious question, though it probably sounded more serious than I meant it to. But here was the truth of the matter: there were only three hundred students at Temperance High School, freshmen through seniors, and this guy didn't look like any of them.

"Jarrod," he said, and I blinked a few times, hoping the name would register. "Jarrod *Doyle*?" he said, raising his eyebrows. "Come on, Lockwood. We were best friends in elementary and middle school!"

The name sank into my memory, and like a stone thrown into a pond, it made ripples. *Jarrod Doyle*, I thought. Jarrod Doyle, who used to play catch with me at recess or pair up with me to run during gym, even though I sucked at anything remotely athletic. Jarrod Doyle, who used to have me over to his place to spend the night watching horror movies before his mom and dad split up and he moved away in the seventh grade, seemingly overnight, as if he'd never existed.

Christ. I did know the guy after all.

"Jarrod Doyle?" I said, trying the name out like a new

3

word in French class. And as in French class, I couldn't help but stutter the syllables a little. "No way. Where the heck have you been?" I asked. "Better yet," I said in the next breath, "what the heck are you doing back here? It's been, what? Five years?"

"Just about," he said, grinning with obvious relief now that I'd finally remembered him. "I'm back home with my mom. Got tired of living with my dad and his girlfriend. Wanted to get back to my roots, if you know what I mean."

I shrugged and shook my head, oblivious to anything but him standing right there in front of me. "No," I said. "What do you mean?"

"Been living up in Cleveland," he said, and threw one hand out like he might be offering me official documents about his previous residence. I looked down, but his hand was empty. "That's where my dad moved after he and my mom divorced. Remember? She went to rehab, he moved up there for a job and took me with him? I thought you knew all this. Hell, I thought everyone in Temperance knew."

I shook my head, surprised that I didn't know, though I should have, really. Temperance was the kind of place where everyone knew everyone else's business even as it was happening.

"Anyway," Jarrod said, "when my mom told me she'd gotten herself back together, I decided to come home for senior year."

"Temperance over Cleveland?" I said, raising one eyebrow skeptically. "You must have something wrong with you."

"No way," said Jarrod. He rocked back on his heels and looked around at the ceiling and the rows of alternating white and blue lockers, our school colors, and took the place in like he was an exile who had finally been allowed to come home. "It'll be nice to be with my mom again," he said, looking down. "And, well, I've missed this place."

Temperance is a town of around three thousand people who work dairy or beef farms, fix cars and tractors, grow corn and soybeans, or work in the last remains of the few factories that have hung on, making paint cans or cabinetry. I reminded Jarrod of all this, in case he'd forgotten, and said, "It's not really the sort of place anyone moves *back* to."

"It's exactly the sort of place someone like me moves back to," said Jarrod.

Sometimes when people leave places behind, they only remember the good parts. But I didn't say that right then.

"So what have you been up to?" he asked, as if I could fill him in on the past five years before the bell rang for first period. Then the bell for first period did ring, and we looked up at the speaker perched in the corner of the hallway like we could melt it down to scrap metal with laser eyes and then keep on talking.

When we looked down again, I said, "What's your first class?"

"French," said Jarrod. "Ooh la la. What about you?"

"History," I said. "You busy after school?"

"Hoping to talk to the coach about trying out for baseball." I noticed only then that he was wearing an unbuttoned Cleveland Indians jersey with a black T-shirt underneath.

"You can do that tomorrow," I said. "Meet me in the parking lot after last period. We can go somewhere to catch up."

"Look at you," he said again, shaking his head like he couldn't believe I was still here, like he'd never left in seventh grade and we'd just spent the night before watching a horror flick in his mom and dad's trailer, which had sat out on the edge of town on an old back road called Cordial Run. "I still remember the thirteen-year-old Aidan Lockwood who couldn't throw a ball worth spit and saw the weirdest shit."

I cocked my head and narrowed my eyes. What did he mean by *the weirdest shit*? Before I could ask, though, he clapped one hand on my shoulder, then walked off in the direction of Madame LaFarge's classroom.

Then the bell rang again and I knew I'd have to explain to Ms. Woodyard why I was late when I got to history. I could already see her waving a finger in the direction of my desk, saying, *Just sit down, Lockwood, so I can get to work on making all of you into informed adults already.*

But even as that exact scenario played itself out a minute later, I was still wondering what Jarrod Doyle had meant.

I knew I couldn't throw a baseball worth spit, but seeing the weirdest shit? He must have been thinking of someone else. He must have been remembering some other friend or classmate, some cousin or someone he met right after he moved to Cleveland. Because the only weird things I'd seen in my life were the birth of a calf when I was eight years old (unforgettably gross, but I couldn't look away) and my grandmother's body laid out in a casket with pearly pink satin lining a few years earlier, her face waxy, overdone with makeup, not looking real at all.

Those things had been weird, yes. Me, though? Average student, bad athlete, nice enough guy, but nothing special. Not really. I lived in Temperance, Ohio, where nothing truly weird happened. Ever.

I moved through that day like I was swimming, taking slow strokes through the hallways, coming up for air in classrooms every so often, listening to the slam of locker doors in this underwater way: everything distant and delayed. And as I swam through the hours, I tried to recall the days when Jarrod and I were kids. I had nothing but patchwork images to work with, though. Vague childhood memories. Laughter over little-kid jokes or stories. Climbing a tree at the edge of the woods behind my house to sit on a limb together and survey my family's farm. The herd in the pasture, chewing on grass, raising their heads and lowing to one another. The gleam of the tin roof on the old yellow farmhouse that had been my family's home for nearly a hundred years, according to my dad, who never had much to say about anything, but when he did, it was always a story about a dead relative or how life was harder back in his day. The sound of Sugar Creek trickling past as Jarrod and I sat on its bank, catching crayfish. My mother yelling whenever we got into something she'd told us not to.

Memories. Just basic memories. The kind of stuff anyone can remember. The kind of stuff that doesn't tell a person anything he really needs to know.

The tree, I remembered then. Jarrod and I weren't supposed to go near it. The tree in the old orchard across the railroad-tie bridge that spanned Sugar Creek. It was an ancient apple tree that had died ages ago, yet somehow it continued to stand, despite a hole in its trunk where a lightning bolt had burned through it, according to family stories.

We'd been told about the bolt of lightning since Toby and I were little and started asking questions about anything and everything we encountered. And because that tree somehow remained standing despite the gaping hole that had hollowed it out years earlier, Toby had once jokingly called it the Living Death Tree, which made us laugh like little idiots, and then both of us had continued to refer to it that way, making our mother sigh and shake her head. At the end of each summer, the Living Death Tree produced a small amount of deformed, rotten apples that dropped almost as quickly as they formed and spread around the base of the gnarled tree like broken Christmas ornaments.

"Stay away from that tree," my mother warned Jarrod and me. "It isn't safe to play around that old thing."

"Why not?" I asked, looking up at her soft face, at her green eyes framed by long auburn hair, smelling the lilac on her skin. In my memories, my mother always looks angelic. But when she spoke, she was never as soft as she looked.

"That's for me to know and for you to find out" was her answer, which was what my mother almost always said whenever Toby and I wanted to know the reasons behind any of her rules and regulations. It meant the discussion was over, *snip-snap*, case closed, and we had better not do what she'd warned against, regardless of whether she'd supplied us with reasons.

"Aidan?" Mr. Johnson said, and I swam up from my memories to find a room full of students around me, all staring at me, some turned around in their desks, grinning, some slowly closing their eyes and shaking their heads sadly, embarrassed for me, waiting for me to say something to end the awkward moment.

"I'm sorry," I said, my voice paper-thin. "Can you repeat the question?"

"I didn't ask a question," said Mr. Johnson. He stood in front of the room at the dry-erase board, marker in hand, twisting the cap on and off, clicking and clicking. "I've just been trying to get your attention. You've been staring out the window for the past few minutes without the ability to recognize your own name."

The room filled with laughter then, and after Mr. Johnson raised his hands like a traffic cop to quiet everyone, I looked at him and said, "I'm sorry. I guess . . . I guess I was daydreaming."

"That's probably why your grade isn't as good as it could be." His voice was dry enough to catch fire with the drop of a single match. "Now, please, Aidan," he said, "try to pay attention."

I nodded once, wanting to seem eager, even though my mind still leaned toward my memories.

Hamlet, I reminded myself upon seeing a quote Mr. Johnson had written on the board in his loopy, almost unreadable cursive. That was what we were reading.

There are more things in Heaven and Earth, Horatio, than are dreamt of in your philosophy.

"Now that you're back, Aidan," said Mr. Johnson, "can you interpret what Hamlet has said to Horatio in this line?"

I squinted at the sentence for a moment, then said, "Things aren't always how they appear, because people don't have the ability to see everything that exists in the universe?"

"Indeed," said Mr. Johnson, pushing his glasses a bit farther up the bridge of his nose. "Indeed," he said again, then looked away to begin lecturing about the crisis of faith and reason that led to Hamlet's seeing the ghost of his dead father.

※

When the last bell of the day rang, I shot up from my seat in study hall to make a fast exit, and as I pushed through the doors with everyone else swarming to escape another day in those fluorescent-light-filled hallways, I spotted Jarrod already leaning against my car, as if he'd left the building ten minutes before the bell rang.

"How did you know?" I asked, jingling my keys in the direction of the rusted-out blue Chevette that had served as my horse-and-carriage since I'd turned sixteen the year before and my brother Toby had handed it down to me, like he'd done with clothes and toys and just about anything else hand-downable since we were little.

"It's the Blue Bomb," said Jarrod. "Your dad's old work car, right?"

"Yeah," I said, nodding. "And then my brother's first car. Man, you have a good memory."

"Not really," said Jarrod, pushing hair away from his eyes. "But it looks like you've got a bad one."

I nodded toward the other side of the car and said, "Get in. The doors don't lock anymore." Jarrod laughed at that, then got in. And five minutes later, after the last bus left, we were on the road like we did this all the time, like we'd been doing this forever.

This was usually the time of the day I'd spend driving

around Temperance on my own, not thinking about school or the work I had to do when I got home. I didn't know why I'd gotten into the habit of doing this after school, but an hour or two on the back roads would usually clear my head, which seemed full of fog most days. On these drives, I liked to pretend that some other life was waiting for me out there, that something mysterious and different from everything I knew was just around the bend. But I wasn't used to having anyone with me on these expeditions, so with Jarrod beside me, it felt different, like for the first time there was some kind of meaning to my aimless driving.

"Do you actually know where we're going?" Jarrod asked after we'd been on the road for ten or fifteen minutes.

"Wherever," I said, shrugging. "Why? Someplace in particular you want to go?" Before Jarrod could answer, though, I said, "Now that I think about it, how long *have* you been back?" It was late October already. School had been in session for over two months, and the wide, toothy grins of jack-o'-lanterns had begun to appear on the porch rails of Temperance's houses.

"Just moved into my mom's place last week," Jarrod said. "It was kind of sudden."

I glanced over, but he kept staring out the windshield, blank-eyed, tight-lipped, not giving anything away.

"Something happen?" I asked. And as soon as the question left my mouth, I felt like a jerk. Five years had passed without a word between us. Somehow I'd almost completely forgotten him, despite once having been his best friend. Yet there I was, prying into his private life, like I had a right to know everything about him.

He answered me anyway.

"Had a fight with my dad," he said, shrugging one shoulder like it might be painful to shrug both. "I think I said this morning that he's got a girlfriend."

"Yeah?" I said, hoping to keep him going.

"Yeah, well, she and I don't really get along," he said, right as I slowed down to edge the car into the center circle of Temperance, which was surrounded by a small grocery store, a gas station, the Dairy Oasis, and Times Square Café, like points on a compass. Inside the circle was a dusty old bandshell, where the wind blew autumn leaves to life, making them shuffle across the steps of the shell like the severed hands of zombies.

"So you don't like your dad's girlfriend or something?" I asked, trying to get more out of him.

"Or something," Jarrod said. "It's more like she doesn't like me. I think she wants my dad and his place for just them, no sullen teenager haunting the extra bedroom. She made me feel weird in my own house, like I didn't belong there."

"Well," I said, "I'm glad you can come live with your mom, at least."

"Yeah," said Jarrod, nodding slowly, a brief pout of doubt twisting his lips.

As I turned out of the circle and onto the causeway, Jarrod peered out the window at the gray-blue waves of Mosquito Lake chopping up and down on either side of us.

"You don't sound as excited about being home as you did this morning," I said.

"Can you pull over here?" he asked suddenly. Then he looked at me, and his eyes were wide open in this way that made it seem like he was asking for a big favor. "You asked if there was someplace in particular. Here," he said. "I want to see the lake, if that's okay."

I slowed down and pulled into a strip of parking spaces on the side of the causeway, where fishermen would park during the summer months before they climbed down the embankment to perch on one of the flat gray rocks and cast their lines out, sipping beer with their buddies and talking about the win-loss records of various sports teams or telling worn-out hunting stories. When I killed the engine, Jarrod didn't wait. He got out and took a pack of cigarettes from his jean jacket pocket. After shuffling a stick out, he lit it with one hand cupped around the flame of his lighter.

"I thought you were going to play baseball," I said, getting out and coming around to meet him. He offered me the pack, but I shook my head.

"Yeah, I am," he said. He sucked in hard, then expelled a thick cloud, and I began to feel even more like I was hanging out with a stranger. "You *can* play baseball and smoke," he said, rolling his eyes at me. "What? Don't tell me that after I left you went on the straight and narrow?"

"Was I ever off it?" I asked, laughing, trying to make it seem like I knew what he was talking about.

Jarrod snorted and brushed the hair out of his eyes, smiling after he sucked in another drag. "I guess you were never *bad*, per se," he said, letting the smoke drift out of his mouth in a slow stream. "Just weird. Not like other people. Not normal."

I laughed again, slow and completely faked, because I still didn't understand what he was talking about, and I didn't want him to know that. I wasn't weird. I was just a benign loner. You know the type. There are a lot of us wandering the hallways of schools around the world, invisible, our shadows always turning the corner in front of you. I kept to myself, turned in homework like a good machine, watched other people doing things together from across the room. Looked down if someone caught my eye, tried not to invite trouble. Maybe being like that is weird for most people, but for me it was how I'd always been. Or at least, it was how I'd always remembered myself being.

We stood in silence for a while, me leaning against the passenger side of the Blue Bomb with my hands in my jeans pockets, Jarrod a few steps in front of me, one hand in the pocket of his denim jacket, the other flicking away ash as he looked out at the waves and the gulls that screed overhead. Beneath those waves were a school and some houses, the remains of an old village where people used to mine for coal, my mom once told me, back when they needed it for the furnaces in the steel mills that used to line the rivers in nearby Warren and Youngstown. When I was little, I used to think of those buildings at the bottom of Mosquito Lake and imagine the inhabitants still going about their business, as if the lake had never been made, their village never flooded to make a reservoir after the coal had all been gotten. My mom used to tell me that there are places like that all over the world. Places we can't see. People we can't hear. She used to say that we'd never know any better by looking at the surface of things. The chop of waves, the flight of the gulls, the lines the fishermen cast over the water—you'd never see an old coal-mining village out there if you didn't already know about it.

When it seemed like Jarrod and I had nothing left to say and that maybe we weren't cut out to be friends like we used to be, I asked the question I'd wanted to know the answer to all day.

"What did you mean earlier?" I asked.

And Jarrod looked over the curve of his shoulder, his hair fluttering in the wind. "About what?"

"About me seeing weird shit," I said. "About me being weird when we were little."

Jarrod flicked his cigarette into the water, where it sizzled before settling in to rock on the foamy waves. "I don't know," he said. "Maybe you weren't that weird. Maybe little kids are weird in general and I'm just remembering *you* being weird, is all."

"How?" I said. "What did I see that you're remembering? Because seriously, I don't know what you're talking about."

He suddenly came toward the Blue Bomb like he wanted to get in and get out of there in a hurry, so I moved out of the way to let him grab the door handle. Before he ducked down to fold himself back into the car, though, he turned to me and took a deep breath.

"You used to have all kinds of stories you'd tell me," he said. "About a white deer you sometimes saw. And about a woman's ghost who talked to you."

I opened my mouth, but nothing came out, not even a laugh. "You're kidding," I said eventually. "Right?"

Jarrod shook his head. "No," he said. "And there were other things you used to tell me about. Like the time Mr. Marsdale died. You remember that?"

Mr. Marsdale had been one of our seventh-grade teachers. He died of a heart attack one night a month or so after school started, and for the rest of that year we had a pretty, just-out-of-college substitute named Miss Largent. "Yeah, I remember Mr. Marsdale," I said, nodding. "What about him?"

"Well," said Jarrod, "the day before he died, you said you saw a man in a black suit come into our classroom and look him up and down like a piece of meat. But no one else could see him."

"A man in a black suit?" I said. "Like a piece of meat?" I repeated. I could feel my brows knitting together, and tried to laugh a little, hoping he'd admit that all this was a long, drawn-out joke.

But before Jarrod put himself back into the car and closed the door on me, he said, "Your exact words, if I remember correctly, were: 'Like a piece of meat he was going to purchase.'"

chapter two

MISSING PIECES

Like a piece of meat he was going to purchase. Those words kept circling the drain in my mind for the rest of the drive back to Jarrod's trailer on Cordial Run, which looked the same as it had five years ago, the last time I'd seen it: a beaten-up, half-rusted white rectangle with a pale yellow stripe of paint wrapped around it like a sad bow. I didn't go in. I just braked halfway down the rutted dirt drive and told Jarrod that I'd see him at school the next morning.

"It was good to catch up," he said, sliding out of the car. I nodded, didn't mention how catching up had mostly made me feel awkward, decided instead to say there was a lot more to catch up on, and that brought out a last-minute good feeling between us. Jarrod wore a half smile as he turned to leave. And really, that was a decent end to a day that had become way too strange.

Fifteen minutes later, after driving away from Jarrod's place in a paranoid panic, I found myself pulling into the long gravel drive to my own house, and then suddenly pressing down on the brakes before I'd even reached the garage. The Blue Bomb's tires spun in the gravel before the car came to an abrupt stop, rocking a little afterward. I shook my head, as if someone had punched me hard enough to rattle me, and realized that I wasn't breathing. Maybe I hadn't been for a minute, because I was starting to gasp like a fish out of water, feeling like I might drown out there in the open air.

I calmed myself down, though, and after I caught my breath, I turned to stare at my house through the grimy driver's-side window. This was the only place I'd ever lived in all my seventeen years, but right then for some reason it felt like I'd just crash-landed on another planet.

The curtains had been pulled tight in all the windows, blocking out the late-autumn light, and the weather vane up on the roof squealed a little as a breeze pushed it a few inches to the west. And in the next moment, as I sat there in my car halfway down the drive, an awful idea came to me: *Something is wrong with me,* I told myself. I could feel it. I could feel something inside me indicate that, the same way the weather vane rooster blew westward with the wind.

We had a two-story farmhouse, goldenrod-colored, with a rusted tin roof that looked like someone had sprinkled it with cinnamon. A gingerbread house, my mom sometimes called it, usually over holiday breaks, when she'd be baking a pie or making a turkey dinner and she'd get nostalgic and start telling stories about how she and my dad met, or what life was like back when she was a little girl. She always said she could remember seeing the Lockwood farm on the bus ride home when she was in grade school. "I think I fell in love with this house before I ever fell in love with your father," she once told me, and my dad had interrupted to say it was her plan all along to marry him and steal the family fortune. "Family fortune," my mother had snorted. "Is that what you call your mother's debts we're still paying off?"

To the right of the house was the barn, where the cattle gathered, waiting for the afternoon grain I'd eventually bring. It was an old barn, built from some kind of wood that hadn't been painted in so many years it had gone gray as driftwood, worn down by the waves of time and neglect. Behind the barn was the pasture, and behind the pasture were the woods that led down into Marrow's Ravine, where my dad and brother hunted during deer season. The golden stubble of a cornfield, already harvested this late in the fall, lay off to the right of the farm, and to the left, Sugar Creek flowed, a trickle dark as tea, separating the house from the old orchard, where the Living Death Tree loomed in the distance like a scarecrow.

"This is my home," I whispered within the quiet of my car, as if I needed to remind myself of something so ordinary. My voice shook as I repeated those words. "This is my home, and I know it," I said.

It felt like there were more words to say, words that were meaningful, words that would somehow set everything back in place. But what those words were, I couldn't recall. And I didn't even know why I was saying any of this out loud in the first place.

"Snap out of it, Lockwood," I told myself. "You're losing it."

Or had I already lost it, whatever *it* was? Because something was off. It was the kind of feeling you get when something is wrong, but the wrongness is so subtle you can't pick out the flaw. A picture-frame-hanging-askew kind of feeling. A hairline-fracture-in-a-window-that-looks-perfectly-fine kind of feeling. I'd lost something, but I didn't know what. And I could only sense that because Jarrod Doyle had appeared out of nowhere and told me things about myself I couldn't remember. Pieces of me, it seemed, were missing.

I finally got myself together and drove the rest of the way up the drive. Then I made myself leave the car and went inside through the back door. Kicking off my shoes in the mudroom a second later, I suddenly understood the feeling Jarrod had mentioned earlier. How sometimes you could be made to feel like a stranger in your own house. For me, though, I was starting to feel more like a stranger in my own life.

I found my mom sitting at my grandmother's old Formica table in the kitchen, a relic from who knows how long ago, reading the news on her tablet—one of the few trinkets of current technology my mom embraced wholeheartedly—as she drank her afternoon cup of coffee. She didn't look up as I came in, just continued tapping and swiping her finger across the glass, even as she said, "Hello, stranger. How was school today?"

And I thought, *Act normal. Act normal and things will be normal.*

"It was okay," I said. "It was, you know, school." She nodded while she scanned the screen in front of her. But as I went to the fridge to pull out a can of soda, she turned away from whatever online article she'd been reading to look at me more carefully.

"Did something happen?" she asked. Her green eyes, the same color as mine, the eyes she always said she gave me, narrowed a little, as if she were trying to see something far away. But I was right there in front of her, of course. She tucked a piece of her auburn hair behind one ear then, as if she needed to move it to hear me better.

I was going to tell her about Jarrod Doyle coming back to Temperance—I was, I really meant to—but something stopped me before I could. A voice, actually. A voice, deep down inside me, suddenly spoke, as if it were traveling up from the bottom of a well, and stopped me cold.

Don't tell her, the voice inside me said, and I shivered as I stood in front of my mom, who sat there blinking, waiting for me to answer. The voice wasn't my own—I knew that immediately—but somehow it was inside me all the same. And it was a woman's voice, which made me feel even stranger.

Don't tell her, the voice whispered for a second time, like it knew I might defy its order.

"No," I finally said, shaking my head. "I mean, no, nothing out of the ordinary. Why?"

My mom cocked her head and continued to narrow her eyes, as if she didn't believe me. "You just seem off a little," she said. "That's all."

"That's because I killed a man on the way home," I said. "Hit and run. Don't check the grille of the Blue Bomb. It's a mess right now. I need to wash it."

She laughed at that, holding one hand to her chest like her heart might jump out of her throat if she didn't, and the crow's-feet at the corners of her eyes grew deeper. She and my dad were already fifty-two when I was seventeen. They looked a bit older than most of my classmates' parents, but I usually forgot about that until I made one of them laugh and their wrinkles showed up.

"You are so bad," my mom said, finally waving me and her suspicions away. That was what my mother always said about anyone who could make her laugh at something she felt she shouldn't, which was one of the few minor talents I possessed. "I don't know who you get your sense of humor from. Certainly not from me or your dad."

"Grandma Bennie," I said after cracking open my can of pop and swallowing a fizzy gulp.

"Not possible," my mom said, shaking her head. "Bennie was serious as the grave, rest her sweet soul."

That was what my mother always said about anyone she liked who had passed on. Their souls were always sweet, and she always hoped they were resting peacefully. My grandma had died two years ago, when I was fifteen, and my mom was right: Grandma Bennie hadn't been much of a stand-up comedian. She'd grown up on a farm out in Cherry Valley, a half hour north of Temperance, and had been forced by her family to quit school at sixteen and go to work in the factory where she met my grandfather, John Lockwood Jr., a man who died long before Toby and I ever came into the world. His photo, grayish-green in color, was preserved in an oval frame on a wall in our living room: a serious-looking guy with a mustache like a handlebar, wearing a button-down shirt, suspenders, and saggy pants. He'd killed himself when my dad was sixteen, the story went, leaving my dad and Grandma Bennie on their own. I'd always hated that picture, because it was the kind where the eyes follow you wherever you stand, judging you, finding you to be small and possibly stupid. Grandma Bennie, I'd always thought, would have needed a sense of humor to live with a guy like that.

"If my humor isn't from Grandma," I said, "then it must be from someone even further back." My mom nodded after I said this, as if to say *Of course,* but quickly and without another word she looked down at her tablet, as if something of great importance had sprung up on its screen.

I didn't stick around to encourage any more weirdness. I'd had my fill for the day. Instead, I let that hairline-fracture-in-a-perfectly-normal-seeming-window feeling lead me away.

I fed the cows a while later, taking time to pat a few muzzles and to rub behind a few fuzzy ears. There were only twenty in my dad's herd, all Herefords—red body, white face—my dad's favorite breed, and they all had names, as if they were part of our family. I could hear my dad's truck pull into the drive as I filled the trough with fresh water, announcing his and my brother's return. My dad and Toby both worked for the county roads department—Toby on a road crew, my dad as a crew leader—hauling coal patch to fill potholes in summer, scraping the roads clean of snow in winter. In spring, they'd get calls in the middle of the night to go out to remote corners of the county to cut up trees that had fallen across roads during storms, and occasionally I'd go with them to help out, to hold a light on them as their chain saws buzzed through limbs like knives through butter and rain spattered against their concentration-lined faces.

When I came back in from the barn, they were already sitting at the dining room table. "Come on, Aidan," my dad said, dinging his fork against the side of his plate and nodding at my empty seat. "I'm famished. Wash your hands and get over here." The Lockwoods were like that: we ate dinner together like a family in a Norman Rockwell painting, only without the overly happy faces populating the table. It wasn't that we were unhappy. We just weren't the best examples of glee.

The conversation during dinner that evening revolved around the roads department, as usual, since my dad and Toby were still stewing in their daily work stresses. That night their complaints centered on their boss, who my dad, in private, always called a corrupt politician. My mom didn't join in. She never took part in these types of discussions. She'd just sit there and listen as she cut her steak or as she lifted a forkful of baked potato. She wasn't much for talk of work, and she was even less interested in politics, which she always called "a petty game played by petty people," in a tone that made it sound like she blamed politics for all the world's problems. She preferred the domestic world: the house, the garden, the farm, her family.

I never had much to say in these dinner conversations either. Like my mom's, my life was limited to just a few social spheres. I'd go to school and then come home to do work around the farm for my dad. And because of that, I wasn't in any after-school clubs, so I didn't have much to add. Probably my dad thought this was normal because it was how he'd grown up. Once a month I'd attend a 4-H meeting he insisted I go to, and I'd sit in a circle of kids from local farms, listening to speakers talk about cuts of beef. This wasn't interesting to anyone except my dad, who hoped 4-H would keep me on the farm as an adult, which I didn't really want, to be honest, so I usually kept quiet at dinner. I didn't want him to know how I felt. I didn't want to invite any arguments. Arguments with my dad were unwinnable.

That night, though, when he and Toby had finished going on about their work frustrations, my mom said, "Aidan had something interesting happen today, didn't you?"

I looked up at her, sitting directly across the table from me, and felt a wave of heat spread across my face. They had all stopped eating and were now staring my way, waiting to hear me elaborate on my mom's declaration. Eventually I said, "What are you talking about?" before I looked down to press the tines of my fork into my baked potato like it was a very important thing that needed to be done at that exact moment.

"Jarrod, of course," my mom said. "Jarrod Doyle is back in town, isn't he?"

"Little Jarrod Doyle?" my dad said, turning back to cut another piece of steak. His knife sawed through the meat and squeaked against the bottom of the plate. "Haven't heard that name in a while, have we? His poor mother," he added, shaking his head. That was what my dad would always say and always do when Jarrod's mom came up in conversation.

"She's doing better, John," my mom said, a little exasperated, as if she was tired of constantly having to remind him. "She's got herself cleaned up. She's been waiting tables over at Times Square Café for a while now. Jarrod's come home to stay with her for senior year."

"Wasn't he living with his dad up in Cleveland?" Toby asked. *Of course,* I thought. Of course Toby would remember this, while I—apparently Jarrod's best friend—had forgotten it.

My dad nodded. "Yeah, Josh took a job up there after he and Libby split."

"Well, Jarrod's back," my mom said, nodding once, like that settled something. "So I imagine we'll be seeing a lot more of him, if he and Aidan turn out to be good friends like they used to be."

I sat there with my mouth hanging open, stunned that my mom already knew. But something like that wasn't unusual for her, really. My mom often knew things before other people. I mean, *really* knew things. Knew things in a way no person should be able to. Every once in a while, she'd wake in the morning and tell us she'd had a dream that she knew was going to come true, and sometimes it did. At other times, she'd stop whatever she was doing to look out a window or to stare down at the floor with lines of concentration etched into her face, and after a moment

29

she'd look up to say, "John, play the lottery tomorrow." Which my dad would do, and he might win a thousand dollars. At times like that we joked that my mom was psychic, but she'd always shake her head and say, "All those words people use to label each other are silly. Besides, psychics are fakes. I'm just a lucky one. That's all."

But to sit there and hear her tell everyone about my day when I hadn't told her a thing about it? *Psychic,* I thought. *She has to be psychic.*

"How did you know that?" I asked.

She looked up from her plate, her face blank as a sheet of paper, and said, "Jarrod's mom called, honey. An hour ago, while you were out doing chores. She said she hoped you and he could spend some time together. He'll be needing friends here again, naturally."

I nearly sighed with relief to hear a rational explanation. And then I immediately started to feel stupid for being so paranoid. But it wasn't as if my day had been completely ordinary in the first place. "Yeah," I said now, nodding, trying to resume a normal tone. "I saw him today. Gave him a ride home, actually."

And that was when my mom laid her last card on the table.

"Oh really?" she said. "Well, why didn't you mention that earlier when I asked how your day went?"

She pinned me with her gaze, and I felt like I was shrinking. Right then and there, I turned into a little kid with my chin barely making it over the lip of the dinner table and my legs swinging as they dangled from the chair.

Weirder than the shrinking feeling, though, was how the room seemed to dim around me in that moment, and how, in the center of the table, a candle suddenly appeared, its flame dancing while my mom leaned toward it, staring into its light as if she were hypnotized by its flickering. And then, where my dad and Toby had just been sitting, there was nothing but their empty high-backed chairs.

I blinked several times, and finally the room came back into focus: the candle disappeared completely, and then my family was back again, Dad and Toby still waiting for me to answer my mom's question. Why hadn't I told her about Jarrod Doyle? their befuddled faces asked.

"I guess," I said, "I guess I forgot to mention it."

"How do you forget something like an old friend coming back out of the blue, Aidan?" my dad said. He squinted as he shook his head, his lips twisting in this way that made me feel like he thought I was probably the stupidest person in the world. That look was the same one his own dad wore in the photo hanging on the wall over in the living room.

"I guess I don't have a good memory," I said, like Jarrod had told me earlier.

"Well," my mom said, "that can be a blessing or a curse, depending on how you view things."

And after that, thankfully, she let the subject go.

I spent the rest of the night up in my room, searching the Internet on my laptop for anything I could find on

Jarrod Doyle. In the end, it was no good. Jarrod was almost completely absent from the online world. No Facebook or Twitter profiles. No blog. Not even an old trail of messages on some forgotten discussion board. I found just one lousy news article from the Cleveland *Plain Dealer* reporting the score of a game Jarrod had won for his high school the year before. He'd pitched a no-hitter, and the writer speculated that Jarrod would be college baseball draft material when he was a senior. Were things really so bad at his dad's, I wondered, that he'd give up all that promise just to move back to Temperance and live with his mom? It didn't make sense to me.

When I hit a dead end online, I went to my bookshelf and looked through an album my mom had started for me years earlier. It held photos and documents from my life inside it. Toby had one too. And there was also the very, very thin memory album that lived on the bookshelf in my mom and dad's room, the one that belonged to our older brother, Seth, who had died from a seizure when he was just five, long before Toby and I were ever thought of, back in the 1980s. Seth had a photo in the living room too, hanging across from the picture of my suicidal grandfather. In his photo, Seth has this real little-kid face, soft and round, with green eyes like my mom and I have. My parents barely ever spoke his name aloud, and whenever they did, tears would spill from my mom's eyes like it was just yesterday she'd lost him.

I opened the album with my name on it for the first

time in what had to have been years. Inside was my birth certificate, an envelope that held one curly lock of dark hair from my first trip to a barber, and photos of me at different ages. In the margins of the pages, my mom had scribbled little notes with a fine black marker.

Aidan at five was a photo of me at my birthday party at a kid's pizza place in the mall out in Niles, surrounded by classmates I still knew because we all walked the same high school hallways. Which made me pause and wonder when, exactly, we'd stopped hanging out, because in the picture it looked like we were all having a good time together.

Aidan at eight showed me playing catch with my dad, probably for the first and last time, since it was evident early on that sports and I weren't really going to happen.

Aidan at ten showed me swinging on a swing set in the park with Jarrod Doyle.

I stopped on that page and slipped the photo out of the binder, brought it closer, smiling as I inspected the image. There we were, after all: two ten-year-olds with our hands gripped around the rusty orange chain links of the swings we sat on. Jarrod was wearing a Cleveland Indians T-shirt and jeans with grass stains on the knees. I had on a shirt with a Superman symbol in the center, but my jeans were crisp and clean. We were looking directly at the camera, smiling like we knew a secret but wouldn't ever tell it. Not to anyone.

I looked at that picture for a while, studying it for clues, but those boys—I could hardly remember them. And as I turned to pages farther in, I started to feel like I was looking at pieces of someone else's life altogether.

A photo from when I'd gone to homecoming with Caitlyn Hornbeck, who was doing a favor for her older sister, who was dating Toby at the time: the four of us all lined up on the front porch in dark suits and pretty dresses. I wasn't really interested in Caitlyn but felt like I couldn't refuse when Toby had already arranged things. "You need to get out more, son," he'd said, slapping my back and smiling like he'd just given me an amazing present. "Caitlyn's hot. Don't mess this up."

I was already messed up, though. I just didn't know how, exactly. And while Caitlyn really was hot, I felt this invisible wall between us. It was like I could see her and she could see me, but we couldn't hear each other, could just see each other's mouths moving in an effort to connect. We spent the night smiling politely at each other through this glass barrier that felt like it had sprung up right behind my eyes. Like I was trapped inside myself, and the me who danced awkwardly with her on the floor was this stand-in, making dumb jokes while I beat against the glass wall, beat against it with my fists and then my head, until my head really did begin to hurt, to throb hard, and I sat down at our table and rubbed my temples, started to rock and rock away the pain, until Toby pulled me up and helped me out to the car to drive me home, a confirmed mess-up.

A blue ribbon I'd won in tenth grade for a steer my dad

had made me raise: "It'll do you good to learn how to look after something other than yourself," he'd said, after signing me up for 4-H without asking. As I stared at that ribbon now, I thought about how wrong he was. I didn't need to look after something else. I needed to look after myself, I realized.

A couple of pictures of Toby and me at his graduation party two years earlier: my dad standing between us, his big arms curling around our shoulders, holding us tight. It was my mom behind the camera that day, instructing us to stand closer. *Act like a family*, she'd said jokingly, and we'd followed her directions like good performers.

Here was all this evidence of my existence spread out before me, but none of it felt like it was mine. None of it felt like it said anything real or true about me. None of it felt like I had made the choices that led to those images. If I searched Google for solid proof of my life, it would probably provide even less than it had for Jarrod. We were just a couple of nobodies.

The longer I tried to sort through things, the more my head began to pulse. At first it had just been this dull thud in the background, so I didn't notice it right away. But after I'd spent an hour scouring Google and looking through old photos like they might hold the answer to a question I didn't even know how to ask, the dull thud transformed, and suddenly bright white lights began to burst behind my eyes like fireworks, sending a hot blade of pain down the middle of my skull.

I could barely stand up whenever I got like this, which hadn't been very often of late, but I managed to make my way from my desk over to my bed, where I curled up in the fetal position and rocked myself back and forth with my arms wrapped around my shoulders, my eyes closed tight, my hands balled into fists.

This was an ordinary migraine, according to my doctor, who prescribed meds that didn't seem to help. The way these seemed to always happen was, I'd be doing something ordinary, like studying or—like I'd just been doing—thinking about random memories. Then suddenly my head would explode and white light would flash through my vision. After that, there was no turning back, and no pills could stop the pain until it was done with me.

Luckily the migraines weren't frequent—I hadn't had a major one since the night of the homecoming dance with Caitlyn Hornbeck—but for a while, back in middle school, mostly, it seemed like all I ever did was have them. My parents used to worry that I'd die from them, like my brother Seth, so they'd keep me home from school for days sometimes, my mom hovering over me, swabbing my sweaty forehead with a cool wet towel, whispering that I needed to let it all go. I never knew what she meant by that, and when I asked once, she cupped my cheek in her hand and said, "Stop trying to hold on to it, honey. Just let it all flow out of you."

Maybe my bad memory was because of my migraines,

I thought now. Maybe they were bombs going off in my brain, exploding my past into bits and pieces.

By the time the pain started to dim this time, I was too exhausted to do anything but listen to the sound of my own breathing. All of my energy was gone. All of it had been given over to the pain as it bucked and bucked, trying to throw me. My breathing was slow and steady, and my heartbeat followed behind. Before I knew it, sleep had pulled itself up to my neck like a blanket, and then I was sinking down into the dark of nothingness, my mind returned to a blissfully blank slate.

At some point in the night, I woke and sat up against my headboard with my brain clear as ice, already clicking away like clockwork, as if the migraine and the exhausted sleep that followed had never happened. I was sure I'd heard something, or someone, in the room with me, in the moment just before I woke. Footsteps had creaked across the floorboards, maybe, or else I'd heard something tap against the window. After a few minutes passed in silence, though, I started to think I must have dreamed it. It was only when I was about to slouch back down into my sheets, relieved to be wrong, that something did reveal itself.

A voice called out to me. A voice called out my name.

Not *a* voice, *the* voice. The woman's voice that had told me not to tell my mom about Jarrod. That voice was in my room with me.

Aidan. Aidan Lockwood, the woman said, as if she were Mr. Johnson trying to snap me out of a daydream.

But the voice wasn't inside me now, like it had seemed to be earlier. I heard it in the room, as if the speaker might be standing right there beside me. When I looked around, though, I found nothing but darkness.

A minute passed quietly before the voice called again. And this time it sounded like it had moved out of the room. Now I heard it coming from a distance, as if it were downstairs in the foyer.

Aidan. Aidan Lockwood.

I climbed out of bed and padded across my floorboards to slip down the hall, floating past the rooms that contained my sleeping family members. Then I was downstairs, looking around for the intruder. When for a second time I found nothing, I decided to open the front door and go out into the chill of late October.

On the front porch I hesitated, holding the door open behind me, worried that I might be going crazy. Above, the sky was indigo and full of clouds backlit by the moon, so that they looked like shadowy creatures floating by. It was either way too late for me to be doing this, or else it was way too early. I couldn't tell which, because I had yet to look at a clock.

Go back, I told myself. *Go back to bed, you idiot.*

But even as I convinced myself, the voice called out again—*Aidan. Aidan Lockwood,* she said—and I turned toward the sound, like metal to a magnet, felt myself being pulled in its direction, as if I no longer controlled my own legs.

The orchard. The old orchard on the other side of Sugar Creek, the creek that cut across the middle of our property. That was where it was coming from. The voice drifted out of the hole in the Living Death Tree like a fog, spread over the entire farm, covering every blade of grass, covering every leaf that dangled on the verge of falling, covering it all with my name.

Aidan Lockwood, the farm itself seemed to call out to me.

I moved through the cold, dewy grass until I reached the railroad-tie bridge that spanned Sugar Creek. It was an ancient crossing my great-grandfather Lockwood had made, according to my dad, back during the Great Depression, when the farm came into his possession. And when I crossed over those old logs a moment later and stood in front of the Living Death Tree, looking up into its canopy of leafless, gnarled branches, the voice finally, thankfully, fell to a whisper.

Aidan, the voice said. *Aidan Lockwood. You are a good boy, aren't you?*

"I don't know," I said. Then I asked, "What—what are you?"

The voice didn't say anything right away.

Then it began to croon what sounded like a lullaby in a foreign language. A mournful song from some other time and some other country drifted out of the hole in the Living Death Tree. I stood there, listening, and felt tears spring to my eyes, as if I could understand those words, as if I could comprehend the sadness in their mysterious meanings.

After a while, the singing stopped, and the next thing the voice said was *Close your eyes, young one. I have something to show you.*

But even as I closed my eyes like the good boy she'd called me, another voice sounded suddenly, out of thin air. This new voice, though, came from behind me.

"Aidan Lockwood," the new voice said, and I turned away from the Living Death Tree to find my mom standing on the railroad-tie bridge, Sugar Creek trickling beneath her, the red morning sunlight edging the frame of our house behind her. She had folded her arms across her chest to hold her robe together, and she wore a pair of old rubber boots that belonged to my dad, which she must have put on in a hurry when she noticed I was missing. They engulfed her legs, and I almost laughed at the sight of her. She seemed like a figure out of a dream or a nightmare.

"What are you doing out here?" she asked. Her lips formed a firm line after they closed on her question, and her eyes scanned me from top to bottom, then back again, making me look down and realize that I was wearing only the boxer shorts I'd gone to bed in. My feet and ankles were streaked with mud. And I was shivering, even though I hadn't felt the cold until my mom called my name and turned me in her direction.

I opened my mouth, but before I could say anything, the voice from the Living Death Tree was inside me again, saying, *Don't. Don't tell her.*

"I don't know," I said, stumbling over my own words, pulling my arms around my chest to match hers. "I think . . . I think I may have been sleepwalking."

chapter three

WHERE ALL
THE GOOD BOYS GO

Jarrod Doyle didn't show up at school the next day, and for most of that morning I felt like maybe I'd dreamed everything that had happened to me in the past twenty-four hours. The voice from the Living Death Tree. Jarrod's memories, which didn't match up with mine. My mother's silence after she'd found me under a dead apple tree in the orchard at half past five in the morning, still in my boxers with mud spattering my legs. I hoped it was all a dream, really, because if it was, then my life could go back to normal. Whatever normal was—even if it was completely boring— I'd take it and be glad to be thoroughly bored.

I was beginning to doubt everything. Myself included.

And then the next day the same thing happened. Or didn't happen. Jarrod wasn't there. Not in the hallways. Not waiting out in the parking lot after school. And the day after that, he wasn't there again. So when Friday came around and I still hadn't seen him, I decided I should probably drive over to the trailer on Cordial Run to make sure he actually existed. To prove to myself that he wasn't some bizarre delusion.

When I pulled down the ruts of his dirt drive and killed the Blue Bomb's engine, the silence of the back roads rushed at me, surrounding my car like a swarm of bees. Living in this part of Temperance was like living in a vast desert. You wouldn't see another person for miles. You wouldn't hear anything but the wind passing through the trees. At certain hours of the day a train would go by, clickety-clacking on a set of tracks hidden in the woods behind the trailer, or you'd hear a tractor grinding its engine from some farm half a mile away. Other than that, just birds and crickets chirping. My family lived only a fifteen-minute drive from this corner of the township, but even in that short distance there was a difference in the quality of the remoteness. Cars would pass by our place on their way out to Niles, for instance, with hourly regularity, reminding us that we weren't so far away from somewhere else. Jarrod and his mom, though, inhabited this great big emptiness of fields and woods and covered bridges. There was something forlorn about it all, living so apart from other people.

I went up the three wooden planks on cinder blocks to the trailer's front door and rapped my knuckles against it, making a trio of hollow thuds. The sound of feet hitting the living room floor like a pair of barbells came a moment later; then the front door squealed open, and Jarrod was standing a foot above me, wearing black sweatpants and a gray sleeveless T-shirt, like he was ready for the gym. His hair was all messed up, like he'd just gotten out of bed, and right before I said hello, he stretched his arms above his head and yawned like a bored lion.

"What's up, Lockwood?" he asked after lowering his arms. Before I could answer, though, he turned around, curling the back of his hand to wave me in behind him. "Come inside. I'm not really into daylight at the moment."

The trailer was a mess. Clothes littered the living room couch and chairs, a multitude of unwashed plastic drinking glasses sat on end stands, and an ashtray threatened to spill cigarette butts onto the water-stained coffee table. Amid all the mess, a completely chemical floral scent from some kind of recently sprayed aerosol canister clung to the air. Earlier that week both Jarrod and my mom had sworn that his mother had put herself back together, but seeing the state of things inside the trailer, I started to wonder. On the other hand, if his mom was working ten-hour split shifts over at Times Square Café, like my mom said she was, then it was Jarrod who should have been cleaning up the place, helping out, especially if he wasn't going to come to school any longer.

"I thought I should stop over to see if you were still alive," I said as I pushed some clothes aside to sit on the couch, its springs squeaking.

"Still alive," Jarrod said, shrugging. He sat back in an old brown recliner, kicked up its footrest, rolled his head around to work kinks out of his neck like a fighter, then gave me a pearly-toothed grin. "What?" he said. "You miss me or something?"

I made a face and rolled my eyes at him. "Or something," I said. Then: "I was just worried that I'd made you up the other day. Had some kind of hallucination. Did you decide to quit school or something?"

"Or something," Jarrod said. "Did my mom get you to come over here to grill me?"

"No," I said. "I haven't seen your mom in forever. But she did call mine the other day after I drove you home."

"Figures," said Jarrod. He rolled his eyes, not at me, but at the idea of his mother. "She worries like she's trying to make up for the past five years all at once."

"Can you blame her?"

"No," said Jarrod. "It's just a lot to make up for in the span of two weeks. That's all."

We didn't say anything for a while. It was like those five years of absence he'd mentioned took up all the air in the room. We breathed in those missing years and exhaled them in awkward silence. Eventually I took out the picture I'd found in my photo album, the one of Jarrod and me sitting on swings as kids, and passed it over to him without comment.

Jarrod grinned as he looked at it. "You always did love Superman," he said, shaking his head. "Where'd you find this?"

"My mom had it in a photo album." I paused, not sure how to say what was on my mind. "I don't . . . I don't know if I can remember everything from back then very well," I admitted.

"No kidding," said Jarrod. He looked up from the photo with raised eyebrows. "What happened? You fall down and crack your head a few years back or what?"

"If I did," I said, "I don't remember doing it."

Jarrod squinted hard, like he was trying to see through to the real me. The me I didn't know anything about. "Really?" he said. "I mean, you don't remember anything? Nothing at all?"

"Well, that's not it," I said. "I can remember things, sure. But I can barely remember you. And there are other things I can't remember, I think, even when I try really hard. Like, most of junior high is gone."

"Good riddance," Jarrod said, and snorted, and I laughed with him, grateful to break the tension, hoping that whatever was wrong with me could continue to be a source of humor.

A minute later, though, I asked the question that had been on my mind since looking through that photo album the night before. "Hey," I said. "Can you tell me something?"

"What?" Jarrod said, lifting his chin a little, looking at me from beneath his furrowed brow.

"Was I—"

I hesitated, and a flare of heat rushed across my chest, up my neck, over my face, like a wave of lava. I felt completely freakish as I tried to figure out the words I needed to ask the question that burned inside me like a live coal.

"Go ahead," Jarrod said, nodding to encourage me, his eyes lit up with what might have been hope that I was remembering something he wanted or needed me to remember.

"Was I, you know, *liked* by people when we were kids? I don't mean popular or anything like that. But, you know, *liked*. Because I found this other photo last night along with that one, and it was a picture of you and me and a bunch of other kids we went to school with—still go to school with, actually—at my birthday party. I don't really remember that party, though, or having other kids around that often, and I haven't been close to most of them for years now. You know, I keep to myself. But that picture. When I saw it, it made me think that at some point things had been different, but I can't remember for the life of me."

Jarrod frowned like he felt bad for me, and I thought I saw maybe even a hint of tears in his eyes, like he was attending the funeral of a good friend who had died in an accident, and was looking down at his dead body, thinking, *That's not him,* the way I'd thought when I saw my grandmother in her casket, all made up with colors she'd have never chosen for herself had she been alive.

"You were liked, Aidan," Jarrod said finally, quietly, firmly. "Everyone liked you, actually. I mean, you and I were best friends, but you weren't what I'd call a loner back then."

I sat there for a while, absorbing what he'd said, wondering why I wasn't a part of things any longer. Then I looked down at my hands, which I'd folded together on my lap like I'd been praying for something, and saw they were shaking a little.

"You tell your folks about any of this memory loss?" Jarrod asked when he saw how troubled I was.

I looked up and shook my head. "No. It's weird, but I didn't realize any of this until I saw you on Monday. I mean, sometimes over the last few years I'd start thinking about something, but I could never hold a thought for very long. It's like this wall will spring up inside me sometimes, and after that I can't see clearly. Sometimes I'll get migraines if I try to think about something too hard. And, well, I get this feeling like I shouldn't tell my mom and dad what I'm telling you right now. Especially my mom."

Jarrod wrinkled his nose and said, "Your mom has always been a little odd."

"What do you mean?"

"You know," he said. "Telling fortunes and stuff like

that. My mom used to go to her after she got out of rehab a few years back, trying to figure out what she should do with herself after she got cleaned up."

"Are you serious?" I said. Jarrod pulled back and looked like I'd accused him of lying, which I guess was true in that I doubted what he was saying. But I couldn't grasp what he was telling me and recognize it as reality. "My mom doesn't do that," I said, shaking my head. "I mean, I've never seen her do anything remotely like that except on occasion, like by accident. At home. With just us around. My dad and Toby and me. We used to joke that she was psychic, but she'd be the first person to tell you psychics are fakes performing for money."

"Well," Jarrod said, "according to my mom, she does. Maybe your mom just likes to keep it on the down low."

"On the down low?" I repeated the words like they were a phrase from a foreign language, squinting as I shaped the syllables.

"I've been in Cleveland too long," Jarrod said, snorting, "or else you don't watch enough TV. Just keeping it under wraps, is what I'm talking about."

"Oh," I said, still stunned, trying to take everything in. "I don't know why she'd do that, though," I said. "I mean, yeah, sometimes she knows things before other people do, but it's always random, and it's usually something not that important. Like she gets itchy fingers and thinks it's a sign that money is coming to her, so she goes to play bingo or something. Stupid stuff like that. Half the time she's joking. She's never been someone who just sits down and tells someone's future."

"Maybe it's pocket money for her," said Jarrod. "Maybe she's ashamed of it and doesn't want you and your dad or your brother to know about it. Anyway, you should tell your dad about not remembering things if you don't want to tell your mom."

"I don't know," I said. "I think telling you has been enough."

Jarrod smiled then. A genuine smile, no teasing grin. Softly, he said, "It used to be."

"What?" I asked, smiling back now, ready for him to deliver a line that would most likely make fun of me somehow.

"When we were kids," he said. "It used to be enough for you to tell just me your secrets."

I suddenly felt awkward again, like we were talking about someone else, this someone else in the past who happened to be me. I couldn't remember the memories he referenced, though, and my face must have shown as much, because the next thing Jarrod said was "You're freezing up on me again, Lockwood. Fine. Let's talk about something else. What's there to do around this godforsaken place, anyway?"

"Not much," I said. "Most people drive out to Niles to hang at the mall."

"Is that where all the good boys go?" Jarrod asked. He lifted his chin as he posed the question, like he was challenging me to not be one of the good boys.

I shrugged. "I don't know," I told him. "My parents keep me busy at home. I don't have a lot of time to run around, really."

He laughed, repeating my words. "*Run around.* Sounds like something your mom and dad would call what everyone else calls *having fun.*" He lifted his hands off the recliner arms and dropped them down hard, like he'd just made a big decision. "Well then," he said. "Let's take a drive out there and find out what's happening. God knows I could use a little running around right now."

Forty-five minutes later, we strolled into the mall like two cowboys busting through the swinging doors of a saloon, looking up and around at the vaulted ceiling, at the illuminated fountains, gawking at the Niles city kids who hung out in clusters at various stations: in the sunken garden, in the arcade, on the marbled steps of the platform where the carousel turned round and round, the horses going up and down, riderless, behind them.

Stepping into the mall was always a bit like going to Disney World. I was used to Times Square Café, the Dairy Oasis, the county fair's two midways, fields of corn and soybeans, Sugar Creek winding through town on its way down to Yankee Lake. The denizens of the mall in Niles might as well have been costumed characters putting on a play. And there were lots of different types of characters, even ones I hadn't anticipated. Like Gilbert Humphrey.

We were in the food court, sitting in a vast archipelago

of white and yellow tables, sipping supersized Cokes, when Jarrod asked, "Is that guy over there what I think he is?"

"Which guy?" I said, looking over my shoulder.

"Don't!" Jarrod whispered. "Damn it, he's spotted us. Here he comes."

"Who?" I said, still not understanding.

Out of the milling crowd of teenagers and mothers pulling children in tow, saying no to all the toy stores they passed, came a local army recruiter. He seemed to materialize a few feet from our table, as if beamed down by a starship, wearing a uniform and a smile, standing tall and proud. "Hey, guys," he said, like we were old friends, and before I could blink, he stood at the edge of our table. "Gilbert Humphrey, army recruitment. You boys look like you're getting ready to graduate."

I nodded. Jarrod shrugged.

"Well, that's great," said Gilbert Humphrey. "That's good you boys are about to make it out into the world. Bet you're glad school's almost done?"

I nodded again. Jarrod shrugged again. "Sure," we said in unison.

"What are you all going to do now?" Gilbert asked, and I could tell immediately where he was going with this.

"I'm not sure," I said. "I figure I'll take the rest of the school year to think it over."

"Good," said Gilbert, nodding. "No hasty decisions." And then, since I'd made myself unavailable, he looked

Jarrod up and down, spotting potential in his athletic form. "What about you?"

"No idea," said Jarrod. "I'll probably do the same as him." He gestured at me with his tower of Coke. We were playing Hot Potato, I realized, throwing Gilbert Humphrey's attention back and forth between us.

"Well, in case you boys don't already have this, here's an information packet." He handed us thick envelopes and we said thanks without looking at them. "We have all sorts of things you guys could do. Want to go to another country? Drive a tank? Amazing stuff out there in the world. Real different from here. And women? Let me tell you about the women."

"Thanks, Gilbert," Jarrod said as he scraped his chair back and stood. "We've got to go meet some friends, but it's been nice." Jarrod looked down at me and I stood up like a soldier who's received an order.

"My number's in the envelope," Gilbert said as we walked away.

And when we finally made it out of his range, I said, "That was awkward."

"Sorry," Jarrod said. "I should have pulled you out of your seat when I first saw him. Those guys can be persistent."

"He'll never get anyone to sign up like that," I said.

"Sure he will," Jarrod said. "Even being that annoying, he'll get people. If this place wasn't full of cattle, though, I don't know how he'd convince anyone."

"Cattle?"

Jarrod nodded. "This whole place—not enough jobs around to give people hope of making a life here, just enough to keep people breeding kids who have nowhere to go but into Gilbert Humphrey's waiting arms. They've got themselves a real army farm here."

"You really think so?" I said. I'd never heard Jarrod sound like this. Like he held some kind of a grudge against the world.

Jarrod looked at me with raised brows, like he couldn't believe I was so stupid. "How does it work on your dad's farm?" he asked. When I didn't answer, he looked almost guilty about even asking the question. "Come on," he said. "Let's just get out of this place."

"Where to?"

"Wherever you want," Jarrod said. "We could go to the moon, for all I care."

We didn't go to the moon. Instead we drove out of Niles. Took Route 422 east to Youngstown, where the little roadside shopping plazas fell away, to be replaced by boarded-up factories and the collapsing remains of steel mills that had been built along the Mahoning River decades before we arrived in the world. This was our inheritance, these shambling buildings. They'd been left behind to rot in the brown fields of dead earth they once loomed over, their insides gutted like the deer carcasses my dad and Toby brought home from their hunts.

"Where are we headed?" I asked Jarrod, who had fallen silent several miles back. Now he sat in his seat with pent-up emotion smoldering inside him. I could almost see the embers and smoke through his eyes.

"Just keep going until I tell you where to turn," he said, nodding his chin straight ahead before turning to look out his window.

I wondered what was on his mind that had made him so sullen so quickly, but I didn't press him. One thing I'd figured out fast about Jarrod was that his moods could take a left turn at any time, without any apparent reason, and usually when that happened he gave off a vibe that said more than words. The vibe said, *Back off.*

So I backed off.

I worried, though, that the reason he seemed able to fall into such a dark place was somehow connected to me. To something I wasn't saying or doing that he wanted me to say, or wanted me to do. Like there was a script out there for us, but I wasn't saying my lines. When I was around him, I felt like a man groping in the dark for a light switch.

We only drove a couple more miles before Jarrod perked up and said, "Here. Take a right here," and followed that up with a few more directions.

I drove off the highway into a residential neighborhood where old narrow row houses stood side by side like faded soldiers, and a few turns later, after Jarrod told me to stop, I had pulled into one of the parking lots of Mill Creek Park.

When I killed the Blue Bomb's engine, I looked over at Jarrod and asked, "Why here?"

"Time travel," said Jarrod. One corner of his mouth lifted into a smirk; then he opened his door and jumped out into the late-afternoon sun.

*

We walked from the lot into a large garden with a round stone fountain at its center. A gazebo was perched on a hill in the distance, and to our right a squared row of hedges held an old-fashioned rose garden inside it like a secret. At the far edge of the place was a wrought-iron railing that barred people from going any farther, and beyond the railing was a cliff that slid down to Lake Glacier, where even that late in autumn we could see a canoe skimming across the surface like a water insect. Otherwise, the place was empty.

"Time travel?" I said, once we were sitting on a bench near the fountain.

"You don't remember what happened in this place?" Jarrod asked. His eyes widened a little, but not like he was angry with me. More like he was trying to pull something out of me. Something I didn't know I had inside me.

I shook my head. I hadn't been in this park for years—it was a bit of a drive from Temperance—and what memories I had of Mill Creek were packed in the vague, cottony cloud of my childhood.

"Why don't you take a look at that fountain for a

minute," he suggested, and I turned to see where he was pointing.

It was an ordinary fountain, as far as I could tell: a circular stone basin with one main font in the center, smaller ones ringing it, their jets sending up a frothy spray over and over on a timer. I wasn't sure what I was supposed to be seeing that was so extraordinary, but just as I was about to say that, Jarrod put his hand on my shoulder and squeezed.

"Just keep looking into the water," he said. "Don't think about anything in particular. Just look. Just see."

I did what he said, even though I thought he was setting me up for some kind of prank. But as I stared at the fountains going up and down, the light began to change, lowering from late-afternoon amber to a lavender dusk. It was the time of day I'd once heard my grandma call the gloaming. It was her favorite time, she used to say, when night and day met for a brief visit, before passing each other on their way to the other side of the world.

The fountain continued to spray, and the sound of its rising and falling began to lull me into a daze. My head was thick with the rhythms of sleep and dreaming, but right before I was about to give up on this experiment of Jarrod's, I saw something—or someone—through the curtain of water.

Two boys. Two boys emerged from around a corner of the rose garden hedgerows to enter the circle of benches around the fountain, and they sat down directly across from us, the fountain spraying between us. The fountain lowered a moment later, and I could see them again. Two kids, no more than twelve or thirteen. One with shaggy brown hair and dark eyes, the other with trimmed curls and green eyes like mine.

They *were* mine, actually, those eyes. Those boys were us—me and Jarrod—I realized as they leaned toward one another to talk conspiratorially, ignoring us, as if they couldn't see their older selves sitting across the fountain.

I opened my mouth to say something, but Jarrod's hand on my shoulder squeezed harder. "Do you see something?" he whispered, hopeful. I nodded and whispered yes. "Good," he said. "Don't say anything. Just keep watching."

The boys were talking about something that upset one of them—the younger Jarrod—and my younger self was telling him not to worry. "It'll be okay," little Aidan Lockwood said, and I almost blushed to hear how I sounded as a kid, my voice still squeaky. "Here," he said to the younger Jarrod, and placed his hand in Jarrod's. "Let me show you, so you'll know how it will be." Then both boys closed their eyes and slumped back against the bench, as if all the life had gone out of them in an instant.

I could tell that wasn't the case, though. I could see that something was happening between them, that they were having some kind of shared experience. On my own shoulder, Jarrod's hand still rested, heavy and warm. And after a minute, the boys opened their eyes and looked at each other. They were smiling now. The younger Jarrod looked relieved by whatever he'd been shown. "So now you know it'll all be okay," my younger self told him. Then they hugged, tight and hard, as if they might never see each other again.

"Boys," someone called in the distance, and they separated to look over at the garden entrance, where a younger version of my mom stood holding her purse open in front of her, pulling out a set of keys. "Boys, we should get going," she said. "Jarrod's mom and dad will be ready to have him back home now, I'm sure."

The boys nodded, then stood and went over to her dutifully. She stroked the younger me on the head and smiled. "What were you two up to over here?" she asked, as if she could sense we'd been doing something we shouldn't have.

The younger me said, "We were talking about the future."

My mom's smile fell into a frown when she heard my answer. Then she nodded toward the parking lot and said, "Okay. Let's go home now."

As they turned the corner of the hedgerow and disappeared from sight, I finally turned to Jarrod—my Jarrod—sitting beside me. "What in the world was that?" I asked.

And Jarrod said, "That was you showing me the future back when we were thirteen."

"No, really," I said. "What was it?"

Jarrod sighed but kept on going. "On the day my dad

got tired of my mom drinking and asked for a divorce, your mom took me and you out here so they could figure out what to do next in private."

His hand still sat on my shoulder. When I looked at it, he took it away like he'd just been burned.

"What was it that I showed you?" I asked. "What did I show you back then?"

Jarrod leaned over, putting his elbows on his knees, propping his head in his hands, upset that I was still, after that revelation, somehow off script. He tilted his face to look up at me, and his hair flopped across his eyes like a curtain. "This," he said. "You showed me this. You showed me us, right now, at this very moment, sitting here like this. Talking."

The trip home felt longer than the one we'd taken to get away from the confines of Temperance. And in the span of time between leaving and returning, though it was only a few hours, it felt like the moon had crashed into the earth, and now every mile of highway I drove down was a desolate stretch of pavement in a world that had come to an end. Because, really, even before Jarrod could get halfway through the rest of his story, everything I thought I knew about the world had truly ended.

He told me that he'd hoped the fountain would jog my memory, because it was special, or at least, it was special to him. He told me that what I'd seen wasn't one of my own memories, but one of his. He'd put his hand on my shoulder because he remembered that I had to be touching someone to show them the things I could see when we were little. "Like what things?" I asked.

And he replied, "Like the future." He said I'd been able to do that when I was little. And he said that I could do something other than see the future. I could show the things I saw to others if I touched them. "You said it was called *reaching across,*" he said now, and I just sat there shaking my head as I drove by the tired little houses that lined the sides of Route 193 like the facades of small towns in old movies. A gust of wind could have blown those houses over, they seemed so flat and unreal right then.

After he finished his story, I stupidly asked if he had some weird kind of power. He laughed at me and said, "It's not me, Aidan. It's you. It's you who can do this stuff. It's *you* who showed me the future."

"A future where you were happy and living with your mom again," I said. "A future where we were still friends. That's what I showed you?"

I looked over, but he hesitated to answer. He seemed worried, began chewing the inside of his cheek nervously, and then he abruptly looked away.

"Yeah," he finally said to the passenger window, where I could see his face reflected in the glass, his eyes downcast. He seemed disappointed in something he wasn't saying. I was up to speed enough on him to tell when he too was going off script. "A future where we were still friends," he said, repeating my words in this way that wasn't believable.

He reached into the pocket of his jean jacket to take out his cigarettes but began patting himself down within seconds. "Damn it," he said. "I'm out."

"Want me to find a gas station?"

"No," he said. "We're almost home, and that was my last pack."

"Last pack?" I said. "Really?"

He nodded. "I told myself I'd quit after I'd smoked the last one. Guess that starts now."

"Why quit?" I asked as we pulled onto his road a few minutes later. The reflective mailbox that stood at the end of his trailer's dirt drive glowed in the distance as my headlights fell on it.

"I guess because you made me feel bad about it the other day at the lake," he said. "And because you're right. I shouldn't smoke if I'm playing ball. I need to save my lung capacity for running bases."

"You're coming back to school, then?" I asked as I pulled down his rutted drive, the Blue Bomb shuddering and knocking like it might fall apart around us.

"Yeah," he said. Then he sighed, long and drawn out, like he was giving up on something other than cigarettes. "I've got to. Otherwise, I might as well go back to the mall and sign up with Gilbert Humphrey."

I put the car in park and turned off my headlights, but left the engine running. We sat there for a while, staring into the dark. Jarrod's mom's car was pulled up the drive a little farther. She was probably asleep already, Jarrod speculated. "Has to get up for an early shift at Times Square tomorrow," he said as he reluctantly grabbed the door handle. The door squealed a little as he opened it, and before he pushed himself out, he looked back at me and said, "What are you going to do about what you saw tonight?"

I looked at my hands gripped on the wheel in front of me and shook my head. "I'm not sure," I said. "I mean, I know what I saw. But I have no clue what to do about it."

Jarrod nodded, then slid off the seat into the dark. Before he closed the door, he leaned down and said, "Maybe you'll see more things now, at least. Maybe you'll see things that'll answer your questions."

"Can't you just tell me?" I asked. "Can't you just share more memories with me?"

He shook his head. "I don't know the whole story," he said. "Just know my part in it. My dad moved a few weeks after you showed me we'd still be friends in the future. I don't know what happened to you after that, because I went with him. The rest you're going to have to find out on your own."

My hands were white-knuckled in the moonlight, clenching harder and harder, and I sighed like Jarrod had a minute earlier.

"Hey," Jarrod said. He ducked his head farther into the car and put his hand on my shoulder like he had in the park, but there was no vision accompanying his touch this time. Instead of reaching across, as Jarrod had called what happened between us in the park earlier, he just used words with me. "Hey," he said again. "I might not know what happens next—that was always your territory—but I *will* help you however I can."

chapter four

MASKS OFF

If I needed help, it was the sort that might make me feel better about my head being so broken. I knew what Jarrod was trying to do, though. I knew he was trying to give me whatever parts of myself he could—to help put Humpty Dumpty back together again—but everyone knows the end of that story. It doesn't really work out.

At that point, I just hoped I might someday look inside myself and not feel like I was staring into a long, empty hallway. At that point, I wanted the clutter of memories. Good or even bad ones, it didn't matter. I just wanted to feel like there was something to me. Something real I could hold on to.

There *was* something, of course; I just couldn't see it. I was as invisible to myself as I was to anyone. I'd have to make myself seeable, then, I decided. And to do that, I'd have to start making new memories instead of worrying about the ones I was missing.

So when Jarrod invited me to a party he wanted to throw for Halloween, I said yes without hesitating. "Yes," I said, nodding once, firmly, like I'd just made a huge decision. And then, after thinking about it a second longer, I asked, "Who else is coming?"

We were in the cafeteria for lunch period. Around us, people were talking and laughing, filling the room with the voices of their incredibly normal lives, lives that all of them could remember with great ease. But at our table in an out-of-the-way corner, everyone felt far away, as if they were on other planets, and we were on a moon base, orbiting at a distance.

"Just a few of the guys from the team," Jarrod said. He took a bite of his pizza, then nodded at someone who was walking by our table behind me.

I looked over my shoulder, and sure enough, it was one of the guys from the team. Patrick Morrison. I hadn't held a conversation with Patrick Morrison since the sixth or seventh grade, most likely, and whenever our eyes met now, it was like he looked right through me.

Great, I thought. *A party. A party with people who don't acknowledge my existence.*

My instinct was to bolt, to just not go in the end, then apologize for not showing up later. But since it was clear to me by then that I couldn't trust my own instincts, I just nodded and said, "Cool," and hoped it sounded like I meant it.

✳

On Halloween morning, as I spooned up oatmeal at the kitchen table before heading off to school, my mom looked over her shoulder as she washed dishes and said, "Hey, if he's not busy tonight, why don't you bring Jarrod over for dinner?"

I swallowed the mound of oatmeal I'd just shoveled into my mouth before shaking my head and saying, "No can do. There's a Halloween party tonight."

"A party?" my mom said, and her eyes lit up like she couldn't believe what I was saying. "I don't think I've ever heard that word leave your mouth before."

I wasn't sure if my own mother had just cut me down for not being the type of person who got invited to parties, so instead of rolling my eyes at her, I just shrugged and said, "Yeah. At Jarrod's."

"At Jarrod's?" she said, her voice going up into even higher frequencies of disbelief. Now that her initial shock had passed, she began to shake her head. "In that old trailer? I can't see how any party, at least a good one, can be thrown in that place."

"Well, it's just a small party," I said, as if I knew any-thing about it. "Me, a few guys from the baseball team, maybe some people from his classes."

"Girls?" my mom asked, turning back to the sink. A

dish squeaked as she wiped it with a wet cloth, and I flinched at the sound of it.

"I don't know," I said. "It's not my party. He just invited me."

"Well, he must be trying to make friends again," my mom said as she set the dish in the drying rack. "Parties will do the trick, for sure. But don't do anything stupid, okay? First sign of alcohol or drugs, you get out of there."

"Mom," I said, looking up from my just-emptied bowl. "I don't think he's going to have alcohol or drugs in his mom's place after what she went through to get off them."

"You never know," my mom said, shaking her head. "Just because his poor mother had trouble with all that and got over it doesn't mean *he's* not going to have his own troubles. Sometimes these things run in families."

I dropped my spoon in the bowl and stood to bring it to her, let it slide into the soapy water and clunk against the sink's bottom. "Did you dream that," I asked, looking straight into her eyes, "or is that a genuinely concerned opinion?" There was an edge to my voice that surprised even me.

My mom's eyes turned to slits in an instant. "Don't you talk to me that way, young man," she said. "I'm just trying to look out for you. It's my job, you know. Being a mother isn't easy."

"I'm seventeen," I said. "I can look out for myself." Then I grabbed my backpack from my chair, thudded down the mudroom steps, and opened the back door.

As I stood there with the door still open behind me, my mom got in one last jab. "You think you know everything, Aidan Lockwood," she yelled from the kitchen, "but you don't know the half of it."

I shut the door on her voice and shook my head at what she'd said. "'Sometimes these things run in families,'" I whispered into the morning air, as if by saying the words aloud and scoffing at them, I might exorcise the idea they held in their syllables. The idea that none of us can escape the problems of our families.

The words turned into a white fog in front of me as soon as I said them, chilled by the late-autumn air. They turned into a fog as thick and white as the one inside me. Then they disappeared.

For the rest of the day, whenever I looked up from a test or away from my teachers, the clock seemed to have moved far into the future instead of keeping the usual school-like time of never-going-to-end. Before I knew it, the day was half over. And in what seemed like the next moment, the bell for last period rang, and I was walking out the doors.

Some people had dressed up because it was Halloween, so it had been a day of costume watching. There was a lineup of mostly bad Lady Gaga renditions and guys wearing plastic claws with their hair slicked up to look like Wolverine. One girl came as Catwoman, wearing a black leather bodysuit, twirling a fake plastic whip like a tail, which got her sent home by the end of first period. A bunch of the school athletes unimaginatively wore their team uniforms. And some teachers managed to get into the spirit. Mr. Johnson was wearing breeches and tights in an effort to look like Shakespeare, and Ms. Woodyard wore a severe nunlike costume that she continually had to explain was a replica of the garb women might have worn at the Salem witch trials. At the end of the day, all of these masked spirits exited the building together, as if in a parade, then drove off in a hurry toward their various Halloween destinations.

Jarrod was already leaning against the Blue Bomb when I got outside. It was weird to see him not smoking an after-school cigarette; apparently, that image of him had been branded into my mind. I think it must have been weird for him, too, because he jiggled his leg up and down and kept playing with a lock of his hair like it really needed his attention. The only time I'd seen him look so nervous was when he took me to Mill Creek to show me one of his memories. One of *my* memories, that is. One of *our* memories, I should say.

"What?" I said as I came up to him, as if just last week he hadn't told me any of those completely unbelievable things. "No costume? Really?"

He looked me up and down before he said, "You're one to talk. Jeans and a flannel shirt? Again? One easily purchased hockey mask and you would have been a hit today, so don't go giving me a hard time."

"On Halloween," I said, "at least originally, masks were supposed to come off, according to Mr. Johnson. But we are for sure the least fun people in this high school regardless. Even Ms. Woodyard came dressed for the Salem witch trials."

"Huh," said Jarrod. "I thought that pilgrim dress was one of her regular outfits."

I grinned, and was relieved to be grinning. Jarrod and I had begun to understand each other's sense of humor—dry and cutting, in his case—which meant we were getting back to being the way we must have been when we were kids, when we'd understood one another in some way that made us want to be around each other. To be friends.

"Need to pick up anything for the party?" I asked. "We have time if you're not ready."

"Nah," Jarrod said, shaking his head. "I've got everything we need. We can head out if you're ready."

"Ready," I said, confident as a businessman, even though I had no clue what the fine print on the contract said.

So we got into the Blue Bomb and headed toward the trailer on Cordial Run, where, when Jarrod unlocked the front door and pushed inside, the door squealing on its hinges, I found the place in what must have been the cleanest state it had been in since we were kids.

The shock must have shown on my face, because Jarrod said, "My mom said I had to clean if I was going to have people over. I told her it was just you coming, but she said that didn't matter." He looked at me after saying that and laughed at his own joke.

"What a guy," I said, and shook my head at him. I'd gotten snagged, though, on what he'd said about it being just me coming, and wondered what had happened to the others. "Didn't you invite anyone else?" I asked. "You said some of the team were coming over."

Jarrod made a face like the guys on the team were some exotic food he'd never try willingly. Octopus or raw fish, maybe. But baseball players? "Nah," he said. "I'll have to hang out with them soon enough, once we start spring training. I figured we could have one of our old horror-flick-marathon nights, like we used to. For old time's sake."

I looked at him for a while, wanting to say I wasn't comfortable with this change in plans, wanting to say I wasn't comfortable doing something we did back when we were kids, because doing that would make me think about all of the *other* things I couldn't remember us doing.

But instead I said, "Sounds fun," and asked, "What do you have in the lineup?"

"I'm thinking we should go for a classic first," he said, raising his eyebrows a few times with real excitement that I was good with his change of plans. "Maybe a slasher. Then we can move on to something current, possibly a supernatural thriller. Those were always your favorites. Or we could watch something so bad it's funny."

"When we were kids," I said, "we didn't watch scary movies and laugh."

I said this with confidence. This much I could re-member.

"Christ, no," said Jarrod. "Back then I *believed* in the boogeyman. And you seeing all kinds of spooky shit sure as hell didn't help convince me otherwise."

I looked down at the orange shag carpeting. It was the same carpet I remembered from when we were kids, and it was probably the same carpet that had been in that trailer before Jarrod's parents had lived there. Looking at it made me feel a little better, because it was something I hadn't forgotten, a touchstone, something that had leaped the chasm between my past and present, making every-thing feel continuous inside me, at least for one brief moment.

Also, it was easier to look at that carpet and refuse to think about what Jarrod had said about me seeing spooky shit back then.

"Hey," he said, his voice softer now. "I'm sorry, Aidan. I didn't mean to bring that up again."

I looked up, sucking in one cheek a little, and said, "It's okay. I'd rather you talk about it than pretend it was never real."

"Thanks," he said, like I'd done him a favor. He stood in the doorway between the living room and kitchen, his arms braced on the frame above his head. "I'm glad to hear you say that. I hate having to be fake around people. I'm glad I don't have to be fake around you."

He turned to go into the kitchen and left me standing

there wondering why he would ever have to be fake with anyone. A guy like Jarrod is usually the sort lifted up on everyone else's shoulders because he can throw a baseball past batters and leave a bit of smoke coming out of the catcher's mitt afterward. At least he didn't see things other people couldn't. At least the thing that made him different was a good thing.

A minute later, he returned with a couple of beers. "Want one?" he said, holding out a sweat-beaded bottle.

I thought about my mom and her prediction that drugs and alcohol would appear at Jarrod's party. A little anti-drinking commercial played in my mind for a second, and my mom was an actor in it, wagging her finger at me. Why did she always have to be right?

I shrugged it off a second later, though. *It's just one beer,* I told myself. And *it's just the two of us, anyway.* And that piece of logic nullified the accuracy of my mom's prediction just enough for me to not care.

I took the cold bottle out of Jarrod's hand then, and twisted the top off like a trouper.

By ten, we'd made our way through two old slasher flicks—*Nightmare on Elm Street* and *Friday the 13th*—and we were just getting to the end of a third movie—*Paranormal Activity*—which had been made like a documentary about a demon-possessed woman whose boyfriend won't stop filming her.

"What an idiot," Jarrod said, shaking his head as the movie ended.

"She kept telling him to stop filming her," I said. "No means no, dude. You get what you deserve."

Jarrod chuckled and took a swig from his bottle. We were on our fifth beers, and I was feeling fuzzy around the edges. A different fuzzy than how I usually felt. This felt like I was somehow lighter, like some kind of pressure had been relieved. This felt like the opposite of those times when a migraine would come for me.

When Jarrod finished his beer a second later, he stood and went to the kitchen to retrieve the last two, then came back with the top already taken off mine. "I don't think you should drive home tonight," he said as he stretched to pass me the bottle. "I couldn't live with myself if you got into an accident after drinking over here."

"I guess I could stay here," I said. "I'd just have to call my parents and tell them."

"Sure," Jarrod said. "Just don't sound drunk when you talk to your mom or she'll be over here in a hurry to get you."

"It sounds like you've had practice at doing this," I said, laughing.

Jarrod laughed too. "Okay, okay," he said. "You've got me. But learn from my mistakes, grasshopper. Practice makes perfect."

So I practiced talking out loud for a while, just to make sure I wasn't slurring my words, which I didn't do at all.

Which surprised me. I'd always expected that the first time I drank anything alcoholic, I wouldn't be able to stand, let alone talk coherently. The beer, though, hadn't hit me hard. Probably because it was the cheapest stuff Jarrod could find in the coolers of the shadiest little convenience store in the next town over.

After all that practice at talking sober to fool my mother, though, it turned out to be my dad who answered the phone when I eventually called. He said staying over at Jarrod's was fine, but he expected me home early enough to help him with chores the next morning. I said, "Sure thing. Will do. Thanks, Dad." And when I clicked my phone off a second later, Jarrod slowly raised his fists into the air, shaking them victoriously, like we'd just won a championship ball game.

"Come on," he said, and got up to lead me back to his room.

While the carpet in the trailer was something I remembered from hanging out there as a kid, Jarrod's room seemed different. It was the size of a matchbox, made even smaller by his bed, which was this huge sleigh-shaped thing that barely fit. It took up most of the space, leaving only a person-sized path to walk around its edges. In my memory, the room had been way bigger. Maybe, though, I only remembered it like that because I'd been a lot smaller.

"You can have the bed," Jarrod said, nodding toward it. "I'll sleep on the floor."

I looked at that narrow strip of free space around the

edge of the bed and said, "No way. That won't be comfortable at all."

"I've slept in worse places," Jarrod said, shrugging. I wondered what he meant, but didn't ask.

"I can sleep out on the couch," I offered instead, turning back to the living room. "I don't mind. Really."

"No," he said. "My mom will come through there when she gets home from work, and if she smells beer on you she'll go crazy. I already put the other evidence in the trash can out back. I don't usually have anything around to set her off, but I figure what she doesn't know can't hurt her."

"It's your call," I said. "But it's also your bed. Why don't I take the floor instead?"

Jarrod opened his mouth, but for a moment he just stood there, saying nothing, as if he'd lost all of his words. A strange look passed over his face. Then quickly he sat down on the edge of the bed, put his elbows on his knees, his head in his hands, and he started to mutter, saying how stupid he was, how he wished he wasn't so goddamned stupid.

"What's the matter?" I asked. But he just kept shaking his head and mumbling about how he was a complete idiot. When that was all I could get out of him, I sat down beside him and put my arm around his shoulders, trying to comfort him. He flinched when I touched him, though, as if I'd tried to stick a knife into him, so I let my arm drop again. "Hey," I said, "what's wrong? Did you drink too much? Are you sick?"

"You should probably go," he said, not looking up from

the floor to face me. His voice had fallen to almost a whisper. "I'm sorry I had you over like this."

"I had a good time," I said, still not comprehending. "It's been fun. I don't understand. Did I do something wrong?"

He looked up from the gloomy position he'd taken, and I could see that he was thinking about something. Behind those dark eyes, some unwanted thought kept floating by, like a fish behind glass, wanting to get out, to be free of his skull. "You don't remember a lot of things, I know," Jarrod finally said, his voice shaking a little. "But I was wondering, do you remember this?"

He took my hand from my lap then, and held it in his. At first I thought that he was going to share a memory with me, the way he had at the park, that he was *reaching across* again. But when no memory came, and his thumb continued to softly caress my knuckles, I looked up and saw him waiting for my reaction. "We used to hold hands like this," he said, "when we were kids. Even when we were almost thirteen. I know it must sound strange. So many other things that used to be normal, you can't remember. But do you remember this?"

I shook my head, slowly, but he didn't take his hand away. I didn't take mine away either, even though I wasn't sure what I was even thinking, if I was thinking anything at all. Holding his hand did somehow feel normal. But I wasn't completely receiving his message.

"Is it there now?" he asked.

"Is what there now?"

"That wall you told me about. The wall that springs up inside you sometimes."

"No," I said, shaking my head, even though I was starting to get nervous enough to almost wish that I had the wall there right now.

"I'm trying to tell you something, Aidan," said Jarrod, his voice growing smaller as he tried to admit something big.

Sometimes I wish I could go back to that moment and wake up right then, to understand everything again, so I could do the right thing, so I could say the right thing to Jarrod. But at the time, my head was still broken.

After it became clear that I wasn't able to say what he hoped for, that I still didn't know my lines, Jarrod took his hand away from mine. "I didn't come back to Temperance because I missed it," he said, his voice now flat as an iron. "I came back after my dad caught me with a guy and kicked me out."

"I thought you left because of your dad's girlfriend," I said, and Jarrod looked over to roll his eyes at the enormity of my stupidity.

"Jesus, Aidan," he said. "I made that shit up. His girlfriend has her own apartment." He stood then, and went over to lean against the doorframe with his back to me. "I was embarrassed by the truth, okay? When I came back here and saw that something was wrong with you, that you couldn't remember some things, I was afraid you wouldn't remember us. Like that. Like the way we were with each other. And clearly you don't."

He sighed, frustrated that I couldn't fill in the rest of what he was trying to say. "Just go," he said eventually. "I'm sorry I had you over like this. I was being selfish. I was hoping if we spent time together like we used to, alone, you'd remember how you felt. Which was pretty dumb of me, obviously. We were just stupid kids back then, anyway, weren't we?"

"Well—" I said, but Jarrod lifted a hand.

"Please don't," he said, still looking down the hall instead of facing me, as if one glance from me might set him on fire. "I'm embarrassed enough. Just go, Aidan. Just go home, will you?"

I didn't want to leave with things so unsettled, but with him not willing to talk any longer, I did what he asked and stood, brushing against him in the narrow doorway as I pushed past. For a moment, a flicker of energy leaped between us, like it had when he'd reached across to me at the fountain in the park, and I stopped there, waiting for him to change his mind. When he didn't say anything, I shook my head, angry, and fled.

After firing up the Blue Bomb and backing down the drive onto Cordial Run, I felt more sober than I'd been before drinking the six-pack. I stuck to the back roads anyway, drove slowly with the window down so that the cold October wind blew against my face as the red and yellow leaves of autumn appeared in the wash of my headlights.

I didn't know how to think about what had happened, about what he'd said and about that weird flash of heat and energy that had sparked between us. I was too surprised. By his confession, by the way I hadn't pulled away from him, even as I started to understand. I'd just sat there and watched him caress my hand like it belonged to him. And then, to top it all off, I'd said nothing after he told me a truth that obviously hurt him to talk about.

I was the one who should have felt ashamed. He'd been open with me ever since he'd come back and made a friend of me again.

But me? I was a locked door. A door even I didn't have the key to.

☆

When I got home, my mom was still up, reading in the living room, the room dark except for the light from her tablet. One of her nightly rituals. A chapter or two of an ebook before heading upstairs. Toby and Dad had made their way to their beds and were probably already off to dreamland.

"Hey," I said as I passed the room, hoping she wouldn't stop me and see that my eyes were glassy or smell the beer on my breath and guess that I'd come home because Jarrod Doyle had semi-drunkenly held my hand while we sat on his bed and he confessed an attraction to me. I couldn't deal with her prying into things even I didn't understand yet.

Before I could make it to the staircase, though, she said, "Aidan, I thought you were sleeping over at Jarrod's tonight. Did something happen?"

"Decided not to," I said from the landing, "so I can get up early and help Dad."

"Well, that's nice of you," she said. "Why don't you sit down here with me for a while, though? I have some things I need to talk to you about."

Here it comes, I thought. The lecture on drinking and driving. And of course she would know that I'd done that, because my mom knew everything going on around her, even when she wasn't there to see it with her own eyes.

"I'm tired, Mom," I said, and feigned a loud yawn. Through the entryway to the living room, I saw the portrait of my suicidal grandfather eyeing me in the foyer, judging my bad acting. I made a face like I would come at his portrait with a large knife if he kept staring like that, if he kept judging. And to my mom, I said, "How about tomorrow?"

"Now would be better, actually," she said.

But I was already halfway up the staircase, pretending I hadn't heard her. I'd sleep peacefully, I told myself as I got into bed, and when I woke in the morning I'd do work for my dad. And after that, maybe I'd get Jarrod to talk to me. If he *would* talk to me, that is. If he could.

If we could talk to each other.

chapter five

THE ANGEL,
THE WHITE STAG,
AND OTHER SPIRITS

"Sleep is a place a person goes to," my mother once told me. "It's not a thing a person does. It's a place where we go to find peace for a little while."

I was a little kid when she told me that, and in the fog of my memory I could still see her sitting in a child-sized chair beside my small bed, leaning over me as she spoke, her hands pulling my comforter up to my chin. I can't remember all the details—I was probably sick or unable to fall asleep for some other reason—but I do distinctly remember my mom brushing my hair from my eyes and placing a gentle kiss on my forehead. I do distinctly remember that, somehow, after her kiss landed on me, my fever broke, or whatever it was that had kept me sleepless went away, and my lids grew heavy, and I then fell asleep fast. *Fell* being the key word. Fell into the place called sleep, where we rest. Where we find peace for a little while.

A white haze surrounded that memory now as I put myself to bed and pulled my covers up to my chin like my mom did when I was little. If I could have kissed my own forehead to put myself at ease, like my mom could, I would have. Heavy eyelids were what I wanted. As quickly as possible, I wanted to feel myself being pulled down into the dark place of sleep, where I could find peace after a night of unexpected and worrisome revelations.

Peace wasn't what I found when I did finally fall into sleep, though. A strange dream came instead. It wasn't one of mine, though, I could tell immediately. Maybe it belonged to someone in my family, or maybe to someone nearby. I had no idea. But wherever the dream came from, it swooped into my room on dark feathers, plucked me up like a baby, and carried me away to another world, where the peace of sleep did not exist.

A world where the scream of an engine burst in my ears, so close, so loud, it rattled my teeth, scraping them top against bottom.

I blinked as I came to, and turned my head to either side, looking around slowly. A row of soldiers sat against the wall opposite me, their faces blackened with some kind of paint; their round helmets covered in netting; their bodies slung with guns, grenades, parachutes; their eyes heavily lidded with worry. Then gunfire began to chatter against the belly of the plane we rode in—that was what it was, I realized as I continued to scan my surroundings—and the bullets rang out like pebbles thrown against a window.

One of the soldiers lining the wall across from me vomited, wiped his mouth with his knuckles, then looked down at his own hand as if he couldn't believe the hand had actually cleaned the spit from his lips without protest.

"Out, out, out!" someone shouted, and the soldiers stood to form a line. "Out, out, out!" someone shouted again, and I looked out the open door of the plane, where the wind whipped through the entrance and ran its hands all over me.

It was dark outside the hatch, black as black can be, but I could hear more airplanes ripping through the clouds around us, could see the flare of their engines, the shadows of their wings forming a bridge of darkness across the sky.

A young man was sitting next to me, fingering the netting that surrounded his helmet like a web. "Out, out, out!" someone ordered again, and the young man stood, his eyes wide with fear, and went to the door as commanded.

I stood with him, I don't know why. I just stood, because there he was, a man in trouble, a man who stood despite being afraid, who looked out over the edge of the open door, where the sky, ruffled like the petals of a black flower, flowed by. To jump or not to jump? That was the question. And I went to him, this young man seized with a sense of duty that emanated like an aura. I took hold of his arm, and when he leaped, I leaped with him.

Into the sky we flew, the wind whipping around us. I didn't think about why I was doing any of this. It was a dream, so I flew into the sky with him, peering down at the dark fields of clover and woods, where gunfire chattered, breaking sparks of light into the night, and people ran through the landscape like frightened rodents.

Then everything stopped for a moment. The air itself seemed to pull us higher into the sky, to pick us up like a kitten by the nape of its neck and return us to where we'd jumped from; then it dropped us again without any warning, and suddenly, throughout the sky, hundreds of white parachutes opened.

We hung there, suspended in the air like white dandelion seeds blown away from their core. And down below, below this soldier and me, a battle had started.

A barn was burning, illuminating the night with its fire. There was a steeple, ringed by the low two-story houses of the village the church served. The men who had flung themselves out of the plane circled the burning barn and the bell-tolling church like moths attracted to firelight.

Where was I?

In the air.

You're in a dream, I told myself.

I was in another world.

Through the black air we drifted, until suddenly a gun-shot rang out, and the young man I clung to grunted in pain. He held one hand against his chest, and when he pulled it away, he found blood there, hot and wet in the cool night air.

Then we hit earth, stumbled, rolling against each other, and came to a stop at the edge of a woods, where we lay stunned, looking up at the sky as the planes cut through the dark on their way back to England.

That was where he came from, I realized. I could pick that up from the current of his thoughts, like picking up a leaf as it floated by on the surface of a creek. The im-pressions of his mind had begun to enter my conscious-ness. But the longer I held on to him, the more I became confused. Couldn't distinguish between his and my own feelings, couldn't tell whose memories were whose.

He'd been in England, training for this moment. That much I knew. I could see the months that had led up to his boarding the plane to jump out into the sky over a field in France. I turned to look at him lying in the grass beside me. As he stared up into the sky we'd just jumped from, the line of his jaw was chiseled against the night, creating a familiar silhouette, the profile of a face I somehow rec-ognized. And I thought, *He looks like my father.*

He tried to stand, got himself halfway up with a good effort of gritting his teeth and grunting. Then he braced himself against the trunk of a tree, pulled a cigarette out of his pack of rations, lit it, inhaled deeply, and exhaled a smoky sigh of relief. When he tried to move away from the tree a minute later, though, something squished inside his boot—the sound of bones moving through jelly—and he winced as pain rang through his body, crippling him momentarily. He stopped, leaned back against the tree again, and waited there, breathing heavily.

In front of us, the trees thinned out and a field opened, spreading toward the horizon. A dirt path cut across the center of the field, leading toward the village I'd seen from the sky. I could still see an aura of light surrounding the burning barn, most likely a mile from where we stood, but I couldn't see the barn itself any longer. I could still hear the church bell tolling in the center of the little town, but I couldn't see its steeple. Instead, I saw the dandelion seeds of young men drifting toward it. I saw one float right into the flames, consumed in the barn's conflagration within moments, as if it had never existed.

Click-clock. The young man beside me had pulled a toy from his pack. *Click-clock* was the noise it made when he pushed on it, this piece of metal painted to look like an insect. A cricket, the army officers called it. I'd seen them before, in the sad and dusty toy aisles of run-down stores in Temperance that carried nothing but pieces of the past for purchase. Bubble-gum cigars, wax lips, lollipop whistles, plastic rings, and crickets. *Click-clock* went the cricket in the young man's hands. Then he looked around, listening hard, but no crickets but the real ones chirping in the meadow answered.

The patch of blood on his chest had spread and grown darker as we stood there. I wanted to do something, but I didn't know how to help him. And since he didn't seem able to see or feel me near him, I didn't know if any of this was real or just a dream I'd fallen into. I was somehow there, though, in this other world, even if that world didn't register my presence.

"Where are we?" I decided to try asking.

"Hell," said the young man after a pause, as if he'd heard me. His voice was so low no steam escaped his mouth. A second later, though, he said it again: "Hell. To hell with it," and I realized he was just talking to himself.

I put my hand on his shoulder, trying to reach across, the way Jarrod had shown me I could do, to put myself inside him. And when I managed to slip inside his mind, I pulled back quickly, shocked by the sensation of the bullet that had cut through his flesh. It nestled in his body, a hot, hard thing, burning and burning like an ember.

He looked up, his mouth open, not knowing what to do, not knowing how to feel about anything. The other men were either in hiding or running ahead to the village, gunfire blasting around them. *I should follow*, he thought. *I should go to the battle.* He tried to take a step in that direction, despite the broken bones in his foot, but before his second step, something appeared in his path, stopping him.

A silvery-white light floated in the field in front of us, moving up the path that crossed the field, coming toward us. The young man looked harder, squinting, and gasped when he saw a white stag emerge from the dark. A white stag with an enormous rack of antlers glinting in the night like a giant candelabra.

I shivered, not from the cold, but from a wave of awe that overwhelmed me as the stag came to stand not ten feet from us. It stopped near the edge of the woods where we waited with our backs against our tree, and looked at us for a brief moment before snorting and shaking its head from side to side as if it were angry, as if it were issuing some kind of challenge.

A moment later, the stag seemed to rise into the air as it jumped past us, so close I could feel its ivory fur brush against my skin. Then it fled into the dark woods behind us.

The young man sighed as he turned away from the burning village to look into the woods, where we could still see the white glow of the stag weaving among the tall silhouettes of trees. Instead of going toward the village, the young man decided to follow the stag's light into the woods. Holding his hand against the hole in his chest, he stumbled forward, the bones in his foot crunching beneath him as he groped after the trail of light that flickered in the white stag's wake.

We chased after the stag for what felt like an eternity but was probably only five or ten minutes. I held on to the young man's arm, tried to balance him, tried to help him carry himself forward. Just once he turned to me and seemed to see me beside him, peering through whatever veil came between us, and said, "Are you my guardian angel?"

"I don't know what I am," I whispered, which was true. "But I'm trying to help you."

When he stopped to catch his breath, which rattled and flapped in his lungs like a frightened bird in a cage, the stag stopped with him. It looked over its shoulder at us, waiting patiently, and the young man thought, *Damn you, quit playing with me.* When finally he gathered enough strength to resume the chase, the muscles in the stag's haunches flexed once more before it leaped, again, ahead of him.

In a small grove in the woods, we found the stag waiting, seeming to ponder the young man as he arrived breathing in ragged convulsions with blood drenching his clothes. The young man blinked as he met the stag's stare, as if he'd been waiting for this moment all of his life, as if Fate had conducted him to this time and place like an usher. The stag's eyes seemed to grow as the young man looked into them, becoming larger, rounder, darker. A person could walk into them like tunnels. He could hide in them like trenches, and no one, nothing, not shells, not gas or grenades, nothing would ever find him in there.

The young man took a step forward but fell as he attempted a second. A shallow stream trickled along the ground, winking with reflected light from the moon and stars above. The stream mirrored the glow of the white stag's antlers too as the stag lowered its head to the water, a cup of light blossoming in the night-soaked forest.

The young man looked where the stag looked, saw the glinting stream before him as a man lost in the desert will see water all around him, the thing that will quiet his convulsions, the thing that will quench his thirst.

Drink, the stag told the young man, and the tips of its antlers touched the water, dimpling the surface, turning the creek into a stream of pure white light.

The young man didn't know if he'd heard the stag or if the stag had somehow put its voice inside him, but he did as he'd been instructed. He crawled the last few feet to the bank of the creek, and there he leaned over to find his own reflection staring back at him. He drew closer to his own image, then even closer, until his face met the face in the water, the two merging into one, and then he opened his mouth to fill himself with himself.

He would die there ten minutes later, his body half in and half out of the creek, the reel of his life rattling to a halt, sputtering.

I looked away, helpless, put my hand to my forehead, and started to cry, even though I didn't know the guy. Started to wonder why I was there, and why I hadn't woken from this nightmare. Started to wonder if I'd be trapped here like a patient in a coma, dreaming this dream, whatever this dream was, for the rest of my life. A ghost forced to witness the lives of others without having one of my own.

And later, when I had time to think about it, I realized

that was what I'd been doing anyway. Going through life like a good zombie. Rise and shine, check off the boxes on the to-do list my dad always left me, then off to school, where I kept my head down and tried not to attract attention. An afternoon drive down back roads, looking for something I couldn't put a name to. A route to some place where maybe my true life existed. Then home again. Water and feed the cows. Dinner. Homework. Bed. Everything I did in the morning done in reverse this time.

The white stag stamped its hoof and snorted as I stood there trying to collect myself, and I looked up again, saw it standing only a few feet away. It dipped its head in my direction and I nodded in return, as if we were either old friends or else cautious, uncertain acquaintances. Then the stag did the most surprising thing. It knelt down on its front legs and spoke to me.

Let me return you to your proper home, the stag said. Its voice sounded in my head, the way the voice of the Living Death Tree seemed to come not from outside but inside me. *This is not your time,* it told me. *This is not your place. You have fallen outside of your own story.*

So I left the young man's body by the creek and climbed onto the stag's wide back, clutching its thick white neck to steady myself. When the stag heaved itself up onto all four legs again, I swayed for a moment, worried that I'd fall. Then it took off in a blink, jerking me backward as it carried me away, farther and farther, deeper and deeper, into the woods around us.

Dawn had arrived without my noticing, and the morning light glowed red and bloody above me. Within the woods, though, every branch and leaf and mushroom ring dripped with dark shadows. The white stag's hooves were as loud as a herd of cattle. On and on it ran, through brush and trees, until we burst out of the woods and arrived in the back pasture of my family's farm, back in Temperance, back in the twenty-first century, where Sugar Creek trickled beside us with a few ribbons of moonlight still swaying on its surface. It was night here, on this side of the world, in this time, in my own story, and the stag knelt once again to let me off.

Your body is in there, the stag said, turning its gleaming ivory rack toward the yellow farmhouse, which looked like a dollhouse from this distance. *Go to it. And be careful not to wander so far again. The world is full of stories. You can get lost if you aren't careful. You can lose yourself if you are unaware. And there are some spirits who would like nothing more than to lure you out of your world and into another.*

"I've already lost myself," I said, and turned my eyes to the ground, ashamed for some reason I wasn't able to name. Maybe it was because I didn't know the first thing about myself. Maybe it was because I didn't know my own story from someone else's. And worse, I didn't know if I could do anything about any of this.

The stag only pawed at the ground, its silver rack swaying slowly as it shook its huge head back and forth.

I will give you a piece of knowledge that may ease your worries, it told me. *You will find yourself again.*

94

Then it turned, slowly, as if it were a large ship changing direction in the middle of an ocean, and took off in a flash of light so blindingly white I had to raise a hand to shield my eyes.

☒

Inside the yellow farmhouse, I drifted upstairs to the room where my body waited in bed with one arm flung above its head. And beside the bed, my mother sat in the chair she'd pulled away from my desk. She was watching over me with her eyes closed, elbows propped on her knees, hands clutching a silver pocket watch that had once belonged to her father: a thing that rarely made a public appearance, since my mom kept it on the nightstand in her bedroom.

Her lips moved over and over, just barely, as if she were saying a prayer. Or maybe she was just repeating my name out of desperation, trying to call her son back to his lifeless body. Whatever it was, it sounded like a spell. It sounded like an incantation.

And then, as I walked the rest of the way in, she turned from the body in the bed to look at this other me standing in the doorway as if nothing were out of the ordinary.

"Now that you're back," she said without blinking, "I suppose we should have that talk."

chapter six

A MAP OF THE STARS

After I slipped myself back into my flesh like a hand fitting into a glove, flexing and stretching my muscles to reawaken, I opened my eyes, blinking over and over, trying to take in my room, which wavered around me like it too might be a vision. I was still reeling from what I'd just experienced, but I sat up in bed with my back against the cool headboard, my knees pulled up to my chest, arms gathered around them, hugging myself, glad to feel something real and substantial. Beside me, my mom cocked her head to the side, curious, and asked, "What's the first memory you have when you think of us? When you think of me and you together?"

I thought about her question for a minute, furrowing my brow as I concentrated, and for some reason, the usual white fuzziness that surrounded my memory whenever I tried to recall something wasn't making an appearance this time.

"The library," I answered a moment later.

"You loved the library," my mom said without skipping a beat, nodding, smiling fondly, clearly happy that I remembered this particular piece of my childhood—that I'd pick this one out when she asked me to think of a first memory—even if my memory of it was still pretty vague. "I used to take you there all the time," she said. "Tell me what you remember about going there. In fact, why don't you just show me?"

She held her hand out, palm up, while the other remained on her lap clutching the timepiece. I looked at her skin, pale in the moonlight falling through the window, unsure whether I wanted to do what she was asking. She *knew*. She knew about what Jarrod had shown me I could do. She knew and was now acting like it was somehow ordinary.

After a few moments passed without me moving, though, she raised her chin in what seemed like a challenging gesture and said, "All right, then. If you won't, why don't *I* show *you*?"

She leaned forward in her chair then, put her pale white fingers on my bare shoulder, and reached across.

※

It wasn't the library my mother showed me, though, at least not at first. Instead, she showed me a day not long after I'd turned thirteen. The day after Mr. Marsdale died.

All through school, the news was circulating. A heart attack while he was asleep the night before. *Blam*, his heart shuddered and he was gone like a snuffed-out candle. I sat through all the talk—in classrooms, in the cafeteria, on the bus ride home later that afternoon—listening to the ebb and flow of conversation around me, wondering if I'd somehow made it happen.

Because I'd seen something just the day before. Something that worried me. And because of that, I wondered if I had some kind of strange connection to Mr. Marsdale's death. I wondered if what I'd done was something more than a prediction of it.

A man in a black suit had come into our classroom the day before, had looked Mr. Marsdale up and down like a cattle buyer contemplating a possible purchase. But no one else had seen this. Just me. I realized that after I'd interrupted Mr. Marsdale during his lesson to say, "Mr. Marsdale, who's that man in the black suit standing beside you?" and everyone in the room had laughed at me behind their hands. I got a stern warning not to be disruptive. Then, later that night, Mr. Marsdale's heart stopped beating.

Somehow I felt like I'd done it, had made it happen. Would he have died if I hadn't seen the man in the black suit come to stand beside him? That awful man with stringy red hair and a beard that animals might have built nests in. He wore a wide-brimmed black hat with the smell of charcoal wafting off it, smoky and dark. Would Mr. Marsdale have died if I hadn't said anything about it? If I hadn't said out loud in class that I saw the man in the black suit standing right beside him?

My guts twisted throughout the school day, and when I got off the bus that afternoon, I ran into the house to complain to my mother. I told her that I couldn't go back there; I told her I felt sick and didn't belong there with everyone.

"What's the matter?" she asked, her hands gripping my shoulders to steady me, her eyes pinched, shaking her head in confusion. "Aidan, where is all this coming from?"

So I told her what I'd seen during history, how the man in the black suit had come into our classroom like anyone who worked at the school might have. Like he belonged there. I told her how he'd looked Mr. Marsdale up and down as if looking at a cow going to auction, as if he were evaluating the distribution of fat and muscle in Mr. Marsdale's body. Would he be a good buy? I told her how I'd tried to call Mr. Marsdale's attention to the man in the black suit, and how no one else but me could see him, and how the man in the black suit had looked straight at me and tipped his hat in my direction before exiting the room, leaving me shaking at my desk, nearly breathless.

When I finished, I looked up, choking on my tears a

little, to find my mother staring out the window over the kitchen sink, entranced by something in the distance, across the creek, over in the orchard. She didn't say anything right away, but finally she turned back to me and said, "He must not have told his story true, then."

"What do you mean?" I asked, blinking away my last tears.

"Mr. Marsdale had a chance," she said, "like any of us do." She stopped then, and her eyes started to look inward to a place where I wouldn't be able to reach her if she retreated any further. I had to prompt her to continue, asked her to go on, to keep her there in the room. "Are you telling your own story," my mother finally asked me, "or are you being told?"

I didn't know what she meant, though, so I didn't answer.

"One day Death will pay you a visit," she continued, "but if you can tell the story of your life before Death tells its version—if you can tell it true—you can maybe keep on living."

"Mr. Marsdale didn't tell Death his story?" I asked.

"He might not have known that he could," said my mother. "He might not have known how to. Most people don't know that trick anymore." She looked over at me standing in the corner, and it seemed as if a breath she'd been holding was suddenly released, filling the room with the scent of peppermint and coffee. "Now you know," she said, "and you can use that trick one day if you want to.

But the thing is, you have to tell your story true, and not everyone can do that."

"Why not?" I asked.

"Because telling the truth is the hardest thing a person can do."

The next day, she let me stay home from school, as if I were truly sick. It was a day spent watching her clean the house from top to bottom, dusting, washing clothes and dishes, vacuuming carpets, feeding cows, filling their trough—an old claw-footed bathtub—with water from a red rubber hose.

In the afternoon we went to the small grocery store off the town circle, where I watched her pick out things we needed. Cereal, oranges, flour and spices, cleaning products. She spoke to everyone we came across: the checkout woman, Margie Wallace; the bank manager, Mr. Keating; several women in the Temperance library, a one-room building with high, dusty shelves that surrounded an open area that held round tables where old ladies gossiped in whispers. They wore white gloves, as if they lived in a different era, as if it were still the forties and fifties of their youth and they were at a wedding party. They stroked my head, complimented my curls and green eyes as if I were a celebrity. But I shrank from their touch. They made me shiver.

"This one's yours, Sophia," one old lady said, holding my chin with the tips of her fingers so that I'd look straight up at her line-mapped face. "The eyes will tell it."

Another clucked her agreement, nodding her cloud of cottony hair. "Those eyes are yours," she said, "if I ever did see them." The women wore pearls and pastel dresses. They smelled of lavender and citrus, of medicine and dusty Bibles. When I pulled away from the old woman holding my chin, she looked at my mom and said, "Why, Sophia, he's sensitive, too. Isn't he?"

My mother nodded. She smiled proudly, brushing hair away from my forehead, and in the next moment she looked down at the floor, as if she was also somehow embarrassed.

My mom selected two books: one for herself, a mystery novel—her favorite vice—and one about dinosaurs for me. I'd gone through a dinosaur phase several months before, but I was now on to ancient Egypt.

"Ancient Egypt?" she said when she found me paging through a book of myths at the end of our visit. I nodded curtly. I was very serious about Egypt right then. Several nights before, I'd dreamed of a mummy climbing out of its tomb to chase me, and I'd concluded that I'd better get myself heavily informed about mummies in case the dream ever happened in real life.

Which it seemed my dreams could sometimes do. Sometimes, it seemed, my dreams could come to life right in front of me.

So we went to the nonfiction section and found a book about the gods of Egypt, Ra and Osiris and Isis and Nut. They had the best names of any gods I'd ever heard of. I liked the story of Osiris, how he was dismembered, how his body was cast to the corners of the earth, how his wife, Isis, journeyed through the world's darkness to retrieve his various parts to put him back together. I imagined her on that journey, alone, finding an ear, an eye, a leg or a finger, placing it in her pocket for safekeeping. One day she would have all of the pieces and she'd put him back together. He'd no longer be lost to her. It was all, in my mind, a ridiculously awesome thing to do.

I loved it.

We drove home that afternoon in silence, me already reading the book, my mother's attention on the road. From the spacey gaze in her eyes, though, I could tell that she was really elsewhere, in some other place and time beyond the car she drove.

When Toby came home from school later, he complained that I hadn't been forced to go back after my meltdown. My mother told him to hush. "You're both treated fairly," she said, "but sometimes people require different things for true fairness."

Toby didn't agree. "Aidan's spoiled," he said, before running upstairs, stomping all the way. And in a way, he was right. My mom favored me. Anyone could see that if they paid attention. When my mom looked at me, she saw a part of herself. I was hers, I somehow understood, just like the old lady at the library had told her. We saw things through the same eyes.

After my dad came home from work that evening, we

sat at the table to eat dinner as usual. Toby talked about the 4-H meeting he'd be attending later that week. He was going to choose a calf from my grandmother's stock after dinner, would raise it over the course of the next year as a project. I was still too young for 4-H, but the following year I'd get to raise a calf along with him. My dad wanted to see his boys raising cattle. He had hopes that one day we'd work the farm together, just like all of the Lockwood men before him. When he talked like that, though, my mom would shake her head and cast him a glance across the table.

"They aren't all meant for that" was all she'd say. Then she'd look down at her glass of wine like she could see the future forming in its bloodred liquid.

Sometimes my dad would argue. Sometimes he'd tell her she was just like her father, who Toby and I couldn't remember because we'd never met him. Our grandparents on our mom's side had died long before we were born, and even before that, my mom had once told Toby and me— after we asked why the house was full of our dad's family photos but none of hers—that she and her father had, as she put it, "had a falling-out." She said she had refused to speak to anyone in her family for nearly thirty years, and from that I learned early in life that my mom was not someone to cross. She could carry a grudge for eternity.

That night, my dad told my mom she was crazy to think she could see our futures spread out before us as if they were maps. "It's foolish," he said, "the way you think you can control everything." I remember thinking how odd it was that he'd accuse her of the very thing she'd just told him he was doing. Trying to decide our futures for us.

My mom didn't argue. She stopped talking and looked out the nearest window. This was how she'd get whenever she and my dad couldn't agree on something. And as she peered out the window at what seemed to be something far away, I felt like she might be doing exactly what my dad had said she couldn't: she was looking at our future selves as they rushed toward us. Here they were, the people we were becoming, about to knock on our front door, hoping they could undo the mistakes we were making at that very moment.

My mom trailed her fork through her mashed potatoes after she turned herself back to the table. She looked up every once in a while to answer a question my dad put to her, or to tell Toby it was his night to do dishes. I could tell she was in one of her moods now, as my dad called those times when she'd turn inward, out of rejection of whatever was going on in front of her, or because something had called her attention away from this world. But later, when I asked her if it was true, if she was in a mood, my mother said my dad didn't understand everything he was seeing.

"They aren't ordinary moods," she said. "They're moods that come on me when I have a presentiment. A message about something that's going to happen." She said that whenever she received one of these, good or bad, she'd always feel a little tired and confused for a while after. When I asked why she'd get tired from that, she said it was from carrying all of those people around with her.

"What people?" I asked.

"The people in the future. You, your daddy, Toby. Everyone in town. And others," she added mysteriously. "There will always be others coming," she said in the tone I knew meant she was trying to teach me something.

"Mom," I said, frightened by these other, mysterious people, frightened by the things she and I sometimes saw. "What are we?"

"What do you mean?"

"I mean, me and you. What are we?"

She pursed her lips, already disappointed with her answer. "Us?" she said, shrugging. "We're just like anyone."

When the sky darkened and stars began to appear, she took me outside to look up at them, tracing their alignments with one delicate fingernail. Hers were not patterns we'd learned in school, though; they weren't constellations I'd ever heard of. "That's the Rose Bearer," she said, pointing to what I'd thought was Cassiopeia. "And there's the Little Man, and that's the Oak Lord bringing him an acorn. And there—the one with its corner star blinking—that star is the Probable Stone."

"The Probable Stone?" I said. Somewhere in the nearby woods, an owl hooted. "I've never heard of that one."

She looked down and said, "You've never heard of the Probable Stone? What on earth are they teaching you at school, then?"

"Nothing useful," I said, and she laughed, knelt down, put one arm around my shoulders.

With her lips beside my ear, she said, "If you're ever lost and don't know how to get home, no matter how dark and lonely it gets, just look up at the Probable Stone and it will show you the way back."

"How can it do that?"

"Why, you just push it three times and tell it a secret rhyme."

"What secret rhyme?" I asked, eyes wide with wonder.

"This is my home," she said, turning me around to look her straight in the face, "and I know it. Even if I go away, it'll still be here. If I lose my way, it's your job to show it."

"Will it really work?" I asked, starting to grow skeptical.

"The Probable Stone has never failed me," said my mother. "Whenever I've needed it, it's always been there."

"When did you need it?" I asked. "When were you lost?"

"That's classified information, Mr. Lockwood," she said. "Just trust me on this one. Look up there and memorize that map of the stars. If you ever need to find me, look at that star right there, touch it three times, tell it the secret rhyme, and it'll show you the way home."

The vision ended, and as it disappeared into wisps of smoke inside me, my mother's hand left my shoulder. "There was a time," she said, "when I didn't keep things from you. But I can't keep you from being who you are any longer. I can see that now."

"Who am I?" I asked, hesitating, as if those words were a foreign language, as if I wasn't sure I was even asking the right question. I was still trying to understand the memories she'd shown me. That conversation where she'd talked about seeing the future and carrying people around inside her: it was like no other conversation I'd ever had with her. I could now see these new pieces of myself inside me, though, could recall the memories she'd just shown me, and I kept touching them, moving them around, trying to push them into the right places in my puzzle. Some snapped into place immediately, but others remained elusive, floating free in the empty space within my frame of patchwork memories.

"You're him all over again," my mom said, shaking her head like even she didn't want to believe what she was saying.

"Who?"

"Your brother," she said. "Your older brother Seth."

I stared at her for a while, unsure whether I should feel uncomfortable about my mom's thinking I was my dead brother reincarnated, or if I should seriously reconsider the idea of reincarnation. Especially now, seeing how everything else I thought I knew wasn't true. Could I be that boy in the framed photo that hung on the wall, that brother I'd never met, staring across the living room at my suicidal grandfather? Sure, we had the same green eyes, the same curly brown hair with flickers of my mom's auburn in it, but otherwise, that boy was a stranger to me.

"I don't mean that you're him, literally," my mom said when my concern must have shown on my face. "I mean that you're like him. He could see things too. But at a much younger age than you started."

"I don't understand," I said. "What's wrong with me?"

My mom shook her head and said, "Nothing. Absolutely nothing is wrong with you, sweetheart. You're fine. But there are things in this world that aren't fine at all. Like that man in the black suit you saw when you were little. There are things in this world that you can see that are dangerous, especially if they notice you watching them."

"The young soldier in my dream tonight?" I said.

"No, not him," my mother corrected me. "He's your great-grandfather on your father's side. And that wasn't a dream. That was D-day, the day itself. You went there, or were brought there somehow, maybe because you've been drinking alcohol tonight and it opened you up to the journey. Not a good idea, by the way, drinking, unless you know how to drink just enough to loosen up. Drink too much and things like what occurred tonight can happen."

"You knew I was drinking?"

My mom rolled her eyes. "You reeked of it when you came home. I could smell you a room away."

"And what was it that happened to me tonight, exactly?"

My mom held me in a steady, serious gaze. "You went back to another time and place, to someone you're connected to in the past. Your great-grandfather. You went there through the world's shadow."

"The white stag told me I fell out of my own story," I offered, and my mom nodded, as if, yes, of course the white stag had told me that. Only natural, really. Of course that was what happened.

"You're going to have to tell me more," I finally said, looking at her with a deliberately hard stare, trying to make her understand how much I needed her to talk to me about these things. "Otherwise, I'm going to go crazier than I am already."

"You're not crazy, sweetie," she said, drawing a firm line in the sand.

"I feel like it," I admitted. "I'm some psychologist's future famous case study in the making."

My mom laughed but waved away that idea. "I can tell you more," she said, taking a deep breath, sighing it out in the next moment. "But it's a long story."

"It's the weekend," I said, shrugging. "You have plenty of time to tell it."

chapter seven

SECOND CHANCES

"So what did she say?" Jarrod asked on Monday, after school was out and I'd caught him in the parking lot. He was afraid to speak to me after he'd revealed his secret. I could tell by the way he'd frozen when I called his name as he made his way to the bus instead of to my car like usual. I hadn't gone to his house over the weekend to talk about his confession. Not after riding the white stag. Not after having a dream that turned out to be a visitation, as my mother had later called it.

If I were to break it all down for Jarrod into the neatest of packages, instead of the ramble I went into after we drove to the lake, it would go something like this:

She said that I'd gone into something called the world's shadow, the back side of here and now, and witnessed something that happened to my great-grandfather. She told me that I come from a line of seers. She told me that my brother Seth had been able to see things too. She said he died because he saw something he shouldn't have. And she said that after I saw the man in the black suit back in the seventh grade, she put a blindfold of some kind over me. "A dust cover over certain memories and abilities," she'd called it, which I guess sounded nice, at least in theory. She did it, she said, to protect me from seeing anything that might hurt me.

"What could hurt you?" Jarrod asked after I'd caught him up on the state of my thoroughly screwed-up life.

"Oh, you know," I said, real casual. "Harbingers of death could mistake me for someone who's died and take me to the other side too early. That's what she called the white stag and the man in the black suit. *Harbingers of death.* I mean, what do you do with that? So anyway, you were right all along. Back when I was a kid, I saw some weird shit. I saw the man in the black suit getting ready to take Mr. Marsdale to Death."

"Whoa," Jarrod said as he leaned back on the causeway guardrail. Behind him, Mosquito Lake was calm. No waves chopped up and down today. The surface was a smooth skin of pewter water. "That's a lot to take in. Makes me want a cigarette just thinking about it."

I took a big breath and released it, then spread my hands in front of me, looking at the back of my fingers as if they belonged to someone else. "Yeah," I said. "I could use a cigarette too." I dropped my hands to my sides again and said, "There's nothing I can do about any of it. We're all just who we are in the end, aren't we?"

Jarrod turned to look at the lake. A single gull skimmed the surface, searching for easy prey. I hadn't meant to say something that would remind him of what he'd admitted a few days earlier, but there it was, his confession, out in the open again, if he wanted to talk more about it. And bringing that up sort of made us even, considering how he kept reminding me of how much weird shit I used to see but couldn't remember.

"I don't know," Jarrod said. He still hadn't turned back to me, so I watched his profile, his eyes downcast, his dark hair curling out from the sides of the baseball cap he wore backward. "I mean, something isn't right." He shook his head as he turned things over in his mind. "You saw things even after Mr. Marsdale died. I remember that. I was only around for another month or two after that happened, but that day in the park, when you showed me a vision of us still together in the future, that was a few *weeks* after Mr. Marsdale and the man in the black suit incident. So whatever she did to you, she didn't do it right away."

I shrugged. "It's been a while," I said. "Maybe my mom's got some of her own memories mixed up over time. In any case, she said she's been letting up on her *influence*—that's what she called it—lately. That it's okay for me to remember again, now that I'm older and able to take better care of myself. But she also said not to bother my dad or Toby about it. She said it'd be best not to disturb them."

"You got your big boy pants on now," Jarrod said, finally turning back to me, laughing. "But I'd still keep looking into things if I were you. I mean, she asked you not to talk to your own dad about it? That seems wrong. I don't want to sound mean or anything, but something about your mom bothers me."

"How can she possibly bother you?" I said, rolling my eyes a little. "You haven't even seen her since you've been back. Which reminds me. She wants you to come over. She invited you to dinner on Halloween, actually, but—"

"But you had other plans," said Jarrod, raising one corner of his mouth and pretending to adjust the fit of his cap by grabbing the bill and twisting it sideways a little.

"I had other plans," I said, grinning back, hoping that whatever tension he felt would start to fade now.

"Well," Jarrod said. One of his eyebrows arched, like the offer of dinner at my house was something he had to think about. "I guess I can do that. Just make sure not to leave me alone with your mom. I don't want you to come back into the room after five minutes and find that she's lobotomized me for my own good or anything."

"Shut up," I said, pushing him on the shoulder, and he got one last laugh in before he looked down at where my hand had touched his arm. When his eyes flicked back up to me, the other side of his mouth had curled too, just a little.

"So go ahead and give her a call," he said. "Tell her she's got a fine-looking young man with a sinful interest in her youngest son coming over, and to wear her pearls so she can clutch them at key moments in the evening."

I let Jarrod's flirtation go without comment, just laughed, shook my head, and told him he was an idiot. Then I pulled my phone out of my pocket to call home and make plans.

After I talked with my mom about dinner, we decided to go visit Jarrod's mom so he could let her know where he'd be when she got home from work later.

Times Square Café sat on the old town circle, just off the causeway, across from a small grocery store and a bait shop. It used to be an old Victorian inn called Diggers, back in the days when the lake wasn't a lake but a coal-mining village. There was said to be a ghost inhabiting the second-floor rooms, the ghost of a woman who was jilted by a miner, who had up and moved to West Virginia the day before their wedding without telling her. "The wedding dress," Jarrod's mom told us that day as she poured us coffee at the bar, "can't be removed. Anyone who's tried to throw it out finds it's returned the next day, hanging over the back of an old chair in the room directly above us."

We both looked up at the high ceiling, where a brass chandelier with crystals hanging off it swayed a little, shaking off dust to sift down toward us like snowflakes. This was the sort of place we had available as a hangout in Temperance: a diner named after one of the most famous intersections of one of the most famous cities in the world, but really it was just this ancient inn filled with kitschy furniture and claw-footed tables. My mom loved the place—she said it had character—but it gave me the creeps.

"Libby, do you care if I eat dinner over at Aidan's tonight?" Jarrod asked after we'd heard the Times Square Café ghost story to its tragic conclusion.

"That's fine by me," his mom said, not blinking. I, however, did a lot of blinking when I heard Jarrod call her by her first name. "Make sure to thank Mrs. Lockwood," she added. "And make sure not to overstay your welcome."

Mrs. Doyle started to sort silverware then, and Jarrod said, "Yes, ma'am," which surprised me even more after he'd just got done calling her by her first name. Then Mrs. Doyle swung around to put the silverware tray behind the bar, and her hair, long and dark like Jarrod's, swayed like a curtain.

She looked younger than I remembered. Less worn out and ruined than the woman I recalled coming to school for a fourth-grade open house with "a hangover the size of a tractor"—she had told our mousy teacher, Mrs. Burroway—and a small flask of whiskey she kept taking out of her purse, then putting back when she realized where she was and what exactly she was doing.

"Don't worry," I said. "I'll get Jarrod back in time to do his homework."

Libby laughed, one short, sharp *ha*, and said, "This one? Homework? All I can do is hope you'll be a good influence on him, Aidan. If he hadn't been the star pitcher for his school up in Cleveland, I'm not sure he'd have been given as many second chances as he's gotten used to having."

"Everyone deserves a second chance," Jarrod said, twirling a spoonful of cream into his coffee. His mom looked at him, her eyebrows raised, halfway between offended and guilty-as-charged.

"Yes, everyone deserves a second chance," she said with her voice lowered a little to challenge him. "But it's also good if everyone does their part to change their bad habits."

Before their jabs became a full-blown battle, the café's front door swung open, and the bell above jingled its old-fashioned greeting. A couple of white-haired guys came in, saying, "Hey, Libby," like they were good friends, and waved from the other end of the room in all its dark-wood-and-ornamental-plaster glory. When I turned back, Jarrod's mom was already moving in their direction with a notepad, slipping a pen out of her apron pocket.

"Why does she stay here?" I asked, once she was out of earshot. "She could make more money waiting tables out in Niles."

"It's close to home," said Jarrod, lifting his cup. "So she saves on gas. And more important, they don't serve liquor here. Libby doesn't even want to carry it out to someone else on a tray."

"I'll give her one thing," I said. "She's disciplined."

"Has to be." Jarrod watched his mom smile with the old men at the other end of the room, laughing at their crusty jokes like they were actually funny. Who knows? Maybe they were. "It's why she wants me to be more disciplined too," he added.

"About drinking?" I asked.

"About *everything*," Jarrod said. He spun around on his stool to face me. He had the same eyes as his mom, like I had my mother's. But where my eyes sparked green, his were dark and murky. "She wants my grades up, my pitching impeccable, and for me to get a college scholarship at the end of the year."

"She's your mom," I said, as if that explained everything. "She wants good things for you."

Jarrod accepted that without comment, and a minute later his mom slipped behind the counter to fill cups for her table. As she poured the coffee in a careful stream, Jarrod said, "Hey, remember when you went to Aidan's mom a while back to ask about your future?"

I stiffened in my seat, and it looked like Libby did the same. She stopped pouring, straightened her back, and glared as if some man had made an unwanted advance on her. "I do remember that," she said, nodding curtly. "Why do you ask?"

"We were just talking about it," Jarrod said, nodding toward me, making me an accomplice in whatever game he'd decided to play here. "What was it his mom told you again?"

"Jarrod." Libby shook her head, wincing. "It wasn't anything. Not what you're thinking, at least." Then she turned to me, as if I had asked the question. "When I got out of the center in Liberty a few years ago," she said, "I was feeling pretty down, as you can imagine. Your mom was real understanding, that's all. She came over a few times to check in on me. Always exactly at times I needed someone to talk to. And she told me not to worry. My stars were looking good, she said. She was being a friend, that's all. Jarrod makes it seem like we were two witches brewing up some kind of magic in the kitchen."

She laughed, and I laughed with her, but Jarrod only grinned, like his mom and I were the foolish ones. Then he brought his cup of coffee up to his lips to sip at it.

"Anyway," said Libby, "I can't talk, boys. We're starting to get the early dinner crowd. The old folks like to get it out of the way before the place gets busy. Jarrod, I'll see you at home later. Aidan, it was good to see you, honey. I just saw your mom the other day, but tell her hi for me anyway."

"I will," I said, and Libby winked at me as she walked away to take care of people.

"*I will,*" Jarrod mimicked after his mom was far enough away. I rolled my eyes at him. "Seriously," he said. "What my mom just told you? That's nothing like how she described it a month ago when I moved home."

119

"How did she describe it then?"

"She said your mom saved her life right when she was about to give up hope. She said your mom took her hand in hers and showed her a future my mom could continue to hope for. It sounded like what you do when you . . ."

"Reach across?" I said.

Jarrod looked down at my hand, which lay on the counter near his.

"Yeah," he said, looking up again, blinking out a small spark of his own nearly extinguished hope. "When you reach across."

"When did she change her story, then?" I asked.

"That's the thing," said Jarrod. "Just a week or so ago. After your mom stopped in here to pay her a visit."

When we pulled down my driveway twenty minutes later, my mom was already on the front porch, waving as if she'd been there since I called, waiting to welcome home a war-ravaged soldier. I hadn't seen her so enthusiastic in a long time. Usually she kept to herself, stayed at home as much as possible, only went out for groceries and to run important errands, made rare expeditions to visit old friends like Jarrod's mom every now and then. When Toby and I were younger, she'd been more outgoing. Never missed a parent-teacher conference, never missed a chance to help out at a bake sale, and took us once a week to the library. Now here she was, a virtual hermit, coming out to greet

Jarrod with a big hug and an "Oh my goodness, you have grown so tall, young man! I can't believe it!"

Seriously, it was cringe-worthy. It was like she was . . . *performing* or something.

It was not only unbelievable because she was usually reserved, but also because not three nights ago she'd seen my spirit outside of my body, returning home after riding a white stag during a war where I'd witnessed my great-grandfather die. Now, suddenly, she wanted to pretend everything was warm, homespun happiness.

Once we got the pleasantries over with and went inside, she had us sit at the kitchen table so we could continue talking as she cooked. It was the time of the day when I usually found her there with her tablet, absorbed in the news of the world filtered through her online portal. But today, she'd already started to prepare a meal. The house smelled of lemon chicken, my favorite, and she'd pulled out a bottle of white wine. It was already uncorked and breathing on the dining room table in an ice bucket.

"So tell me what's up," she said. Before we could answer, though, she opened the oven door to peek at the pecan pie and added, "It's so good to have you back home again, Jarrod."

"Thanks, Mrs. Lockwood," Jarrod said. He dipped his head in her direction politely, even though her back was turned to him. "It's good to be back."

"I'm sure it is." She closed the oven and came over to sit with us at the table then, where she put her hand on

Jarrod's forearm and said, "I'm so glad you're home with your mom now. She's missed you something awful."

"We're doing good again." Jarrod nodded briefly, then moved the arm my mother had been patting to scratch his chin. When he lowered his hand again, he said, "I always thought I'd find myself back here someday anyhow."

"Really?" My mom raised her eyebrows a little. "What made you think that? I would think that most young people who leave this place don't ever look back."

Jarrod didn't say anything for a second. He just met my mom's waiting stare. I could see him trying to figure out an answer. He knew she was more than an ordinary mother making dinner. He knew she'd done something to change the way his mom remembered things recently, same as she'd messed with the memories of her own family. And he knew what my mom had told me about harbingers of death and the world's shadow. So there my mom sat, lifting a cup of coffee to her lips, sipping it while keeping her eyes locked with Jarrod's.

"I guess," he finally said, "that living in a city didn't really take with me."

"Interesting," said my mom. Then she stood and went to pull plates down from a cupboard. Looking over her shoulder as she reached up to the shelves, she said, "I've always felt I wouldn't want to live anywhere but Temperance. We must be kindred spirits that way, you and me."

Jarrod gave her a friendly grin. But when she turned back to the cupboard, he looked at me and made a face that said *Your mom is a total alien.*

Twenty minutes later, my dad and Toby came through the back door, knocking their work boots off in the mud-room, hanging up their coats. When they stepped up into the kitchen and saw Jarrod at the table between my mom and me, my dad got a big smile on his face and said, "Why, Mr. Doyle! It's been a while!" and held his hand out for Jarrod to shake.

My brother followed suit, and before long they were all sitting around the dining room table as my mom and I brought out the food. Toby had already caught Jarrod up on the local high school baseball scene, which Toby still followed. He said he'd heard Jarrod was pitching some mean games up in Cleveland, and Jarrod said, "Well, I've got a good fastball, but I need to work on my curve."

"Everything straight down the center, no looking back, just like your father," said my dad, grunting afterward. Jarrod was the kind of son he could have easily been proud of, like Toby. "Josh was always a straight shooter," he said, "in life and in baseball. How's he doing, by the way?"

Jarrod sort of flinched at the mention of his dad, or maybe he flinched at the mention of being *straight down the center* when in reality he wasn't straight at all. But I guess you wouldn't notice a flinch that slight if you didn't know his dad had thrown him out because he'd been caught making out with a guy in his bedroom. I felt bad, sitting there, knowing his secret. It seemed to gather behind him now, like a dark cloud he hoped no one would notice. But I did. I noticed. Every day I saw his secret follow him around, like some mangy mutt he'd been too nice to.

Jarrod glanced my way, as if he was worried I'd tell everyone, but I looked down at my plate, where my mom's chicken and rice waited, and let him recover. I knew the truth about why he'd come back, but I also knew something else: that he wanted me. That he wanted me to want him back in a way I wasn't sure I could. It was almost as if I *had* to not look at him now, knowing all that, so he could go on being normal with my family.

He told my dad that his father was doing fine—still working at the car factory, still going to Indians games, despite record losses—and when he was finally back in a good rhythm of talking about all things baseball, I looked up again, slowly, to watch him when he wouldn't notice me looking.

He was so animated, not hesitant, like he'd been initially. I found myself watching the curve of his jaw as he spoke, the line sharp as a sickle. And the way he kept brushing his hair from his eyes. How he waved his fork around to illustrate whatever he was talking about. He was . . . I didn't know. I wasn't sure how to express in words about what I felt right then. Especially about another guy. For as long as I could remember, I'd assumed that one day I'd run into some girl who jarred me out of my haze—maybe on one of those after-school drives down the back roads of Temperance, or maybe once I'd discovered my true destination during one of those drives, the home I was looking for—and everything for the rest of my life would just fall into place, like it does for most people.

But here I was, feeling something else, a vague and possibly dangerous emotion. I wasn't on one of my back road drives, though, and there was no girl waking me up from the spell of confusion I'd been under. There was this guy instead, this guy who had called my name in the hallway, this guy who had made me look up and realize that nothing around me was what I thought it was. Not even myself.

It was while I was staring at Jarrod, trying to sort through those unexpected and confusing feelings, that I noticed something other than me was out of place in that room: a shadow, a real shadow, that didn't belong to anyone in our house.

At first it seemed like the light in the room dimmed, as if the flow of electricity through the house was about to wink out. And then the shadow suddenly slipped out of a corner of the room to come and stand behind Jarrod's chair. At first it was just this dark, vaguely human shape, but as I continued to watch, the shadow took on full definition, a hazy layer of color, developing like an old-fashioned photograph, antique and blurry, until I could make out the figure of a woman.

I opened my mouth, but I couldn't manage to say anything as the shadow put her hands on Jarrod's shoulders and leaned down to whisper in his ear. He just sat there, talking with my father and brother as if he didn't feel her behind him, as if he couldn't hear her spinning her voice inside him, the voice she sometimes spun inside me.

Who was she? And what was she telling him? If she

had her way, would Jarrod eventually wake to find himself standing under the Living Death Tree in the orchard?

"What are you doing to him?" I finally managed to say.

And everyone at the table turned to look at me.

"Aidan?" my dad said, his face a mess of confusion. "What are you talking about?"

The woman's shadow disappeared in an instant, like smoke clearing after a magic trick, and my mom, looking more startled than anyone else in the room, said, "Yes, just what are you talking about, Aidan?"

Toby held a forkful of chicken in midair and looked at me like I was a crazy person. But when I turned to Jarrod, he only looked at me with his dark steady eyes, undisturbed by my outburst, waiting to hear what I'd say next. And I knew right then that whatever I said, he'd be on my side.

"It's just," I said, trying to think of an alternate explanation for my outburst, since the truth would not have gone over well with anyone but my mom, and not even her, really, since it would have brought up the sort of things she'd asked me not to mention to my dad and brother. "It's just that you guys are talking Jarrod's ears off. Give him some breathing room, or he probably won't come back to visit."

Jarrod laughed at this answer, and the tension in the room evaporated. "Oh, don't worry," he said. "I'll be back, as long as your mom promises to make dinner again. This is delicious, by the way, Mrs. Lockwood."

My dad laughed too, now that he'd been prompted to find my outburst humorous. And with that, I knew I'd escaped what could have been an explosive moment.

My mom turned her attention to Jarrod now, saying that he was quite the charmer and that she'd make him a meal whenever he wanted. "As long as you can guarantee that my son won't bite everyone's heads off in the middle of dinner," she added, turning to raise her eyebrows at me, as if she couldn't believe my behavior. Then she speared a piece of broccoli with her fork, fast and sharp, like a hunter going in for the kill.

I let the comment go. And I waited. Waited to get through the rest of dinner. Waited to get through dessert. Waited to be excused from chores that night, since I had a guest over, so Jarrod and I could go up to my room to hang out like we were completely normal seventeen-year-olds, away from everyone else for the evening.

"What was that all about?" Jarrod asked after I'd closed my bedroom door behind us a little later. "Something raised your hackles back there, didn't it?"

I slipped my hands into my pockets and looked out my bedroom window at the dark line of trees behind the pasture, where I'd exited the woods on the back of a white stag a few nights before. "Yeah," I said, nodding. "I saw something down there. In the room with us."

"What was it?" Jarrod asked. I could feel him step

closer as I stood with my back to him, heard the creak of floorboards beneath his feet, as if he were sneaking up on me like the shadow had snuck up on him.

"There was a woman down in the room with us," I said. "I saw her doing something to you. I don't know how to explain it. She came out of the corner to stand behind you. She leaned down and whispered something in your ear. That's when I freaked out at the table."

"You're kidding me," Jarrod said. I could almost feel his breath on the back of my neck as he formed his words behind me.

I shook my head. "No," I said. "She went away after that, but I know what I saw. She was doing something to you. She was . . . *telling* you something. But in whispers. I couldn't hear her."

Moonlight glinted on the dewy November grass, so that it sparkled like a field of stars below my window. I thought of the Probable Stone, the star my mom had pointed out in the memory she'd given back to me. I wanted to find it right then, to touch it, to ask the star to take me home again, wherever home was. Because where I was didn't feel like home any longer. It couldn't be home, so full of mismatched memories and shadows that hovered in corners. My house was haunted. But by who, or what, I didn't know.

Sometimes it felt like it was maybe me—my old self, the one I'd forgotten—doing the haunting. Waiting for me to turn around and see who I used to be.

"There's no one else for me to trust," I said. "Not even my family. I've never been able to talk to my dad. And even though I love my brother, we've never been really close, you know? And my mom. Well—" I stopped there for a moment, shaking my head and wincing a little, not wanting to feel the hurt and anger that welled up whenever I thought about her these days. "I don't know who she is anymore," I continued. "There's just you. You're the only person who doesn't feel like a stranger right now. Even though I haven't seen you in years, even though I can't remember everything about us, I can feel you inside me, in all the memories I can't recall anymore. There's just you."

I couldn't face him as I said those things. It was too hard to say something that made me feel that vulnerable. So I kept looking out the window, where in the glass I could see a reflection of Jarrod's face hovering over my shoulder.

"I'm glad you can trust me, Aidan," he said. "But if we're going to be completely honest with each other, I have something else to tell you."

"What?" I asked, hoping it wouldn't be some other huge problem for me to figure out. I had enough of those to handle.

"I told you that my dad kicked me out because he caught me with another guy."

"Yeah?" I said.

"Well, that's true. But it wasn't really completely innocent on my part."

"What do you mean?"

"I mean," said Jarrod, "that I set myself up to be caught that night."

"Why?" I asked. I could see my own brow furrowing in my reflection in the window.

"Because," said Jarrod, "my dad wouldn't let me move back in with my mom, even though she's been clean and on track for a while now. And I needed to get back here somehow. To help you, if I could. So I brought that guy home after picking him up outside a club one night, and I made sure it was when my dad would be coming home from his night shift. I made sure we were . . . well, you know, not quiet. So my dad would come in and see us like that."

"How did you know I'd need your help?" I asked, shaking my head, unable to comprehend why he'd go so far out on a limb for me. Unable to comprehend how he even knew I'd need him.

"Because one of the things you showed me when we were thirteen was this time in your life, when you wouldn't know yourself any longer. You didn't understand how it would happen, but you knew it would. You showed it all to me. And you asked me to come help you remember things if I could."

"You're kidding," I said.

"I'm not," said Jarrod. "For a while after my dad moved us to Cleveland, I'd think about you and all that stuff. With each year that passed, I started to tell myself maybe

I'd imagined all the weird things you were able to do and see, all the things you'd shown me. But at the end of this summer, I dreamed about you, and I hadn't done that in a long time. When I woke up, I couldn't get the dream out of my head. I felt like you'd sent it to me, like a message. A few weeks passed, and I kept having dreams about you. And I saw you like you are now, not like the thirteen-year-old I'd left behind. So I knew they were more than ordinary dreams. That's when I brought that guy home so my dad would discover the truth about his perfect son and send me to live with my mom since he couldn't stand to look at me any longer."

"And here you are," I said.

"And here I am," said Jarrod.

I turned around quickly to tell him what an idiot he was for taking that kind of a risk, and he was right there, his face inches from mine, waiting for me, waiting for this moment, like maybe all those years ago I'd shown him this moment happening too, and he'd positioned himself to be ready for it. His warm breath fluttered against my lips, and it smelled of peppermint.

"I saw this moment in a vision you showed me once, a long time ago," he said now, confirming my suspicions. His voice was low in his throat, almost like he was frightened of what he was saying. His eyes were dark, and something in them glittered.

I struggled with how close we were, with how I was almost pressed up against the window with only an inch or two between us. But I managed to overcome my fears and tell him what I had to.

"If I showed you this exact moment years ago," I said, "then you know what to do next, don't you?"

I could feel my body trembling and tried to calm it.

Jarrod nodded, but he didn't do what I thought he would, not right away. Instead, he said, "Are you sure about this?"

And I nodded, closed my eyes like that might help me go through with it blindfolded. I'd been blindfolded for years by then anyway. I was used to not seeing.

"I don't know," Jarrod said a second later. "You seem afraid."

"I *am* afraid," I admitted, but I opened my eyes again, looked at him for one long moment.

"There," he whispered now. "That's better."

Then he put his hands on my cheeks and leaned in to kiss me.

There was a moment in that kiss where I felt like I'd been thrown over the side of a ship into the depths of the ocean, and I split into two people: the me who'd been thrown overboard and the me watching myself falling down and down through the dark blue water, unconscious, floating, my arms flung out like a jellyfish, formless, my eyes closed, drifting down and farther down to the bottom of an endless nothing.

I'm going to drown, I thought. *I'm going to lose myself entirely.*

And then my drowning body opened its eyes, looked

from side to side, saw the glimmering of sunlight filtering from above, and began to swim toward it, pulling upward and farther upward in long strokes.

I opened my eyes an instant later, inhaling deeply as Jarrod and I pulled away from each other.

"What do you think?" he said, blinking his dark eyes, stroking my cheek with one fingertip. "Is this okay?"

I could have answered him with words. I could have said "Yes, it's okay," and "It's more than okay."

But instead, I just nodded, put my hands on his cheeks like he'd put his on mine, and threw myself overboard a second time.

chapter eight

IN THE
WORLD'S SHADOW

November would be good. I kept telling my-self that it *had* to be good after the insanity of October. So life wasn't what I thought, I told my-self. So what if I could sometimes see into the fu-ture or the past? So what if I could unintentionally slip into something my mother called the world's shadow if I wasn't careful? So what if I'd gotten up on the back of a harbinger of death, as my mother called the white stag, and rode it home through time and space? So what if I'd seen another har-binger of death walk into my seventh-grade class-room on the day he planned to claim the life of my teacher, and couldn't remember because my mom had hidden some of my own memories from me? So what if I'd made out with a guy in my bedroom while my family watched television in the room below?

So what?

November would be good, I told myself. It had to be. Otherwise, I was going to self-combust.

Over the last few weeks, the leaves of Temperance had changed from yellow and red to the deep brown of late autumn. Throughout the day, the wind would strip them from the trees, one by one, and float them through the air until they gathered at the foot of our porch steps, spread them across the expanse of the high school parking lot, or line them up along the windowsills of houses. Leaves got caught beneath windshield wipers, and whenever rain came and I turned the wipers on, the leaves would fly up and away after being released, to drift through the air like paratroopers.

Wherever I looked, it was a golden-brown landscape I moved through.

Winter was coming down the line, though. I knew it when my dad and Toby took a day off work to go hunting and came back with a young buck, which they hung from the basketball hoop on the front of our garage to drain its blood, staining the gravel beneath the hoop a sticky black for weeks to come. And I knew it when my mom started to decorate the house for the coming holidays.

Jarrod and I spent the first half of November trying to figure each other out. Since he understood what we were doing together better than I did, I let him take the lead. And because of what my mom had done—cut me off from parts of myself—I felt like I was speaking a foreign language. *You, me, this thing between us.* I didn't always know what to do or how to do it, but I moved toward this feeling Jarrod created in me just by being near him. I touched his chest. Looked into his eyes. He stared back, and his lips were rough against mine.

This wasn't how it was supposed to be, though, was it?

Nothing, *nothing* I'd been told—by my family and teachers, by books and TV—none of it meant much to me any longer.

And I had to figure out a way to live with my mom without hating her for messing with my head and lying to me, even though she said it was for my own protection. What a *parent* thing to say. That excuse, like everything else, didn't mean much to me.

"Let's take it slow," I told Jarrod, even though I wanted to pack a bag and hit the road, ride to some other place where I could kiss him on a street corner. Go someplace where we could figure each other out without worrying that anyone was looking at us, staring. Places like that existed. Temperance just wasn't one of them. It was hard to ignore how different life here was from what we saw on TV and the Internet. Guys and girls were the norm here. If there was anything other than that, I'd never seen it. It was hard not to think that the right life for us was probably elsewhere.

"Don't worry," Jarrod said, stroking my arm, raising goose bumps. He took my hand, looked at me through the locks of hair falling across his eyes, and said, "I'm not going anywhere."

But how could I know that for sure? Hadn't he gone away before? And hadn't my mom made me forget important things? It seemed to me that nothing could be certain, that people couldn't be trusted, not even your own family. Life could change your circumstances and whisk you away, or else someone could do something horrible to you, maybe without you even realizing it. And when you did realize it, they'd say, *It was for your own good.*

"It's just that I don't know how to be myself," I said. I was holding on to his hand like if I didn't, I might float up through the air, into the clouds and into outer space, and then I'd keep on floating until I reached a planet with a gravity strong enough to hold me. This world, this town, my family, it all felt like I could put my hands right through it. Like there was nothing here but smoke and mirrors.

"You don't have to know how to be yourself," Jarrod said, running his thumb across my knuckles. "You just *are* yourself. You don't think it. You just feel it."

"But everything I feel," I said, "none of those feelings can be real if I've been lied to. That's what she's done to me. She's made my whole life into a lie."

"She messed up," Jarrod said, shrugging. "All of our parents do. They think they're doing good things for us, and sometimes they are. But other times, they're doing things that are just convenient. I'm sure my mom used to think one more sip of whiskey would calm her nerves so she could take better care of me. I'm sure my dad thought by kicking me out, he'd kick the queer right out of me. People fuck up, Aidan. Your mom's no different just because she's—I don't know. What the hell is she? Did she explain that to you, at least?"

"You mean, what the hell are *we*," I said. "Her and me both." I wanted him to remember that I was as strange as she was so he didn't blind himself to that and then later change his mind about me. "And no." I shook my head. "She didn't explain any of it. Said she doesn't know what we are, just that we're like anyone. Said she thinks most people can do what we do, if they would only let themselves."

Jarrod made a face like what I was saying was pure garbage.

"Yeah," I said. "She's still lying. I know she knows more, she just won't tell me."

"Maybe it really is for the best, then," Jarrod said, sitting up against his headboard and stretching out his arms. He'd been lying beside me for the past hour, working me through tangled feelings, probably hoping we could do something far more interesting. But he listened to me; he asked questions.

"How can it be for the best?" I asked. "You're starting to sound like her now."

"I don't know, Aidan." He got out of bed, running his

fingers through his hair. "It's just that whatever's happening here, it's big. Maybe it's best not to know everything. I know that sounds like a cop-out, but you're already freaking out about what you do know. Finding out more might be enough to crack you." He came to stand near where I sat on the edge of his bed, bent down on one knee, then put his hand in my hair to ruffle it a little. "And I don't want to see you break," he said. "Not after just getting you back again."

It was weird to find myself in this position. Especially with my family. Not because I was secretly having a relationship with Jarrod while everyone assumed we were just friends, but because of the secret I kept for my mom. "Don't bring up any of the things I've shared with you to your dad or brother" was what she'd said after I'd ridden home on the back of a white stag, when she'd finally talked openly about the things I was starting to see and hear that autumn.

"But don't they already know?" I'd asked.

"Toby doesn't," she'd said, shaking her head vigorously. "He never had the sight you have, not to that degree, so it's best to just leave him be. Your father once knew about all of this, yes." She'd looked down at her hands, where her fingers slowly twisted together in her lap, fidgeting.

"What do you mean, *once knew*?"

And she had looked up with her lips pursed, unable to

meet my eyes, and said, "I helped him forget some things. The same way I did with you."

"Mom," I'd said.

But she'd hushed me. "It's better this way," she said. "Our lives are much better separated from the things I hid from you and your father. Please, Aidan. Help me keep it this way. I just want us all to be happy."

Grudgingly, I'd agreed. What else could I have done, really? Run and told my brother I'd seen our great-grandfather in the war that killed him? Run and told my dad that my mom had somehow made him forget things, that she'd done something to make him remember his life differently from the way it had actually occurred? They would have looked at me like I was crazy.

So the days passed as if they were normal, and then Thanksgiving came around just in time for my family to really get some good practice at being ordinary. We spent that day in the usual way—watching the parade on television, eating turkey, mashed potatoes, gravy, stuffing—like any average American family, even though my mom and I sat across the table from each other withholding a secret from my dad and brother while we ate slices of pumpkin pie. Our eyes met every so often, but my mom was always the first to look away, which made me realize just how much she required my silence.

It was only a couple of weeks later, when everyone had just gotten used to the idea of December, that the house phone rang in the middle of the night. Across the hall, I heard my dad's voice, thick with sleep, say, "Snow? Really? That much? This early?" And his voice kept going up and up as he spoke, drifting across the space between us, slipping beneath my doorway, like the voice of the Living Death Tree seemed to manifest right there in my room sometimes, a disembodied presence.

Snow usually didn't fall this early in December, and never that much when it did. But when I got up and went to the window, sure enough, it was falling fast and thick over the fields and the back pasture. It must have been falling like that for hours, too, because the ground was covered and my car had become this amorphous whiteness sitting in front of the garage. I looked down at my phone: it was five in the morning and the town was already buried in nearly a foot, according to my local weather app.

When I heard my dad buckling his belt and zipping up his coat, I left the window to go downstairs, arriving just in time to see him close the front door behind him. Snow still floated in the entryway where he'd been standing. The flakes hung in midair for one long moment, almost suspended in time, before they drifted to the floor and turned into drops of pearled water.

My mom, too, was awake already. I found her in the kitchen, sitting at the table with a glass of water, her hair draped over her shoulders in uncombed strands. When I first came in and saw her under the fluorescent glare of the kitchen light, the fine lines that crowded the corners of her eyes seemed to cut deeper than usual. A bit of makeup usually hid the age that had crept up on my mom over the past few years, but without that polish she looked more worn down than I was used to seeing her.

"You should go back to bed," she said, putting her glass down when she saw me in the doorway. "They're going to cancel school soon anyway."

She was right. The house phone rang again not twenty minutes later. My mom took the call, listening to the recorded message from the principal, even though she already knew what was coming.

Before she'd even had a chance to shout the news to me from the kitchen, the weatherman on the news station I'd put on in the living room predicted that the snow would keep coming for the next few days. And after hearing that, in true Midwestern mother fashion, my mom decided we'd better stock up on necessities before things got worse, and she drove off ten minutes later, headed for the grocery store, where I was sure a mass of Temperance's parents were already gathering.

The first night of any string of winter days my dad was gone because of work was almost always a magical experience, at least initially, because his absence let the rest of us do whatever we wanted. Toby would watch TV without having to fight with my dad over the remote. My mom would open a bottle of wine and lie in bed reading a mystery novel, sipping from her glass until the bottle was empty. Me, I'd wander down into the basement, a space we usually avoided because my dad kept his woodworking machines and taxidermy tools down there and he didn't want us messing around with them. These were hobbies he indulged in whenever he had free time. I liked to go down there when he wasn't around to examine the things he made below the floors where we lived out our daily lives. Running my fingers along the leg of a stool still clamped on the lathe, stroking the back of my hand against the fur of a deer's preserved muzzle, both made me feel like I was somehow trespassing, but also like I was able to understand something about my dad, who was quiet and didn't share his thoughts with anyone too readily, unless he was angry, and then everything he thought, good or bad, came spilling out of him. The things he made in the basement were like hieroglyphs found in an Egyptian tomb, and I ran my fingers over them, hoping to somehow know him better.

After the first day of snow, he'd usually come home and the roads would be clear and everyone's lives would go back to normal. We'd eat dinner and he'd fight with Toby over the TV, and my mom would only have one glass of wine at dinner.

This snowstorm, though, was different. The first night passed in that magical absent-dad way, but in the morning, when he hadn't come home to pick up Toby, my mom called the roads department, worried. No one was there to answer her call, though. The answering service came on instead, telling her to leave her name and number, saying that someone would be in touch as soon as possible. They were working as fast as they could.

She called my dad's cell phone afterward, and luckily he answered. "The snow won't quit," he said. "Me and the other guys have our work cut out. Stay home. Tell Toby not to answer his phone if a supervisor calls. Or else you answer and tell them he's sick. I don't want him on these roads."

When another day passed without my dad coming home, my mom began to stop in the middle of doing things. She'd look out a window suddenly, as if she'd just heard my dad's truck pulling into the driveway, but who knows what she saw out there. Phantoms, maybe. It was never my dad. The driveway was always empty.

Toby got the tractor started on the third day and drove it fifteen miles to the roads department, ignoring my mom's pleas for him to do as his father said and stay home. A few hours later he returned, covered in a layer of frost that had formed on him as he drove out in the open air. Looking like a snowman as he stood before us in the kitchen, he said, "All the crews have been called in and are overnighting it. There are a bunch of trees down, and the roads are almost impassible in some places. Dad said he'd be back as soon as he's able."

Which made my mom sigh, relieved to know that he was okay.

When he didn't come that night, though, when my mom had to later pack his dinner away in the refrigerator, her

144

forehead started to crease with concern again. I began to worry too. Jarrod had texted several times over the course of that day to say, "Hey, your dad just drove past my place with his plow," letting us know that he was out there in the world, safe, doing his job. But now those occasional notifications were cold comfort.

On the fourth day, my dad called near midnight to tell my mom that the storm seemed like it was never-ending, and that was when she and I stayed up together, avoiding the stare of my suicidal grandfather, watching the hands of my grandma Bennie's old cuckoo clock slowly sweep across the hours.

"This isn't natural," my mother said to finally break our silence. She looked out the front window at the rolling hills of snow, at the buried bushes, at the trees sheathed in cases of glinting ice. Everything glinted under the cold glare of a full moon. We were like those small figures of people in snow globes, I thought, trapped in a tiny town under glass.

"What do you mean?" I asked her.

"I mean, someone's done this," she said. "Someone's wished this into being."

"What?" I asked again. It was the first time she'd talked openly—without any coded references—since she'd made me promise not to tell anyone about the things I'd been hearing and seeing since October. I was hoping I could find out more now, while an emergency distracted her from keeping her secrets.

"There's a wish behind all of this," she said matter-offactly, as if she were my physics teacher talking about gravity. "A wish that comes from sorrow and anger. Can you see the tears behind the flakes as they fall?" She pulled back the curtain a little more, to show me, and I pressed my face closer to the window.

I couldn't see anything like tears falling behind snowflakes, but I knew they were there if my mother said she saw them. "Wishes made in sorrow or in pain are powerful creations," she said, dropping the curtain again. "Sometimes they come from people who are too caught up in their feelings to realize what they've even done."

"A wish," I said, "can actually be made?"

My mother nodded, her lips pursed in thought, as if she didn't like the idea of wishes but had to acknowledge their existence. "Curses, too," she said. "If a person knows how to bring them into being."

"How?" I asked.

She shook her head, eyes heavily lidded. "It's too much to explain right now. I've got to deal with this blizzard."

"How?"

She turned back to the window then, and I noticed her fingertips rubbing against the palm of her hand nervously. "I have to go into the world's shadow to change this," she said. "And I'll need you to look after me. Here, at home. I might be gone for a while. And if I'm not back in a few hours, I'll need you to wake me."

"You can do that?" I asked, thinking of how, not long ago, I'd been unexpectedly swept away to a battlefield in

France during World War II. "You can go there when you want to? Like, on purpose?"

She nodded, eyes closed, like she was ashamed of all the things she still hadn't taught me. "You can," she said, opening her eyes again. "But you shouldn't do it unless you absolutely have to."

"Why won't you tell me about these things?" I asked, throwing my hands in the air, shaking them with each word that I said, the same way my dad did whenever he got angry. "Why don't you trust me?"

"Aidan," she said, "it's not you I distrust. And I don't have time for this right now. I have to change things. This blizzard has been caused by someone, and I think your father may be in danger because of it. Will you or won't you wake me if I don't get up on my own in a few hours?"

"I will," I said. "That's easy enough."

Her face was grim, but she nodded, grateful for my agreement. "If I don't wake at first," she said, "you'll have to keep trying. Shake me. Throw water on me if you have to."

"Are you sure you want to do this?"

"I have to," she said. "This has nothing to do with wanting."

We climbed the staircase together then, and before she stretched out on her bed, she took the old silver pocket watch, the one her father had given her, and clutched it in her hands.

I took a seat on a chair beside her nightstand, watching

as she stared up at the ceiling, breathing deeply, as if she were about to plunge underwater, stroking the round case of the watch like a favored pet. Then she began to count backward from one hundred, stating the numbers slowly, solemnly, as if she were recalling the words of a spell. And when her lips parted to finally say "Zero," her eyes closed abruptly, and the word flew out of her mouth like a snow-flake, melting in midair.

After that, she was gone. She was there on her bed, but I could tell she was gone. And her body remained behind, an empty vessel. Like I must have been gone, like I must have been still as stone, looking like a person who'd died in his sleep, when I'd parachuted into a forest in France with my great-grandfather Lockwood. I sat beside her like a guard now, wondering how I'd make it through the next couple of hours, wondering who could have sent a blizzard to endanger my father, like my mom suspected, frustrated that I couldn't do anything. Frustrated that my mom wouldn't teach me about the things I needed to know in order to actually help.

My mother had done this on purpose, I reminded my-self then. She'd gone into the world's shadow by willing it. What else could she do—could *I* do—that I didn't know about?

She kept too many secrets, my mother, and I kept bump-ing up against them like furniture in a dark room.

I went up and down the staircase several times for a while after that, before I realized I was pacing. *One hundred to zero,* I was thinking as I reached the upstairs landing for probably the fourth or fifth round of anxiety-driven stair climbing. *Just lie back and close your eyes. Slip inside like a shadow. Like slipping a hand into a glove.*

I stopped pacing then. I was tired of feeling useless. Tired of having this ability and not being told how to use it. I'd gotten back from the world's shadow once before. I could do it again, I figured.

I headed straight to my room then, where I stretched out on my bed and looked up at the crack etching its way across the ceiling, and stared at that dark crevasse for a long time, breathing deeply, like my mom had done before she went under.

The longer I stared, the wider the crack seemed to grow—to widen, to deepen—until suddenly it was a chasm above me, a dark canyon with wind howling through it, pulling me up toward it, lifting me higher and higher, closer and closer, like a person possessed by a spirit.

Everything that made up the ordinary world I moved through, all the laws we're forced to live by, natural and man-made, felt like they'd been undone. The crack in the ceiling was a space I could fall into if I wanted, if I'd only let myself fall upward into the sky above.

I began the count backward from one hundred then, and closed my eyes to the world as I reached zero—

—only to open them again in the world's shadow.

At first there was the boy. The dog came after. There was the boy and then there was a black Lab trotting behind him. Then the boy slapped his hip lightly in signal, and the dog hurried to catch up and walk alongside him. He was a squinty-eyed kid, fifteen or sixteen, wearing blue jeans and a brown barn jacket with a sheepskin collar warming the back of his neck. He was walking through the back field, a field I would have recognized in any season, because it had always been what I saw spread out beyond my bedroom window, though this particular season was not the winter I'd left behind me, but autumn, and the tree line at the back of the field blazed with color.

"Be careful, now," a voice called from behind the boy, and he turned to look at the back of the yellow clapboard house, where his mother sat on the stoop snapping the last of the beans from her summer garden. Bennie. My grandma Bennie. Only much younger than I'd ever seen her. She had a face already worn out by the world, with lines around her dark eyes and early gray curling into her brown hair. "And make sure your father knows it'll be time for dinner soon, if you can drag him out of there when you find him," she said.

The boy nodded. He was waving goodbye to her even as he turned back to the woods, to trudge through the rain-sopped field in his gum boots with the black dog trotting beside him.

There was a sun that day too, hovering over the trees on the horizon, orange and bleary, smearing the sky with its brassy oils. There was a slight wind at the boy's back, gently nudging him into the amber-lit forest. And there were the usual movements of squirrels and birds and rabbits, chatter and singsong, the shifting of brush and leaves as creatures turned themselves invisible at his approach. The dog, however, could sense them. It lifted its black nose, turned its ears in one direction, then another, every time it heard some tiny thing scuttle into a cold hole or into one of the ant-hollowed logs that littered the trails of the forest. The dog left the boy's side to circle around for a while, patrolling, until the boy slapped his hip again and the dog returned, tail flicking back and forth, and peered over its shoulder at whatever it had wanted to apprehend.

The boy went to these woods often; so often, in fact, that he had brought them into his mind over a long period of time and could now walk through them in his dreams. He pressed his face against his pillow each night, after feeding and watering the cows in the barn with his father, and walked through the world contained within him: the world his father and his grandfather had known before him. This land. These woods. He walked the footpaths they had worn into the earth during their years here, over the bridge and into the orchard, where the Living Death Tree scratched at the sky with its spindly black branches. Then down the lane he went, from the pasture to the woods, following paths only he and his father and grandfather could see spread out before them.

The farther into the woods he went, the bigger the

world seemed to grow around him. The sunlight thinned as the trees twisted together, enclosing him in their shadows. And somewhere inside that private world, down in the ravine at the back of the woods, was his father.

There had been crying that day too, earlier. The boy was not able to stop thinking about it, and I watched the moments replay in his mind over and over as he walked. His mother's sobs, a burst of strangled pleas, the way she'd sounded as if her life were in danger. The boy had come down from his tiny attic bedroom to find his mother on her knees in the living room, her face buried in her old-too-early hands. The door in the mudroom slammed then, making the house shake, making the boy look up for a moment before his mother let out another sobbing sound and he turned back to her, saying, "Mom? Momma?" and she lifted her red face to finally look at him. "Was he saying it again?" the boy had asked her.

"Just give him some time," she'd said, nodding. "He'll walk it off in the woods. Give him some quiet."

An hour had passed, though, and the boy's father hadn't returned, which was why he'd decided to set off to find him, to bring him home to his bean-snapping, worn-down-too-early mother, who he loved more than anyone in the world, who sometimes made him wonder what had ever made her marry his father, a steelworker who drank half his paycheck on the nights he received them, then came home to smash the glass of the picture frames that held photos of their family members, like his father's own mother, Grandma Plumie, who the boy missed sorely. Grandma Plumie had been gone for three years now. And in those three years, it seemed the boy's father had only grown more distant from everyone, had grown into a stranger, as if he and the boy had never known one another, held conversations, as if the father had not made the boy from his own body with the boy's mother.

After Grandma Plumie's funeral, after Aunt Ethel took half of Grandma Plumie's jewelry, then left without a word, the boy's father had woken one morning to find that, somehow, he'd been cast as an actor in a life he could not remember making.

He began calling the boy John instead of Johnny, in a tone that dripped battery acid, as if John were the name of a constantly returning door-to-door salesman. He began to tell the boy's mother that he'd made a mistake by marrying her, that his own life was one great big mistake, that his own father, who had never come home from the war in France, who had died over there, should have never made him.

"This world," the boy's father would say. "This world isn't worth spit, I tell you." And when the boy's mother said, "John, don't talk like this," the boy's father would cry and say he was sorry and that he was a coward. He'd never done anything right. He hadn't gone to fight in a war like his father had; the army had refused him, said he had a slight curvature of the spine and a murmur in his heart, and that he was too old, really. And though all of his wife's younger brothers had gone to Vietnam for a war that was unwinnable, they'd still done their duty. They'd done something honorable, even though all but one of them died over there, just like his father had died in the service of his country.

And on top of that, he was losing his inheritance. The farm. He had taken to selling it off in pieces. One parcel when he needed to buy a new tractor. Another when he needed a new car. Part of the woods, even, had been sold off to loggers after he'd gambled away the last of the savings his father left him.

More and more often, the boy would find his father in dark corners of the house, his head buried in the palms of his hands, shaking. And once, when the boy went out to feed the cows, he'd stopped pouring the grain into their buckets when he heard an odd noise come from above and realized quickly that it was someone crying, someone up in the hay mound. Whimpering, really.

That day he left the barn and went to his bedroom in the second floor of the yellow farmhouse and watched from his window, waiting to see who, if anyone, would eventually emerge. And when the gate did finally swing open, it was his father, wiping his eyes one last time before he turned to lock the gate behind him.

At the edge of the ravine—their destination—the boy and the black dog came to a stop to look down the footpath that led to his father's tree blind at the bottom, where the boy could find his father anytime he disappeared from the house now. He was down there again. The boy told the black Lab to sit, to stay, and the dog went down on its haunches like a statue while the boy carefully picked his way down the slope to the bottom of the ravine.

It was when he reached the bottom that the boy spotted his father sitting against the base of his tree, his legs crossed, a revolver held against his temple. The boy froze, afraid to move another inch, not wanting to disturb him, not wanting the gun to go off. Just a while ago he had asked his mother, "Did he say it again?" after he'd found her in the living room, sobbing. "Yes," she'd said. His father had said it again. The thing he'd been saying for weeks now, it seemed. That he was going to correct the mistake God had made of him. Now, here in Marrow's Ravine, was the first time the boy had actually seen his father appear as if he might actually do what he'd been threatening.

The boy looked up to the side of the ravine, to the black Lab waiting for him on the ridge above, its pink tongue lolling. And then, suddenly, beside the dog, he saw the curve of wide white antlers appear before the broad white head bearing those antlers followed. There was a creature up there, a creature the dog didn't seem to notice, and it stared down at the boy with eyes so dark and so cold, it seemed like it could see right into the center of the boy's soul.

It was when the boy turned to look up at the top of the ravine that his father noticed him. The boy's father lowered the gun from his temple then. And at that very moment, when it seemed the man might return to his senses, he shook his head wildly, the hatchet of his nose shifting back and forth, and said, "I'm sorry. I'm sorry." Then he flashed the gun into his mouth and pulled the trigger.

The sound of the gun exploded in the boy's ears, pushing every other noise—every bird's call, every squirrel's chatter, even the trickling of Sugar Creek itself—out of Marrow's Ravine.

And after the echo of the blast and the ringing of the gunshot began to sift back down from the treetops, a deep stillness remained, quietly filling the place like a fog, as if the woods themselves had been shocked into a resolute silence.

The boy stood there, staring, his eyes wide, his lips parted for the sharp breath he'd taken right before he watched his father's unstrung puppet of a body slouch against the base of the tree, head slumping against the shoulder. Gone now. Gone from him.

I stood there with him, my own eyes wide, my own mouth hanging open, shocked into silence, until I heard my father crying, and turned to see him fall to his knees, covering his face with his hands. I watched my father, younger than I was now, place the back of his hand against his eyes to wipe away tears that wouldn't stop coming. Watched as he heaved and sobbed at the foot of his own father's body.

I couldn't stop myself any longer. I reached out from the shadows I hid within, reached out to try to touch him. To put my hand on his shoulder. Tried to take his hand from his eyes, to hold him, to bear some of his grief for him. But no matter what I did, I couldn't get through to him. It was just like our life together back in my time, back in my world: he couldn't see me.

I knew he sensed me, though, because a second later he said, "Sophia? Is that you? Are you still up in New York with your father? If you can, would you do that thing? That trick with the star? Would you come home right now? I need you so bad."

I furrowed my brow, confused. What trick was he talking about? It sounded like the story my mom had told me about the Probable Stone, the star she said could lead me home if I ever needed it. So she had told my father, too, back when they were high school sweethearts. Because how else would my sixteen-year-old dad seem to know my mom could do some trick that would let her come home to Temperance from some other place with a snap of her fingers? Seeing that he knew that all those years ago, though—it didn't make sense. Why had my mom taken all of that knowledge she'd obviously once shared with him and made him forget it?

I couldn't probe to ask that question. I couldn't get that answer from my dad's younger self. Because even as I knelt beside him and clutched his shoulder, trying to reach him, a curtain of rain began to fall around me, harder and harder, colder and colder, and then the vision of my dad faded altogether.

✵

I woke back into my body, back into my bedroom, completely drenched, to find my mom standing over me with the watering can she used on her houseplants, pouring water on me as I lay there.

She was shaking her head, her lips curled in anger. And when I was done blinking the vision out of my eyes, she said, "I cannot believe you, Aidan Lockwood. You promised you'd watch over me. I could have been hurt. I could have been trapped if something bad had happened. And you could have been trapped in there too, seeing something you shouldn't be seeing."

"I'm sorry," I said, and sat up against my headboard. "I just wanted to help, and you won't let me. You won't even teach me about the things I can do."

My mother scoffed. Seriously, she scoffed, then turned to look out my bedroom window, as if she couldn't stand the sight of me any longer. After a long pause, she turned back and said, "I took care of my business in there. The blizzard is over. What happened to you while you were in there? Did you even direct the journey or did you just let anything come to you?"

"I saw something," I said, relieved she was done hammering me for trying to follow her.

"What exactly?"

"I saw Grandpa," I said, which made her flutter her eye-lashes in disbelief. "Dad's father," I specified. "Grandpa John, in the picture downstairs."

My mom raised her eyebrows at that one and released a held breath. "Really?" she said. "And what did he have to tell you?"

"He said he was going to correct the mistake God had made of him," I whispered, and my mom's face fell as if I'd just told her someone she loved had died unexpectedly.

I told her the rest of the vision then. Told her about seeing my dad as a sixteen-year-old. Her mouth quivered into the hint of a smile as I described him to her, de-scribed him as the boy she'd fallen in love with as a young woman. But as I neared the moment when my grand-father actually pulled the trigger, my mother said, "Stop. I know this part of the story. I know all too well what happens next."

"What does it mean?" I asked. "Why was the white stag there again?"

"You saw it in the world's shadow when you visited your great-grandfather in the war, too," my mom said, nod-ding. "But I don't know what it all means." Which I didn't believe for a second.

"You have to know," I said. "I *know* you do. There are all kinds of things you won't tell me. Like, how did you stop the blizzard?"

"Aidan," she said, but I could tell she was just about to lead me down a path away from what I wanted to know.

"And why do you think someone made it happen?" I said, continuing to press her. "Better yet, *who*?"

"Aidan!" she said, and her eyes began to narrow.

"It's not fair to keep these things from me!" I shouted. "I deserve to know what's going on here too. I'm a part of this, whether you like it or not."

My mom squinted at me then, and the angry curl returned to her lips. "Don't talk to me about what's fair," she said. "You don't know what other people have gone through—what other people have *sacrificed*—to protect you and give you this life. Maybe you had this vision for a reason that has nothing to do with the white stag. Maybe you needed to see what you saw so you can understand why your father is who he is, why he does so much for you. Maybe you need to think about how it would feel to lose your father at such a young age, like your dad did. He took care of your grandmother and this farm after that happened. He took care of me after we got married. And he's taken care of you and your brother, never giving himself a chance to think of any other life for himself. How fair is that, Aidan?"

I didn't answer. I sat there, silent, ashamed, until she huffed, angry that I'd managed to push her this far. And in the next instant she stormed out, shaking her head, as if she couldn't believe she'd raised a son as ungrateful as I was.

※

The next day I drove over to Jarrod's to pick him up for school like usual, now that the roads were clear and the blizzard was over. But when I arrived, instead of waiting for him, I turned off the Blue Bomb's engine, went up to the door, and knocked until it swung open and Jarrod stood before me.

"Is your mom home?" I asked.

He shook his head. "Working a double to make up for all the days off during the blizzard."

"Good," I said, and stepped up to stand beside him in the doorway, our faces inches from each other. "Why don't we skip school today? Horror movies and making out sounds better."

Jarrod laughed, as if he couldn't believe what I'd just proposed. Then, when I didn't laugh with him, he said, "What? Is my good boy turning bad on me?" When I only grinned in answer, his face changed to something more curious, and he said, "I thought you wanted to take things slow. To be careful."

"That blizzard," I told him, "was sent here by someone or something, according to my mom. She's the one who stopped it."

"Okay," he said, waiting for me to go on.

"So, you know," I said. "That someone or something is apparently out to get my family. It seems we have enemies. Enemies who can conjure up blizzards. I figure I better not waste any more time, if something like that is really out there."

"Wait," Jarrod said. "Are you saying—"

But I didn't let him finish. I put my hand over his lips for a second and said, "Horror movies and making out." Then I removed my hand only after I'd leaned in to kiss away whatever question he'd almost asked me.

I didn't know the answer to that question anyway. I didn't know much about anything, really—not nearly enough about my own family, not enough about the secrets my mother kept from me, not enough about myself or whatever else I might be capable of doing—but when I put my hand on his waist and pulled him closer, I knew exactly this one thing:

Him and me. Together.

chapter nine

THE TRAIL OF
MY FATHER'S BLOOD

At school, Jarrod and I shared smiles that held secrets. No one knew about us—not the *us* we were beyond those hallways and classrooms—and I figured that was probably how we'd continue to be, as long as we lived in Temperance. Or at least as long as we were in high school. But I was starting to understand that we could be who we were together, regardless of whether we stayed forever in a town as small and changeless as ours. If my mom decided to go psychic on me, though, and read those particular thoughts, she would disagree. She had always been a true believer in Temperance—she said the people here were the salt of the earth—but they would probably have been more like salt rubbed in a wound if they knew my and Jarrod's secret.

Small towns in remote corners of the world are really quaint, unless you don't fit into them. Then they're just small.

I'd never really had a friend here, not like Jarrod. Or at least, I couldn't remember any after my mom pushed them away from me, blocked them from seeing me, the same way she'd blinded me to the invisible world. The salt-of-the-earth people of Temperance my mom always defended had mostly treated me like I was invisible over the past five years, except for those times when I spaced out in class, thanks to my mom screwing my head up, and then I was all too visible and everyone got in a good laugh.

When I thought about it—when I thought about it so hard my brain would start to tremble toward a migraine—I knew that if Jarrod hadn't come home, I'd have been lost forever, aimlessly driving my car around town in circles, hoping I'd find my real life waiting just around the corner of this false one my mother had given me. I would have never found myself without Jarrod to help me remember that I wasn't as thin as paper. To help me remember there was more to me than even I knew.

I stopped telling myself that things would get better, like I'd been doing for weeks at that point. And I thought that was wise of me, considering the fast turn my life had taken into Seriously Weird Central. Now I told myself to get ready for whatever was coming next. Because things *were* coming—I could feel that the same way my mom felt things hours, days, weeks, or years ahead of time. Only these things were not good. Whatever was coming for my family was done playing with us. The next time it came, it would do its worst.

In early January, my dad and Toby started gearing up for their last go at deer season. They did this every year, hunting together down in Marrow's Ravine, where my dad and his father and grandfather had all hunted.

My dad's stand was a well-traveled route for deer—there was a buck or a doe each season, guaranteed meat in the freezer, another rack hanging on one of the walls of our house, if it was something special. And if you had an old man who had claimed a place that never failed to bring out the deer, you could count yourself lucky to inherit that place when his hunting days were over. That was how my dad got his place in Marrow's Ravine, just a mile trek back through our woods and down a steep slope to the center of that forest.

He'd inherited the spot from my grandpa John, the man whose eyes constantly followed me around our living room. When my grandma Bennie was still alive, living down the hall in the extra bedroom, I once asked her what he'd been like. "He was a shy fellow," she'd told me. "Never did well talking to most people." She smiled then, looking beyond my shoulder at the tree line behind the fields of clover in our backyard, and said, "That's what I liked about him. He was all mine, when I had him."

This stand of his, this place that must have been a crossroads for deer in northeastern Ohio, had been handed down to him by his father, the man who had jumped out of an airplane on D-day, a man who had chased the white stag into the woods until he found death waiting for him in his own reflection.

My mom and I were often alone those first two weeks of January. And as my dad and Toby drifted through the woods and crouched in tree stands, I started to ask her questions. Questions I hadn't been able to ask when they were around because of my promise to keep her secrets. "Can you tell me more?" I asked one evening, before they'd come home from the woods.

She was sitting in a wing-backed chair in the living room, reading something on her tablet. When I asked the question, she looked up and stared at me, blank-faced, possibly annoyed, before saying, "What is it you want to know?"

"Whatever I need to know," I said. "You can't sit there and deny that something is out there looking for us. You've said so yourself. And besides, I'm putting things together on my own. Things are finding their way to me. Whether you're going to help or not doesn't matter."

She placed her tablet on the table beside her, then turned back to me with a pinched expression. "What things *exactly* are finding their way to you?" she asked, almost as if she didn't believe me.

"You gave me back the memory of the man in the black suit," I said. "And I met the white stag in the world's shadow. I watched my great-grandfather die. I watched Grandpa John over there shoot himself." I turned to look at my grandfather's portrait for a moment, met his eerie stare, then turned back to my mother. "There's plenty coming to me. And I know there's more. I just want to understand. I want to know how I'm a part of everything."

"I've already told you," my mother said flatly. "The man in the black suit and the white stag are agents of Death."

"But . . . why? Why did I see *them*? Why not some skeleton wearing a hooded cloak and carrying a sickle?"

"There are as many harbingers of death as there are different kinds of people in the world. They come in forms people have given them over the years, depending on how they see them. The white stag runs through your father's family. Ironic, isn't it, for a clan of hunters? It carried you home because you have Lockwood blood running through you. It recognized you. And when you die, you'll either be led across the way by the stag or by the agent from my family. Old Black Suit. Whichever one holds more sway with you will come."

"I want the stag," I suddenly found myself saying.

"Why?" my mother asked, cocking her head to the side, curious.

"It didn't seem as creepy as Old Black Suit."

"Old Black Suit," my mother said, "may be unnerving, it's true. But at least you can reason with him. The stag—well, let's just say it's the agent for your father's family for a reason. Like the Lockwoods, the stag can't be swayed beyond its purpose."

"Thank you," I said, "for talking to me like this. I mean that."

Instead of saying you're welcome, though, my mom simply pursed her lips before asking, "Is there anything else, then?" as if she were a sales clerk at a store counter.

"You never told me how you stopped that blizzard," I said, not letting her tone offend me, trying to press her for as much information as possible.

My mom sighed and looked down at the tablet on the end table, as if she'd rather be reading. When she looked up again, she said, "It's complicated, Aidan."

"Why can't you just tell me what we're dealing with?" I said, and I could hear my voice climb a little higher.

"Because it will change everything I've done to protect you. It's not possible. Just bear with me a while longer. I'll fix things right, I swear."

"Then why don't you start by teaching me what I can do?" I asked. I'd been burning to ask her for weeks now.

"Aidan," she said, "you don't want to know these things. Trust me. Trust that I would put all of this down if I could."

She looked at the Christmas tree in the corner of the

room then, at the strings of lights still glowing and the ornaments still hanging off the branches. "We should probably take that down," she said, "shouldn't we?"

Another closed door, I realized. Another dead-end discussion. I could have continued to press her, but I knew by my mom's tone that she was finished, that the only thing I'd get from her after this point was either going to be a moment of pretending to be close like we'd been when I was a little kid, taking down the tree, rehashing holiday memories, or else a heated, hurtful argument.

So I nodded, agreeing to help take down the tree, agreeing to let her change the subject.

I spent the next hour with her, removing the satin bulbs and gingerbread, the cords of lights and the ornaments constructed with toothpicks and Popsicle sticks—things Toby and I had made back in elementary school. That I had ever been so small, so young, so unknowing, was hard for me to believe. Where had all the time gone, and how did it go so quickly? Or had it gone anywhere? Had it instead taken on a particular shape? Had we somehow molded time into these childish ornaments with our tiny hands and stored it that way, held inside them?

My mom had difficulty getting rid of things that had to do with her kids: photos, essays, finger paintings, athletic trophies, 4-H ribbons. So when I commented on how the ornaments we'd made as kids were shoddy and should probably be thrown away, she said, "One day you'll want as many of these things as you can get." And when I asked why, she said, "Because they'll remind you of who you are when you forget yourself."

"I've already forgotten myself, though," I said, and she looked at me through the branches like I'd just slapped her.

A fight was about to break out, but I'd made a fair assessment of my life right then, I felt. Hadn't she admitted to hiding memories from me? Hadn't she avoided telling me more when I'd asked just an hour earlier?

Before she had a chance to argue, though, the back door slammed open so hard it shook the entire house. A second later, Toby burst into the living room where we'd been plucking candy canes off the tree branches. His face glistened, his cheeks were flushed red, and his eyes were filled with terror. His lips trembled as he tried to speak, and when he finally got his mouth open, he shouted the words "He's dead! Oh my God, Dad's dead!"

My mother didn't panic when Toby burst into the room with those words spilling out of him; she didn't lose one ounce of control. She simply put the candy cane she was holding back on the branch and said, "Calm down, Toby. What's happened?" And when Toby was able to explain that our dad had fallen out of his tree stand and wasn't moving, my mom went straight to the kitchen to call Sheriff Barrens to tell him about what might have occurred down in Marrow's Ravine. There were a few tears in her eyes as she spoke, but her voice held steady. "Yes, well," she kept saying, over and over. "Yes, well." She finished the call by saying she was going down to the ravine to see about the truth of the matter, and that she'd meet him there. Sheriff Barrens must have told her not to go, though, because she said, "I'm sorry, but you know I have to do this."

While they spoke, Toby sobbed on the couch, hunched over, fists tucked into his armpits. He was wearing his orange camouflage snowsuit and hunting hat with furry ear flaps. The suit was covered in mud, as if he'd stumbled and fallen into water, making me think of our great-grandfather drowning in that creek in France. "Toby," I said, "what happened?" But he only shook his head. Snot dripped from his nose, and no matter how many times I asked, he wouldn't answer.

I'd never seen my brother like this before. I'd never seen him so reduced, so afraid.

When my mom came back from talking to the sheriff, she sat beside Toby on the couch and put her hand on his shoulder, gently, as if he might break, as if her touch would call him back to us. "You need to calm yourself," she said, taking off his orange cap and pushing away the sweaty hair from his dirt-speckled forehead. "You need to calm yourself so you can take us back to your father. We need to find him. We need to help him right now."

"I can't," Toby spat through gritted teeth. "I fell half-way down the ravine when I went to check on Dad. I lost my phone in the fall or I would have just called you. I think I either twisted or broke my ankle."

"Show me," my mom said, and Toby reached down, gritting his teeth harder, and his face turned an angry red color as he pulled the boot off.

The flesh of his ankle was purple and swollen. My mom felt around it for a while, squeezing gently in different places, asking what he could feel and what he couldn't, asking if he could move the ankle in certain ways. It reminded me of the jellyfish squish of bone I'd heard in my great-grandfather's foot after he'd landed from his plane jump. When my mom was done, she looked up at Toby and said, "It's not broken, I think, just badly sprained." Then, turning to look up at me, she said, "Aidan, you'll have to come with me."

"Me?" I said.

"I can't do it alone," she said. "I need you to help me find your father."

Her tone was remarkably calm, but I'd never heard her say she needed me before, not like this, not with this carefully hidden dread in her voice.

I nodded. "Okay," I said. "Let's go, then."

"He's not dead," my mother said as soon as she closed the mudroom door behind us and the cold air began to fog around our warm bodies. I looked at her—bundled in a thick barn jacket and a black men's stocking cap, a blue scarf twisted around the bottom half of her face—and could see the severe expression in her eyes that meant she wouldn't allow any other idea to exist as we began to silently trudge through the snow a moment later.

I listened to our boots crunch through the icy crust with each step that we took and tried to imagine a world in which my dad was no longer alive. It wasn't possible. Toby had to be wrong. He had to be.

After my mom and I had been trudging on like that for a while, lost in our own heads, I decided to finally break our silence.

"How do you know for sure?" I asked, giving her a sidelong glance. "How do you know he's not dead?"

"Because," my mother said, not missing a beat in her step. "I would have felt him leave this world. And besides, he's been hidden, protected."

"Protected from what?" I asked, but my mom just stared for a second like I'd said the stupidest thing in the world.

I didn't say any more. I kept my head down and pulled one leg in front of the other, over and over, punching through the snow. My breath came out in plumes as we pushed back through the frozen pasture, back through the ice-crusted lane that would take us into the woods.

"Do you know where we're going?" I asked when we did finally reach the edge of the woods a while later, in the same place where, several months earlier, on a cold autumn night, the white stag had knelt down to let me slide off its back.

"I have a general idea," my mom said, "but I haven't been down to Marrow's Ravine in years. When's the last time your father took you?"

I thought about it for a second. The last time Dad had taken me down to Marrow's Ravine had been a year ago, when I was a junior and he and Toby had been excitedly talking about going back to screw steps into their trees and climb into the branches to set up their stands. My mom had stood in the living room watching them gear up for the journey, and unexpectedly she'd suggested that my dad take me with them. "What for?" my dad had asked, looking from her to me like there was something wrong with both of us. "Aidan doesn't hunt."

"Maybe he'd just enjoy the walk," my mom had offered. "Maybe he'd enjoy seeing what you two see back there."

My dad had grudgingly agreed, nodding and chewing his bottom lip like he'd been forced to pick a not-so-likely classmate for a gym team. But I'd suited up quickly, not wanting to annoy him further, because he and Toby were already almost ready. Then we went back through the pasture and back through the woods, with the trees stretching up tall and dark around us, until we reached the edge of the ravine, a mile or so from our back doorstep. Then we climbed down the side of the ravine, using the spots where my dad's and his dad's and his granddad's feet had worn a trail of steps into the earth over their decades of hunting, to find the tree my father would use for his stand. Toby's place was on top of the ridge, where he could look down and see my dad at the bottom. The plan was, if a deer got past my dad, it would run up to the ridge, where it would think it was safe, and then Toby would have a chance to take it.

"It's been over a year," I told my mom. "I've never come back here in winter, not since I was a kid and Toby and I used to play down there sometimes."

My mom brushed a strand of windblown hair out of her face as we pushed farther into the woods. "We'll have to keep our eyes open, then," she said. "These eyes"— she pointed back and forth between our eyes with two fingers—"and this eye too," she added, pointing from her forehead to mine.

We drifted for what seemed like forever, lost in a vast white desert where none of our eyes seemed to do us any good. After a while, my mom seemed to be on the verge of giving up hope. I could tell she was worried that my dad's condition was getting worse, that every second that passed made it more likely he would slip out of his body and leave this world behind him. I could see her thoughts as she formed them, as if they were no more than strands of yarn, a cat's cradle inside her mind instead of strung between her fingers. Usually my mom had all kinds of shields up to guard her thoughts and feelings. Now, though, with her attention focused on my dad, seeing into her mind was like looking through a pane of glass.

We stumbled through snow-laced underbrush, licking our chapped lips, blinking ice out of our eyes, until finally I found a set of deer tracks, a pair of holes punched through the snowy crust. And there were flecks of blood in the snow too, as if maybe the deer had been hit, and the tracks remained, as if no amount of snowfall could erase them. I looked up from the tracks, turned in the direction they came from, and for a moment I thought I saw a deer running toward me, as if it were charging right at me. I startled as it came at me, jerked to the side a little, but before it could reach us, it broke apart like smoke and I could only hear the ghost of its hoofbeats as it passed, drumming and drumming as it ran in the direction of the farm.

"Did you see that?" I asked, turning to my mom.

She shook her head, squinted at me for a second. "What did you see?" she asked.

I didn't want to tell her I'd seen a ghost deer, that I'd heard its hooves as it ran past. If it was the white stag, it might be a sign that things were bad for my dad. So I told her I'd seen a glow coming from up ahead, that it might be where sunlight broke through the woods because the ravine widened and separated the tree canopy. She nodded and said that sounded like a smart idea, and from there I took us in the direction the deer tracks came from. Clutching her coat tight near her neckline, my mom let me take the lead. And after another twenty minutes, we'd done it. We'd reached the ridge that looked over Marrow's Ravine.

I could see my dad from that high up, even through the snow flying in my face, even through the branches of the trees that sprouted up on this side of the ravine. He was facedown in the snow, one arm flung out at an odd angle, and the falling snow had already begun to cover him.

My mother gasped, then covered her mouth with her hand while tears formed and streaked down her wind-chapped face. She put her other hand on my shoulder to steady herself. "You did good," she said without looking at me, without removing either hand from where it had settled. Then, after she caught her breath, we began the climb down.

On the way, I kept wishing that I had stopped my mom from bringing me with her. I kept wishing that I'd called Jarrod and asked him to come over. Right now, he could be holding me as he told me none of this was really happening, that what I was about to face when I reached the bottom of the ravine was all in my head. I wanted him to tell me that I was crazy. Crazy, at that point, would have been preferable to the reality in front of me.

But my wishing was futile. I didn't know how to wish something into or out of existence. My mother had refused to teach me. So instead, I found myself holding my mom's hand, helping her pick her way down the side of the ravine. It felt like I was watching it all happen from outside my own body, like it had felt when I'd fallen into the world's shadow and watched my great-granddad fall through the air over a French battlefield. My breath came faster, then harder, and steam poured out of my mouth like smoke from a stack. I could hear my own heartbeat as we reached the bottom, and I could hear it stop for just a moment, skipping a beat when we came to stand next to my father.

We found him almost directly below his tree stand, his rifle emerging from a crust of snow a few feet away, his shape still visible, like the curves of a body beneath a white sheet. A trickle of blood had leaked from his mouth and was frozen against his bristly jawline. And when I saw the blood, I let out a gasp like my mother had when she'd seen him from above. My breath curled away in wispy tendrils as reality settled inside me like a dark seed, one that would take root and grow a black and thorny vine around my heart in the days to come.

It was then that I noticed that the tracks I'd followed to the ridge were down here too, around my father's body. It looked as if the deer that had made them had found him before we did, had circled him, sniffing, trying to make sense of the human at the bottom of the ravine, the steam lifting from his body. There was a trail of blood in the snow between the hoofprints, a thread of red leading away from the spot where my father lay motionless. My mother didn't seem to notice it, but I saw it clearly. It led up the side of the ravine in the direction we'd come from and was surely the blood I'd seen half a mile back.

My mom bent down to place one hand on my father's shoulder, but her legs gave way beneath her and she fell to her knees in one fast motion. She let out a short, sharp moan then, and touched the back of my dad's head. "Oh," she whispered, shaking her head, trying to deny what lay in front of her. "Oh, my love, we had time left. I was saving it up. I had heaps and heaps of time saved for us."

We stayed for a while like that, my mom kneeling in the snow next to his body, my head bowed as if I'd found myself in a vision, silent, unable to participate in the events going on around me. Eventually my mom looked up with her mouth open, her lips trembling, as if for the first time in her life she didn't know what to say.

"We have to go," she managed to say. "We have to go back so we can get him home before nightfall. I won't leave him out here like this."

The walk home felt longer, and slower, especially having to climb the side of Marrow's Ravine instead of picking our way down. I held my mother's hand most of the way up, leading her to the safe places to plant her next step, and eventually we reached the top, exhausted both by the climb and by the constant awareness we had to maintain on our way up. I could see how easy it would have been for Toby to stumble and fall, especially thinking that our father was dead or dying. He was lucky, really, that he'd done nothing more than sprain his ankle badly.

We followed our own tracks back through the woods in silence. Every now and then, I'd try to catch a look at my mom with a sidelong glance, and her face was always hard, red, and angry. She looked like she might tear a bear limb from limb if one happened to cross our path. I almost hoped we'd run across the sheriff on our way back, just so I wouldn't be alone with her in her barely contained rage. But he was nowhere in sight, so I stayed quiet as we trudged back through our own footprints.

Until we came to the place where I'd noticed the deer tracks—tracks my mother hadn't been able to see when we'd gone back to find my father. Tracks she still couldn't see as we returned. Tracks with the trail of my father's blood winding between them.

Then she stopped suddenly and turned to me with that angry red face and said, "You saw something here, didn't you?"

I shook my head, not wanting to make her angrier than she was already.

"Yes, you did," she said, nodding, trying to encourage me now with a softer tone to tell the truth. "Tell me, Aidan. What did you see when we were on our way down there?"

"A deer," I admitted. "A deer like a ghost. It just came right through here, then disappeared in a puff of smoke."

"The stag?" she asked.

"It was fast," I said. "It didn't seem as real to me as when I've seen it in the world's shadow. But it could have been. It happened so quickly."

My mother looked around, trying to pierce the veil of the present into the past, to see what I'd seen. "I don't understand," she said. "I don't understand why you would see that and I wouldn't."

"It might have been nothing," I said. "It could have been entirely random."

I put my hands in my armpits to signal that I was cold standing there, to see if I could get her moving again, but she didn't budge. Instead, she stared at me hard for a long moment. And then she said, "Don't keep things like that from me, you hear?"

And in a moment of complete exasperation, I said, "Why not? You keep things to yourself. You hide things from all of us."

She breathed out of her nose heavily then, squinting at me like I was a stranger who had offended her. Clearly I'd become one of those children whose parents look at them one day and suddenly realize they've become their worst enemies.

"If you see things that I can't," she said a second later, "I need to know what they are, or we may never get to the bottom of this. Whatever happened to your father doesn't feel like a simple accident to me. Okay?"

"Okay," I said, and stood there, not knowing what else to say, afraid to say anything. Afraid that I might choose the wrong word. A word that might attract whatever had killed my father. At least, I thought, she was giving me a rationale with her orders. Much better than how she usually responded when questioned. *That's for me to know and for you to find out.* Maybe, I thought, we could work together, if she could just see me, if she could recognize me as an adult.

"Okay," I said again, nodding. And then we continued our trek home.

＊

When we finally reached the house, we found Sheriff Barrens waiting with Toby, and after we made arrangements for the sheriff to go back and bring my father home, I called Jarrod.

"Did you know this was coming?" he asked on the phone.

"No," I said. "Neither did my mom. She swore she'd know if my dad had died, but she didn't."

"If one person in the world would know something like that," Jarrod said, "it'd be your mom. I'm sorry, Aidan. I don't know what to say. Can I do anything?"

"You can come over," I said, thinking of the wish I'd made earlier, the wish that would have erased this day and left me sitting on my bed with Jarrod, him holding me, telling me everything would be okay.

"I'll borrow my mom's car" was all he said before disconnecting.

When Jarrod showed up twenty minutes later and rang the bell, my mom reached the door before I could. And when she opened it and found him standing on her front porch with his hands in his pockets, his mouth hanging open a little because he'd expected me to answer, she said,

"Why are you here?" as if he might have done all of this, as if he had caused my dad's fall. And all Jarrod could say was how sorry he was for her. How sorry he was for all of us.

"I asked him to come over," I said from the landing between the first and second floors.

My mom turned to look up at me. Her face was white, as if all the blood had drained out of her in the last few hours, and her mouth was open in surprise, like Jarrod's. When she looked away from me and back at Jarrod, she mumbled, "You were the only one. The only one who wasn't a part of the story."

"Excuse me?" Jarrod said.

My mom walked away, though, shaking her head, leaving the door open and Jarrod standing on the front porch with his black stocking cap pulled down over his ears and the snow falling gently around him.

I shook my head as she walked out of the foyer into the living room, where she'd built a fire. She'd been staring into the flames since Sheriff Barrens left, as if the orange and red licks charring the logs might hold the answers she wanted. "Come on up," I said to Jarrod after she was out of sight, and I waved him toward me.

When Jarrod came into my room with me, he closed the door gently and said, "What did your mom mean back there? About me being the only one who's not part of the story?"

"I'm sorry," I said, shaking my head, unable to believe

how rude she'd been, and for no apparent reason. "She's been like this since we found him. She's not making much sense right now."

"That's understandable." Jarrod pulled his arms out of his coat and hung it on the back of my door, then came over to sit with me on my bed, just like I'd wanted, and we leaned back against the headboard together. He put one arm around my shoulders and squeezed me close, put his chin on top of my head, kissed my hair softly. "How about you?" he said. "How have you been?"

"It wasn't just an ordinary accident," I said immediately.

"What do you mean?"

I still saw the trail of blood leading away from my father's body, that thin red ribbon. It had wound up the side of Marrow's Ravine and through the woods, a crimson thread on the snow. The thread my father had left for me to follow, I'd already decided, the thread that would lead me to discover who, or what, had killed him.

"I want to go with you," Jarrod said after I told him what I was going to do.

"I don't think you can, actually."

"Why not?" he said, pulling back to look me in the eye, to challenge me a little.

"Because," I said, "I think the trail is going to lead me somewhere you can't follow. Somewhere *not here*. Somewhere not in this world."

"Then I don't want you to go there," Jarrod said,

squeezing me tight again, as if he might weigh me down and keep me on this earth if he just held on to me.

I buried my face between his neck and shoulder, felt the heat of his skin against my face, kissed him gently on his collarbone. And when I looked up, I said, "I don't think either one of us has a choice. I have to do this. And you have to let me."

✳

Three days later, this would happen:

After the calling hours, after the funeral, after a couple of my father's friends from the roads department and one of his hunting buddies took up the handles of the casket with me and Toby, after my dad was lowered down into the earth, after my mom and Toby and I had deliberated over whether we would actually toss our handfuls of dirt on top of his casket, eventually letting the clods drop and watching his casket then be covered over with flowers, I went back to the woods again, back to follow the trail of my father's blood.

His figure was still etched into the snow where he'd fallen, as if it were a permanent feature in the landscape now, and I knew it would always be there when I looked at the base of his tree in Marrow's Ravine, knew that where he'd fallen would forever be a marker of his absence. I stood there for a while, staring into the void his body had made in the snow, and wished that I'd never promised my mom I'd keep secrets from him. Secrets about myself that mattered. Now he was gone, and he'd never have a chance to know the real me. Never.

Back home, my mom was sitting at the dining room table with a white candle lit in front of her, like I'd seen in a vision while we ate at that table as a family a few months earlier, before I could understand the things I'd begun to see and hear. She was searching the world beyond this one, trying to locate my father, wanting to make sure he was okay, trying to find answers. She'd been looking for him since we'd found his body, but she hadn't been able to find his spirit in the days that followed. "Where is he? Where has he gone?" she kept muttering, even in front of Toby, who she'd asked me not to talk to about things like voices and visions. Now, it seemed, all of her rules were broken, and she was the one breaking them.

We'd gotten into a fight before I left that morning to head back to Marrow's Ravine. I was shrugging on my coat while she sat there, clutching her father's silver pocket watch like it might be a cross or a string of prayer beads, looking like a zombie as she stared into the flame of her candle. "You said not to bring up things like what you're doing around Dad and Toby," I told her.

"Hush," she said without looking away from the candle. Just that.

"You always hush me," I said, continuing to push the issue. "You always tell me to keep quiet."

"I asked you to not say anything to them for your own protection," my mother spat.

"Well, that didn't work out for anyone," I said, "did it?"

My mom slowly turned away from the candle to give me a fierce stare. "What are you trying to say here, Aidan?"

"I'm saying you made me promise not to tell Dad about what was happening, for our own good, but he died anyway. And now he'll never know me. Not the real me. Not the me you hid from everyone."

"Aidan," she said. "Something outside of my control is happening here. You can't blame me for that."

"Maybe you never had any control to begin with," I said. "Maybe I shouldn't have ever trusted you after I found out how much you lie."

Then I turned and left, slamming the back door behind me.

My mother had gone blind to the invisible world, apparently. She couldn't contact my father's spirit. She couldn't see the thread of blood I'd seen back in the woods when we'd found my dad's body. Now I knew that the invisible trail had been left there just for me. A secret message written in blood for one particular set of eyes to see.

From the place where the thread started, where my father's blood had leaked from his mouth after the fall, I began to follow the trail back up the side of the ravine, back through the woods to the place where I'd first found hoofprints. And from there I followed the thread as it unspooled further, leading me back to the edge of the woods, back through the lane to the pasture, where suddenly the thread veered in a wide arc and I followed it over the railroad-tie bridge that spanned Sugar Creek, until finally it disappeared into the hole at the bottom of the Living Death Tree.

When I looked up from the trail of my father's blood and stared at the gnarled old apple tree in front of me, the voice inside its hollow core said, *I've been waiting for you. Come in.*

And I got down on my back, assuming that resistance at this point was fairly futile.

The snow crunched beneath my weight as I began to slide backward along its surface, and then my head slipped through the hole at the bottom of the tree, which seemed to grow bigger and bigger as I pushed inside it, wider and wider, accommodating the width of my shoulders, until I had somehow fit myself inside the tree entirely, and then—

—I was falling through darkness.

chapter ten

SORROW ACRE

In the dark, falling through the silence, I screamed. Screamed like I'd never screamed before. Screamed until my voice flew out of my mouth and floated like a silk scarf through the thousands of miles of dark above me.

Then I landed, and the world shuddered.

When I opened my eyes, I had to blink over and over, had to put my hands to my face to make sure my head was still there, that I was still real. Light had returned suddenly, so bright I felt shot through with arrows and crumpled up in a ball on the ground, feeling like one of my migraines might surge through my brain at any moment and wreck me completely.

No surge came, though. Instead, I lay there, not moving, helpless to do anything but wait and watch, helpless to do anything but listen to the voice that whispered in my ear in that bright white void I'd landed in, unable to climb out.

This is the story, the voice of the Living Death Tree said. *This is what binds you.*

Then another wave of light washed over me, even brighter, blinding me once more.

And when my vision returned, this is what I saw. This is what she showed me.

A young man strode down a coal-patched back road lined on either side with towering silver maples. Light fell across their branches, oozed down to the tips of their leaves, collecting like sap, dripping. I stood beneath them, watching the heat and dust rise from the tar-spattered road in waves.

The young man wore a wide-brimmed hat to shield his face from the sun. He took it off, though, when he stopped to look at the land that spread out before him. After wiping the sweat from his brow, he waved at an old man sitting on the front porch of a farmhouse, who nodded in return, then raised his hand, signaling the young man to come join him in the cool shadows. And by the time the last embers of light dipped below the tree line at the back of the farm that evening—the orchard, the corn, the hay fields, the creek that wound through the center of that place, even those ancient maples lining the road—everything the young man could see, he owned.

His name was Lockwood, he told the Hodges family: two sallow-faced elderly parents of a too-skinny adolescent daughter. They wanted to go down to West Virginia, where they had family, they said, and where they'd heard there might be work available in coal mines. Running a farm, Hodges said, wasn't worth it when the drought burned your crops, and what the sun didn't burn, the grasshoppers devoured. They were already two payments behind with the bank, so Lockwood was able to buy the place from them for a song. Then off the Hodges family went in a rust-eaten green truck with its bed full of sticks for furniture.

Lockwood watched as they disappeared down the road in a cloud of dust, a clatter of gears grinding within the ancient vehicle. Then he turned to his farm and started to work it.

He was from somewhere up in New England, people in Temperance said after he'd been around town awhile, though none had heard this come out of Lockwood's mouth, and he didn't sound any different from them. He'd been the child of a minister, some said. Where he got his money, no one knew, but he arrived with enough to buy the Hodges farm when the Depression had grown so terrible that no one had cash any longer, not even hidden under their mattresses. There were whispers that he must have robbed his father's church before leaving. There were whispers of an argument between the father and son that had sent him packing. And though no one could trace the whispers back to a credible source, they lingered, as whispers do, as the voice of the Living Death Tree lingered in my own ears, telling me this story.

Each morning Lockwood rose before the sun did, and each night he returned to the house after the sun dipped below the horizon. He sowed fields and cut hay on days when the sun was strong and the wind dry, and when he wasn't tilling he was working to get his first corn in, to pick through his orchard, taking bites from the occasional apple as he climbed through the branches. He repaired the falling-down barn, painted the paint-flaked white house a goldenrod color, and after his first harvest, he'd made enough money to acquire a few necessities: two cows, a bull, and a wife.

He had one of the town girls in mind, a young woman he saw on her way to church each Sunday. Her name was Pluma Winchell, but everyone in Temperance called her Plumie. Her name reminded him of feathers, of smoke, of soft rose petals. All things that tickled, and indeed he was tickled each time he saw her walk through the town green with her mother, coming or going to church or the butcher. Her mother would slap Plumie's arm whenever she caught her cutting looks his way. "What are you looking at, girl?" she'd say. But that only made Plumie smile even harder.

He took Pluma Winchell for a wife the following spring, after the winter melted and the orchard blossomed. And when Lockwood brought her home, she exclaimed at the beauty of the apple blossoms that fell around her, dusting her shoulders. "Like snow," she said, only they held the warmth of the sun and the fragrance of early summer.

In their second year together, Lockwood became a father to a son, John Jr., and soon after, he purchased several neighboring farms when the banks foreclosed on their previous owners. The hands he hired to help as his own farm grew were sometimes the men who had owned the pieces of land he'd acquired. Most were immigrants with made-up first names like Mike or Charlie and real last names like Drbyniewski or Kubja who had dreamed of owning something in America. Now they scrabbled to survive and worked for what Lockwood offered, and with their help his harvests grew even larger.

By his third year, the farm ran like clockwork. Hay twice in the summer, apples and corn in the fall. He switched one field over to oats and Plumie started a vegetable garden between the creek and the house, putting up jars of tomatoes and carrots and green beans in the cold stone cellar. The bull Lockwood bought the year before had got the two cows with calf, so his livestock doubled. Things were going well, even if some of the hands were said to gather in one of the taverns near Mosquito Lake on weekends and complain that Lockwood had stolen their property.

A land baron, some called him, and from my place in the shadows of their story, I winced, trying to recall where I'd heard those words. They rattled around in the back of my memory like forgotten coins in a pocket. And when I picked them up to examine them, I remembered being a child at some school function for my brother Toby. I was no more than eight or nine, and the father of one of Toby's classmates was sticking a finger in my dad's face, arguing about something to do with the baseball game we'd been watching. I can't remember what sent them into an argument, but at some point during their fight, the man told my dad he wasn't better than anyone else in Temperance just because he'd come from a family of land barons.

"What did he mean?" I'd asked my dad as we walked away from the field not long after, making our way back to the Blue Bomb.

"Don't worry about it, Aidan," my dad had said, putting his big hand on my shoulder. "He doesn't know what he's talking about."

When I thought about it now, it didn't make sense. My dad and Grandma Bennie had had to sell off most of the farm in parcels over the years, just to get by after my granddad put a gun to his head and left my grandma to take care of a farm and a son on her own. We'd lost all of the land my great-grandfather, the real land baron, had purchased.

Lockwood. Great-Grandfather Lockwood. Now he stood on the railroad-tie bridge he'd laid across Sugar

Creek when he first arrived, and watched as the sun sank below the silhouettes of the trees at the back of his property. *There has to be something else,* he thought as he crossed the bridge to wander the fields at twilight. I could hear the faint voice of his father in the recesses of Lockwood's memory, the minister he'd stolen from to come here, to buy this property. The gloaming, Lockwood's father had called the hour when the boundary between worlds was thin and the fae folk could be seen on the horizon.

Behind his father's back, Lockwood had laughed at those stories, had laughed at how they'd come from his father's mouth. Imagine a minister believing in such things! But looking back, Lockwood didn't hold it against his superstitious father either. With the distance between them now, he was able to even find it a little charming. To think he had come from such a family! To think how he had somehow escaped them to make a better life than the one he'd been given!

He failed to remember that he'd stolen from his family in order to make this better life.

One evening in late summer, he drifted through the cornfields, their stalks taller than his head, their leaves brushing his face and shoulders. They were whispering of their pleasure in the soil, but Lockwood couldn't understand their vegetable language. And when they finally fell away from him, he found himself at the back of his property, at the edge of the woods, where he put the cows to pasture. The cows and their calves weren't there at this hour—they were back in the barn, their eyelids lowered—but something at first glance made him think one of them must have remained behind. It stood in the shadows of the oaks and hickories, snorting at him.

Lockwood was about to clap his hands and holler for the cow to move up the lane to the barn, but before his hands could meet one another, he froze, gasping at the creature that stepped out of the shadows. It was no cow after all. There, where the pasture met the woods, stood a white stag with antlers that branched out and farther out into a twisted ivory candelabra. The stag that had let me ride it home from another place and time, the stag that had let me ride it back to my own story.

The stag's eyes were round and black, its fur silver-white, and the tips of its antlers glowed in the purple evening shadows. Lockwood blinked as he dimly recalled a story his father had told him, a story in which this creature existed, a story Lockwood had never believed.

There is more than this, the stag told him. Just that, nothing else. It was as if the creature had emerged from the woods to deliver this one message as a warning. And for one long moment, as Lockwood stood there, open-mouthed and staring, he thought he might be dreaming.

Then the stag lifted its tail and kicked away, back into the woods, gone, as if it had never existed.

The vision began to shimmer then, and darkness filled my eyes like black water.

Do you remember this story? the voice asked me. I shook my head in the dark and said no, I didn't. I'd never seen any of this. Not that I could remember.

I showed it to you, once, she said. *I told you this story when you were still a boy.*

"When?" I asked.

When you were thirteen, the voice told me. *When you were awakening to the invisible world around you.*

"I don't remember any of this," I said.

Then I will show you once again, the voice said. *I will show you what should not be forgotten.*

The dark retreated. Light filled my eyes again. And in the center of that light, I saw a young boy. A dark-haired boy with green eyes and a streak of dirt smeared across his sweaty forehead.

A boy, the tree whispered, *who was slowly and secretly becoming a criminal.*

The criminal's name was Dobry Jablonski. Twelve years old, he lived with his mother on the edge of Temperance in a one-room shack his father had built shortly before dying. For years after emigrating from Poland, his family had lived in a mining town over the border in Pennsylvania, but they'd left a year earlier to finally start a farm of their own in Ohio, to start the life they'd dreamed of making.

Lies, Dobry Jablonski thought. *This country is full of them.* He hadn't been able to convince his father of this, even after they'd lost their land, or his mother, even after she began to take in other people's laundry, and all because they'd chosen to sail across the Atlantic and dream their lives into something better. But over time Dobry had come to notice how the dream of a better life didn't happen for most people, no matter how hard they worked, perhaps especially for those who worked the hardest. He would have complained to his mother about this, as he'd complained to his father, if only she hadn't lost her husband so recently. He didn't want to deplete what hope she might have left for their future. Hope could keep people going, he knew that, and he wanted his mother to keep going, despite how he felt.

Dobry was the man of the house now. His father had told him this while coughing up blood into a dirty handkerchief on his deathbed. That was months earlier, when the farm still belonged to them. Now Dobry worked for the man who had bought his father's farm when they could no longer make payments. Now he worked for the man who paid the wages of a slave.

There is no difference between this country and where we come from, Dobry thought as he stashed a basket full of apples at the edge of the orchard. He would walk past it later, after work, and take them home. *If this man wants to pay me a slave's wages, I will do what I must to compensate.*

Tall wooden ladders leaned into the green canopies

of the orchard, and the hands climbed up and down the rungs in dirty trousers held up by suspenders. Each picker held a sack in front of his stomach, with a rope strapping the sack around his neck. Arms outstretched, they reached into the light of the golden evening, past the thick leaves of late summer, to pluck the fat apples from their stems. Others wandered between the trees to deposit the apples in barrels Lockwood had placed near the corncrib. But Dobry had other plans. After leaving his stolen apples at the far edge of the orchard, he ran back to continue picking.

From the bedroom window on the second floor of the house, Plumie watched the boy at the edge of the orchard, stealing apples from her husband. She held the curtains apart only a few inches. Her breath was held at that moment, but the sheer blind swayed before her. It was I, a ghost standing next to her, who disturbed the curtains.

The dark-haired boy with green eyes and skin pale as chalk was stealing. Plumie had been watching him hurry away in the late afternoons with a sack full of apples for weeks now. She hadn't told her husband because the boy looked sick and the apples would do him good, she figured, and anyway, her husband didn't pay the boy enough but to buy a scrap of meat at the end of the week and minor provisions like salt and flour, perhaps a sweet to suck on for an hour. Her own children didn't want for anything. Plumie saw this as a fragile condition worth maintaining, but her heart still skipped a beat whenever she saw Dobry Jablonski scurrying away for the sake of a few apples. There he was now, returning, sack empty, to climb into the trees, to pull down the fat apples for the Lockwoods.

When Plumie turned to go downstairs, I followed her, taking the steps I took every day of my life down into the kitchen. Plumie needed to feed her daughter. Ethel would be hungry at this hour. The girl was a much easier baby than John Jr. had been. Initially Plumie had thought there would be some kind of strange competition with a girl for her husband's attention—this was something Plumie's own mother had told her to watch out for—but Ethel could not have cared less about her father. He was so rarely around. Off hunting, planting, cutting, raking, slopping manure into the spreader. And there he was now: Plumie saw him through the kitchen window while Ethel sucked at her breast. He was coming up the lane from the woods. Beside him, sunlight glinted on the rippled surface of Sugar Creek.

When Ethel finished, Plumie put her in the crib and went out to meet her husband. But when she looked through the gate of the barn, where she'd assumed he was headed, he wasn't there. And he wasn't in the lane where she'd seen him through the kitchen window a few minutes earlier. She turned toward the orchard then, and found him trudging across the railroad-tie bridge. She had to raise her hand to block the sun, though, and by the time she got the light out of her eyes, he had disappeared into the red-globed trees, where the hands could be seen stripping the apples away from their limbs.

A moment later, five crows fluttered out of the trees like an omen and cut through the blue air to land on the other side of the hay field, looking back at the orchard and nodding together, as if they knew something bad was about to happen. And only seconds later, Lockwood emerged from the orchard holding Dobry Jablonski by the shirt collar, slapping the back of the boy's head to make him move faster. The boy fell several times on the journey, went down on his hands and knees in the dirt and the ruts that led toward the barn. But Lockwood pulled him up, again and again, until they were in Plumie's garden, near her rhubarb. As they passed her, the boy managed to give Plumie a pleading look, like a nervous cow on its way up the chute to be slaughtered, and Plumie said, "John? John, what's the matter here? What's happened?"

Her husband didn't answer. He only moved toward the barn like a slow black cloud, full of thunder.

Once in the barn, he tied the Jablonski boy's hands to a post with binder twine that scratched at the boy's wrists and bit into his skin even as Lockwood knotted it tighter. Plumie came to watch them from the front gate, her hand at her heart, which fluttered like the crows had. Something terrible was about to happen. "John," she said, trying again to reach him, to reason with him. "What are you doing? This is a child. Have you forgotten?"

"You'll be sleeping with the cows tonight," Lockwood

told the boy, ignoring his wife's pleas. "And tomorrow you'll go to Warren to speak with the sheriff. What do you think about that, little thief?"

When Dobry Jablonski didn't answer, Lockwood spat at the boy's feet.

He unlatched the gate, still ignoring Plumie, and went back to the orchard full of anger and righteousness, to deliver a lecture on the villainy of thievery, to teach the Slavs and Poles and whoever else worked on his farm a lesson.

Plumie whispered into the air, as if God might hear her. "Oh please, oh please, oh please," she whispered. And each plea flew away like a crow, silent, sleek, and mysterious.

Word spread quickly that night, from household to household. Families who rarely spoke across their respective divisions talked of what had happened in the Lockwood orchard. Fathers and mothers warned their children not to steal, not here, not if they knew what was best for them. They scolded children who didn't even work for Lockwood. They scolded children who didn't work anywhere at all. Dobry Jablonski would be made into an example, and they knew this. This was exactly Lockwood's intention, to have everyone in Temperance distribute this warning for him, as he'd assumed they would.

Lockwood wandered around the house that night, oiling his rifle, occasionally peering out the window at the barn, where the Jablonski boy sat in manure, his legs splayed in front of him, his hands tied around a pole at his back. People had been tried for less, had gone to jail for less than stealing apples. Lockwood knew this, and he didn't care that he might seal the boy into a dark fate by taking him to see the sheriff in Warren the next morning.

At ten o'clock Lockwood joined his wife in bed, where he fell asleep as if nothing of great importance weighed on his shoulders, as if any other ordinary day had come to its inevitable end. Later I came to stand over them, the sleeping figures of my great-grandparents, and watched their mothlike breath hover over their parted mouths, watched the dip and rise of their stomachs as they inhaled and exhaled in unison.

Lockwood's dreams were busy that night. I watched them pass through his mind as his body slept. He dreamed of the white stag he'd seen at the back of his property. He dreamed of the stag lowering its head to take a long drink from Sugar Creek. When the stag had finally quenched its thirst, it raised its head and turned to look at him.

There is more than this, it told Lockwood.

And then Lockwood woke, sitting up in bed before me, shivering in a cold sweat.

Breakfast first, he thought, splashing his face with water in the washroom. Then he'd put the boy in his truck and drive over to Warren. He'd have one of the hands manage the farm for the day. He'd give instructions to the letter and the work would get done as if he'd overseen it himself, especially with the Jablonski boy's fate weighing on the pickers.

Plumie had breakfast ready by the time he got downstairs. She fed him eggs and bacon and toast and coffee. He drank the coffee black and bitter, the steam curling into his flaring nostrils. After finishing, he rubbed bits of egg out of his mustache and stood to leave.

Outside, while he sat on the porch to pull his boots on, he looked up to find a woman walking down the dusty road. She wore a scarf over her head. A *babushka,* the Slav women called them. Her skirts were nearly in rags; he could see that even from this distance. Her arms were folded under her breasts, as if she was sick or frightened. But if she was frightened, it did not stop her. She came toward him without hesitating, barefoot, turning off the road into his dirt drive and walking up the front yard to meet him.

Lockwood stood on the porch looking down at her. "Morning, ma'am," he said. "What can I do for you?"

The corners of the woman's mouth were turned down, and her eyes were glassy. Lockwood figured this must be the boy's mother. She had the same pale skin and green eyes. And what she did next nearly shocked him. It was something he'd never seen before. The woman got down on her knees before him and, in a thickly accented voice, begged for the life of her son.

"Get up," Lockwood said, trying to pull her from the ground. "Get up, woman."

But she would not rise. "It costs me nothing to beg," she told him. "I already lost everything years ago. In Poland, my family was better. My father was a healer. We were respected, you see? Here, we are nothing. Things can change for the worse, not just better. I understand this now. If you did not know this already, I will tell you. My son is all I have in this world. His father is dead. If I do not have my son, I die also. Please. I beg you. I ask only for you to give me my son and he will repay twice what he took from you."

Lockwood did not immediately answer. This woman—Eva Jablonski, if he remembered her name correctly—was something else. He was reminded of a different world, of a different time, when peasants knelt to beg for their lives or for the life of another. He thought of some of the tales his father had told him as a child. He thought of how the lords in those old tales displayed their lordliness by pardoning or by setting a task before a beggar to earn what they wanted. And wasn't he a kind of lord now? he thought. Wouldn't it be right to make a pact with this woman who asked for something without shame?

"I'll make you a deal," he told Eva Jablonski. The woman narrowed her eyes but held his stare. Lockwood turned to face the orchard, pointing toward it. "If you can pick that orchard clean by the time the sun sets, I'll give you back your boy."

Eva Jablonski turned to face the orchard, assessing the task set before her. She blinked twice, nodded wordlessly, then stood again, gathering her skirts about her, to trudge toward the trees.

Lockwood did not mention that nearly a quarter of the apples had been picked yesterday, that it had taken an entire day of five hands working together to clear just that one corner of the orchard. He had made the pact, and now he would see, as any lord would, if she kept her end of the bargain.

All that morning Eva Jablonski climbed the orchard ladders deep into the branches of the trees, picking apples. The sun rose higher, grew hotter, and as the farm's hands arrived, Lockwood informed them that there would be no work for them that day. They crossed the bridge over Sugar Creek anyway, and called up into the trees to Eva, asking her what had happened.

Eva did not linger with them. She simply said, "I pick these apples, Dobry comes home," and continued picking. The others looked at each other, wide-eyed, and started to climb the ladders to help. "No," Lockwood said from behind the ring they'd formed around the tree Eva inhabited. "She must do this alone."

Though they couldn't help Eva Jablonski pick the orchard, the hands rallied around her, carrying cups of water up the ladder to her occasionally, once two pieces of crusty bread. She stuffed the bread in her mouth and guzzled the water while still picking. Water sluiced down her chin, washing away trails of grime. "Good work, Eva!" someone shouted up to her. Someone else said, "Keep going!" But Eva didn't acknowledge their cries. She continued picking, placing the apples in the bag around her neck, carrying them to the barrels by the corncrib with clockwork precision.

Sometime in the early afternoon, Lockwood gave permission for the boy to be brought to the orchard, bound, to watch his mother work for him. She was not aware of his presence as he watched her struggle, sometimes becoming entangled in the branches, sometimes nearly falling, in order to save him. He cried, silently, the tears washing down his dirty face, as his mother heaved herself from tree to tree. She was not healthy; this much he knew. She had the same sickness that had killed his father. He could tell by the way she lumbered with the sacks of apples, coughing, wheezing harder as each hour passed, that she would soon not be able to pick any longer.

By five o'clock that evening, Eva Jablonski had cleared more than half the orchard. This in itself was a feat no one had thought possible. She had a quarter of the trees left to pick before the sun set. She had two hours left, three at most, and many men began to beg Lockwood to accept what she had done so far as payment for her son's transgression. Lockwood sat on the edge of the corncrib, chewing the stem of a daisy, and shook his head. "We've made a pact," he told Eva's supporters. "It would only be an offense to her if I changed the rules now."

By seven o'clock that evening, Eva Jablonski had picked nearly all of the apples in the orchard. The barrels were full to overflowing. The woman was hunched over in a terrible way. Sweat beaded and fell down her brow. Her mouth hung open; her tongue lolled like the clapper in a bell. "Only a few more, Eva," her supporters said from below. "Keep going, only a few more."

She fell into a pile of rags and skin and bones at half past seven, when the light was amber, glazing over the orchard like honey, and shadows had begun to spread. No one moved to pick her up. They waited, breaths held, hands at their mouths. And after a moment, the woman looked around, blinking, narrowing her eyes as if she'd gone blind, then somehow pulled herself up and went on to the last tree.

"She's going to do it!" a woman shouted, smiling from within her babushka.

Another mother, thought Lockwood. He wandered beneath the last of the apple trees, shaking his head at the marvel that was occurring. *The fierceness or stupidity of mothers,* he thought. Which of these traits did Eva Jablonski exhibit? He himself was unsure whether he'd do what Dobry's mother was doing, if it were his own child who was endangered.

Eva Jablonski picked through the apples in the last tree until the sun was nothing more than a red sliver on the horizon, lowering. She picked, then bagged the apple, picked, then bagged the next, heaving and sobbing, murmuring a nonsensical prayer. By the stunned and confused faces of her friends, it seemed not even those who spoke her language could understand what she was saying. And just as the sun lowered to the other side of the world, Eva Jablonski plucked the last apple from the last tree in the orchard.

She held the fruit in her hand, held her arm high in the air, and a bellow of exhausted strength flew out of her. People began to cry out. "She has done it!" they shouted. "She has done it!" And even Lockwood himself applauded the woman's tenacity, clapping his hands together slowly, shaking his head in admiration.

Everyone waited for Eva Jablonski to climb down and embrace her son, but slowly the arm holding the apple sank; then the woman's legs gave way beneath her, and she fell several feet before she was stopped halfway to the ground, caught in a tangle of branches. Her body hung in the tree for several moments before those below realized she was not moving, and finally a woman shouted, "Get her out! Quickly! Someone help her down from there!"

Someone untied the woman's son, and Dobry ran to the tree. His wrists red and raw from the twine that had held him, he climbed up to her and put his face next to hers but could not feel her breathing, could not hear the pulse of her blood. "Momma," he whispered. "Momma, get up." But Eva Jablonski remained still.

Two big men climbed up to fetch the woman's body. They pulled her down and laid her out on the ground beneath the tree, where everyone crowded to look at her for a long moment. Then, after they understood that Eva was dead, they picked her up and carried her away, back to her ramshackle one-room house at the edge of Temperance.

Before they left, Dobry Jablonski turned back to Lockwood and stared hard, his green eyes flashing. "You killed my mother," he said, and his voice had turned rough, as if he had become a man in an instant. His voice scraped with anger. Anger that was large, and growing larger by the second. Anger that was too large for a small boy to contain.

Lockwood shook his head and said, "We made a pact, your mother and I. You should be proud of her. She kept her side. She has paid for your freedom."

But Dobry Jablonski continued to stare at Lockwood, who seemed unnerved by the boy standing in front of him, refusing to leave with the others. He was rattled enough to take from his pants pocket a silver watch and stretch it across the space between them, placing it in the boy's hand. "Take this," he told Dobry Jablonski. "May it be a help to you in your future."

Dobry's eyes never left Lockwood's. They held his gaze throughout the entire transaction. And then, as Lockwood slowly but surely backed away from the boy, Dobry lifted one finger, pointing it at the man like a wand, and with an air of finality in his hate-steadied voice, he said, "You will grow old before your time. You will die in a place where no man will be with you. Your land will be taken from you, and your sons and their sons and their sons will wither until your name has no meaning."

There was magic in those words. It nearly shimmered in the space between Dobry's finger and Lockwood, like heat rising from a coal-patched road in summer. The silver pocket watch in Dobry's other hand gleamed, as if possessed by a spark of magic.

Lockwood cocked his head to the side, then spat on the ground between them.

The boy said no more. Eventually he turned to leave, and followed the caravan that carried his dead mother down the back roads, back to their home.

Lockwood did not give the boy's words too much attention. But later that night, he awoke, soaked in his own sweat, from a dream of the boy and his green eyes staring at him as he recited those same words.

Old before your time.

You will die. Alone.

Your sons will wither.

And in the dream, the boy's mother, Eva, rose from where she lay tangled in the branches of the apple tree, to pluck the words out of the air and tuck them deep inside a fold of her ragged skirts for safekeeping.

The sound of thunder cracked the sky open like a pocket watch, and Lockwood jumped from his bed to see lightning illuminate his bedroom window. He crossed the room, feet cold on the bare floor, to pull back the curtains and watch the coming storm.

Lightning flashed again, creating momentary cracks in the sky. And each time a bolt flashed, the barn and the orchard and the creek were briefly lit up below. Lockwood thought he should check on the cows. But just as he was about to go downstairs, he saw someone outside in the storm. A person. A person down in the orchard. The silhouette of a person standing beneath the swaying limbs of the apple trees.

Lightning flashed once more, and there she was, a woman standing beneath the tree Eva Jablonski had died in. When the lightning disappeared, the landscape winked out of existence, leaving Lockwood in the dark of his room, shaking his head. Another flash appeared moments later, but this time the bolt cut straight through the heart of the tree, setting the leaves on fire while smoke poured from the hole the lightning had cut through the trunk.

Lockwood ran downstairs and out of the house, barefoot, the rain soaking him, and crossed the railroad-tie bridge over Sugar Creek into the orchard. The woman he'd seen there—had she been hit by the lightning? When he reached the tree, though, he found no one. Licks of fire still crackled across the limbs while the trunk continued to smoke in the night.

The Jablonski woman. This had something to do with her; Lockwood was sure of it. But he shook his head after entertaining that thought. Was he turning into his foolish father now? Somehow believing what the Jablonski boy had said? Believing that curses had power? Believing that he would die alone in the middle of nowhere? Believing that the family he was making would die in the soil he'd planted them in?

The people of Temperance would come to call this plot of land Sorrow Acre. In time, though, they'd forget the reasons behind that name, and they would forget the woman who died as she toiled for her son's life. They would pack up all of their regrets and blissfully forget all that they could forget, protecting themselves from the sorrow that filled the soil and the trees in this place like a poison. The pact Lockwood had made with Eva Jablonski had guaranteed this, Lockwood realized. Eva had kept her end of the bargain. And one day he would keep his.

On the horizon, a creature of mist and shadow moved along the tree line, its eyes dark and glassy, its antlers flickering. Lockwood couldn't see it this time, but he sensed its nearness, as he sensed my own presence in the nearby shadows, the same presence he'd feel when I was with him several years later as we fell through a night sky in Europe.

He was already making plans. How to find the creature, how to kill it. He didn't know why, but he sensed the ill will the creature held for him. A war was about to begin in Europe. Rumbles and rumors of it had already begun. He would go there when they called for him to fight. He would go there even if they didn't call for him. And several years later, he would meet the creature again, in its own woods this time, on the other side of the Atlantic.

He would find it once more, after I'd flung myself out of the belly of an airplane with him. And after he found the stag again, he'd take the first step along the path each of his sons and grandsons would eventually take after him, until they had all withered and the name Lockwood no longer held any meaning.

Do you understand now? the voice asked as the vision began to disappear into wisps of smoke around me.

I was down in the dark hollow of the dead apple tree, blinking the last of the vision out of my eyes. I felt the earth beneath me again, smelled the dank odor of decaying wood, the mustiness of rotten apples, and quickly pushed myself out of that hole, sliding out onto a skin of ice, inadvertently making a blurry snow angel behind me.

This is your story, Aidan Lockwood, the voice said. *Do you understand me?*

I sat up to lean back against the trunk of the tree the woman had died in, caught in the web of gnarled branches strung above my very head, and nodded.

"If I understand you right," I answered her a second later, "then your name is Eva Jablonski. And your son cursed my family."

chapter eleven

THE LOGIC
OF GHOSTS

"What did she say then?" Jarrod asked later, after I'd gotten up from the ground in a hurry, after I'd refused to stay and listen to the woman in the tree any longer—she had said she had one more thing to show me, but I'd shaken my head, said no, said I'm sorry, said it was all too much—and had run across the railroad-tie bridge, returned to the house, passed by my mom at the dining room table whispering my father's name like a mantra, gone past the open door to Toby's room, where he sat in a chair with his bad ankle in a brace, staring out his window as if he might somehow see my dad appear at the edge of the woods to reveal that everything that had recently happened to us simply wasn't true. After all that, I'd called Jarrod to ask if I could come over.

Half an hour later, I was stretched out across the cushions of his couch with my head cradled in his lap. Staring up at his face was way better than staring up at the ever-widening crack in my bedroom ceiling.

"She said that she didn't make the curse," I told him, and described how the woman had shown me the dream my great-grandfather had had on the night she died in his orchard. How she'd shown me the moment her son, Dobry, had made the curse, how she'd reached out from the branches that held her dead body and plucked his words from the air, tucking each one into the folds of her ragged dress for safekeeping.

"So," said Jarrod, "she just, what—enforces it? How long has it been?"

"From what I can guess," I said, "about eighty or ninety years, give or take."

"That's one hell of a grudge," said Jarrod.

"I think it's what killed my dad," I said. "And I think it's also probably what killed my brother Seth."

I turned away from Jarrod to stare across the room at the television screen. In the blank gray eye of his mom's ancient TV, this hulking thing that sat on the floor surrounded by a huge cabinet, I saw myself reflected: my head in Jarrod's lap, his broad chest above me, his fingers playing with my hair, his other hand stroking my arm. In that antique TV, it all looked like a romantic scene from some old black-and-white movie, only with two guys on the couch instead of a man and a woman. Despite the warmth of the reflected image, though, and despite the warmth of Jarrod's body, I felt cold enough that goose bumps had risen on my skin as I told him what I'd learned.

"You mean your brother who died of a seizure?" Jarrod asked. He'd seen Seth's picture in the living room when he was at my house for the first time months before, had asked if Seth's picture was a photo of me as a little kid. When I told him the truth, when I told him Seth was a brother who had died before I was born, Jarrod had blinked and stuffed his hands into his back pockets as he looked at the picture once more, this time considering it more thoughtfully, trying to imagine what it would be like to have a sibling you'd never even met. When he turned back to me a second time, he said only that he thought my mom's features were dominant in my family.

And I'd thought, *Unfortunately.* If it weren't for her, after all, if I were more like my dad, I might not have ever seen a vision or been pulled into the world's shadow. I might never have spoken to a ghost who lived in a tree and kept a curse that would inevitably destroy my family.

"My mom used to always say Seth died from a seizure," I told Jarrod now. "That was her story. After I started to see and hear things back in October, though, her story changed. She said Seth had seen something he shouldn't have."

"Like what?"

"I don't know," I said, shaking my head in Jarrod's lap. It was the woman in the tree, I thought. She'd spoken to Seth, I figured, just like she'd called out to me over the last few months. It had to be that. Or it had to be *something* like that. She'd shown Seth the vision she'd shown me. Or she'd shown him something else. A white stag or a man in a black suit wearing a wide-brimmed black hat and a scraggly red beard, his face craggy and pitted. She showed him something that would kill him, or she'd killed him herself somehow. I was sure she had something to do with it.

"So why would the woman tell you that story?" Jarrod asked. "Why wouldn't she just let the curse take you, too?"

"I don't know," I said. "I felt like she would have if she could have. But something was stopping her. There's something she can't do to me. I could feel that. I just don't know what's stopping her, or why."

"Listen to us," said Jarrod, "trying to figure out the logic of ghosts, when clearly they have to be pretty irrational to stick around here for so long holding grudges. Why try to make sense of them?"

I turned to face him again, relieved to see a corner of his mouth rise into a smile. He ran his fingers through my hair in one long stroke a second later, then leaned down to kiss me. His hair brushed my forehead, and his lips were strong. They tasted of cinnamon and were sweet like sugar. I could have kissed him like that forever, just to feel safe, just to close my eyes and see nothing else in this world, just to feel nothing else in this world but my skin against his, his breath on my collarbone, my fingers tracing the cage of his ribs as he enveloped me.

Nothing felt more right than that. Nothing felt more right than the two of us. I just didn't know how to make us work beyond the shelter of this trailer on the far edge of town. I didn't know how to make us work beyond the secrecy of my bedroom. And I worried that what we had together, this fire between us, could be put out by others if we were visible. If we let anyone see us.

When Jarrod pulled away, I said, "*You* have to be pretty irrational too, to stick around here for so long, you know."

"Around Temperance?" he said, grinning, waiting for me to turn what I was saying into a joke of some kind.

"No," I said. "Around me." And I wasn't joking. I couldn't muster an ironic tone, because I believed what I was saying. That I wasn't worth it. That I had too many problems. Even if he was gay and his dating pool limited by being in Temperance, he could have found someone else. Someone whose family wasn't so messed up.

Jarrod's smile disappeared then, but his hand found mine and squeezed, hard, tight, like he would never let me go.

"Being in love isn't irrational," he said. "It only looks that way to people who have never felt it."

"Is that what we are?" I asked. "In love?"

For a moment after I put the question out there, it filled

219

the room like a fog. I tried to see the two of us the way anyone else might if they were to open the door of the trailer right then. I tried to see myself lying beneath Jarrod, my hands drifting under his shirt to slide across the warm skin of his back. Then I wasn't trying to see, wasn't imagining anything at all, as my hands did find their way under his shirt and began to travel up the warm skin of his back. Then he was leaning down, kissing me harder than before, and I put my arms around him, kissing him harder too, like we were in this ridiculous kissing contest or something. Who could obliterate the other one with his lips? Who could show the other one he wanted him more? Then he was fumbling with the button of my jeans, until suddenly he released it, and then both of our mouths parted, as if we were somehow both surprised at this conclusion. Then we closed our mouths again, put them back against one another.

In love. It felt like a real possibility. It felt like it was more than a possibility, actually. Like it was maybe our destiny, if you believed in destiny. The way Jarrod sometimes talked, and the way I was turning down paths I never knew existed, I was starting to believe. I thought back to the vision I'd shared with him when we were in middle school, the one I'd shown him in Mill Creek. The one he would eventually show me. What had I really shown him that day? *A future where we were still friends,* he'd said when I'd asked him that question a few months earlier. Then he'd looked out the window of the Blue Bomb as we drove home, as if he was embarrassed by something he couldn't admit.

That wasn't the truth, of course, and I could see it now. He'd played down that vision. I'd shown him something more than our friendship lasting into the future. I'd shown him something more like this, something more like now, where the two of us were alone in this ramshackle trailer on the outskirts of town, him squeezing my hand as he pulled away from a kiss to finally answer my question: "Is that what we are? In love?"

"Yes," he said, low down in his throat, like he didn't want any argument about it. And then the fog of my question began to evaporate, the air to clear between us. "That's what we are."

Jarrod began to slip his hand around my waist, to pull at my jeans, to peel me open. I didn't know what to do—other than what we were already doing—and stopped him to say as much.

"Don't worry," he said, brushing his thumb against my cheek. "I can show you."

If ghosts weren't entirely logical, neither were human beings. *Some* human beings, anyway. My mother, for one, had stopped making sense months before, even though I suspected there had to be some kind of method to her madness. But madness might have been the problem in the end. After my father's death, it seemed like my mom stopped making sense even to herself. It was always candles and a fire roaring in the fireplace now, as if she couldn't see anything outside of the flames she constantly stared into. It was as if the material world had dropped away from her abruptly, and she kept falling now, falling away from a reality she couldn't face.

When I came home from Jarrod's later, my mom wasn't in the living room staring into the fireplace, though. And she wasn't in the dining room staring into the flickering light of a candle. The house was silent except for the creak of the floorboards as I stepped across them. But as I started up the stairs to the second floor, I heard muffled voices, and when I reached the top step, the voices became clearer. Words slipped beneath my brother's closed door and skittered across the hallway like mice.

I stepped closer, quiet as I could, until I was at the door with my ear pressed against it. "Try harder," my mom was telling Toby. "You had to have seen something more. Something else. You're able to do that, you know? If you try hard enough, you can see things other people can't. You're a lucky one, Toby, like your brother and me. You just have to give yourself permission."

"I don't know what you're talking about, Mom," Toby said, and I heard a note of totally-freaked-out ringing through his voice. "I've told you everything," he continued. "I was up on the ridge in my stand. Dad was down in his. I could see him from above. Right before he fell, he raised his muzzle-loader up to his shoulder like he was going to shoot at something. But there were no deer around, as far as I could see. There wasn't anything. It was just snow and the wind blowing more snow. We hadn't seen anything all day but some squirrels digging around in the drifts. Then Dad shot, and then the next thing I knew, he was clutching his chest like all the air had gone out of him. Then he started to lean forward, like something was pulling him over, like he was struggling to stand. Then he fell from the tree and I started to climb down mine to go to him. I'm telling you. That's all I saw. That's everything."

"Well," my mother said, "I suppose this is partially my fault."

"How?" Toby asked. "What are you talking about?"

She was silent at first. Then, quietly, she said, "I should never have blinded all of you. I should never have told that story."

"Please, Mom," Toby said in the weak voice that only came out of him in his most anxious moments. Which were rare, almost nonexistent, or at least had been up until the past few weeks. "I don't know what you're talking about. You're scaring me."

I thought about opening the door and interrupting; I thought about bursting in and demanding she tell us what she was going on about with this story she kept mentioning, like she'd done the night Jarrod came over. But right as I grabbed the knob, I heard her stand and scrape Toby's desk chair back into place before saying, "You don't have to be afraid, Toby. I'm going to protect you. I'm going to keep us all safe."

The floorboards creaked as she came toward the door, and I turned to go back downstairs. I only made it to the midway landing before the door opened, though, and I turned around fast, put my hand on the newel post, and pretended I was just then coming up.

"Hey," I said as my mom closed Toby's door behind her.

She didn't say anything at first, just stared down at me as I came the rest of the way up. When I reached the top, she said, "You have something in your eyes," and reached out as if she were going to pluck a speck of dust away from my eyelashes. I flinched and backed up to the edge of the staircase, as if she were about to hit me, and she dropped her hand. "Why are you looking at me like that?" she asked. "I wasn't going to hurt you."

"My eyes are fine," I said. "I'm just tired."

"You shouldn't be going out all the time," she said. "Your father would be upset if he knew how often you're not at home now. He'd be upset if he knew how much time you spend with Jarrod."

I flinched again, this time at what she was implying. She knew Jarrod and I were doing more than playing video games and studying for tests. She knew everything, unfortunately. And she knew that my dad would have been ashamed of me if he'd known. Guilt was her weapon of choice tonight, but I refused to let her work that kind of magic on me.

"I still get my homework and chores done," I said in my defense. I wasn't going to let her use my dead father to guilt me from beyond the veil. No way should she get to say what he'd think or feel about anything, I figured.

Especially since she hadn't been able to find his spirit over the past few weeks of her constant scrying.

She shook her head and said, "That's not the point."

"What *is* the point?" I demanded.

"The point," my mother said, then stopped midsentence to stare at me, her eyes frozen somewhere between anger and confusion. "The point," she repeated, still unable to complete her answer.

She turned quickly then and retreated to her room, clicking the door shut behind her, as if she'd realized she would have only shamed herself if she'd finished that sentence.

"Yeah," I whispered, alone in the hallway again. "I kind of figured."

At school, since my dad died, people had started to treat me a little differently. They'd started to see me. To nod in the hallways, to say hello, to ask how I was doing. After all the years I'd spent being invisible, I didn't know what to make of the attention. Why had they all changed so suddenly? Was it because my dad had died in a hunting accident? In a town like Temperance, where more than half of the junior and senior classes were absent on the first day of deer season, there would be sympathy for something like that. People would think, *That could have been me or my dad.* They would see me now because when they looked at me, they'd see themselves.

Or was it because I was always hanging out with Jarrod Doyle? Jarrod had joined the baseball team and was off-the-charts better than the other players. And because of that, he'd started to scale the ladder of popularity without much effort. Had I been lifted up into the range of everyone else's vision because he'd taken an interest in me?

Maybe it was both of those things. Sympathy for a guy whose father died while hunting, respect for a guy who a popular, seemingly normal person like Jarrod had taken under his wing.

Whatever the reason, it didn't matter. I nodded back, returned their hellos, smiled at their smiles, said I was fine, thank you. I did and said Normal Things. But it was too late to truly become friends with people I'd hardly spent any time with in the last few years. I mean real time. Not just forced to occupy the same space for several hours at school five days a week. *You were liked,* Jarrod had said when I'd asked if I used to have friends, back before my mom did something to mess up my head. Any one of these people might have once been a friend, and I just couldn't remember. And neither, it seemed, could they, thanks to my mother. On top of that, each time I tried to search inside myself for the memories she'd hidden from me, a flash of white pain would burn through my brain like a bolt of lightning.

Like the bolt of lightning that burned through the trunk of the Living Death Tree, hollowing it out from top to bottom.

I didn't let this depress me. There were only a few months of classes left, and I didn't want to play the role of the nobody who suddenly becomes everyone's friend right before graduation. Those kinds of endings to books and movies always seemed dishonest. As if the point of life was to be liked and accepted. I didn't need to be liked or accepted. I needed to know and to accept myself. And when I dug down through the muck of my mixed-up memories and feelings, the only person I could say I wanted to be around right then was Jarrod. Everyone else? They were paper people. They were the background to my life. Jarrod was the foreground.

At lunch, I told Jarrod what I'd overheard in my brother's room when I got home the night before. I told him how my mom had been acting and about the strange things she'd been saying to me and now to Toby.

"I'm sorry, Aidan," he said, shaking his head across the table. "But it sounds like she's completely lost it. You might have to get together with your brother and see if you can get her to a doctor. Like, you know, a psychiatrist or something."

"I don't know." I looked around the cafeteria as if I might find an answer on the faces of the other students. "I think she's making some kind of sense," I said, turning back to Jarrod, "but I don't have enough information to understand. It's like she's having a conversation with people who should already know what she's talking about. But Toby and I don't have a clue. She told Toby how she should have never told *that story,* just like she told you that you weren't a part of the story. Remember?"

Jarrod nodded. "When she said that, I just figured she thought I was intruding on you all when she needed some privacy. I thought it was understandable, considering what had just happened with your dad."

"What story is she talking about, though?" I asked, more of myself than of Jarrod.

He leaned back in his molded plastic chair, folded his thick arms across his chest, and raised one eyebrow at me skeptically. "You know, Aidan," he said, "if you want to find out, you're going to have to do something you ordinarily wouldn't."

"Like what?"

"You're going to have to go snooping," said Jarrod.

"Snooping?" I said. "But where?"

"Around your house," Jarrod said, spreading his hands in front of him as if this were as obvious as the trays with the remains of our lunch sitting in front of us.

"But there's nothing there I don't see every day of my life," I said. "What could I possibly find?"

"What if there's something you see every day of your life and you just don't realize it holds the answers?" One corner of Jarrod's mouth rose into a grin; then he put his elbows on the table and leaned over our trays, coming closer and closer, until it seemed like he was going to kiss me right there in the cafeteria in front of everyone.

I must have frozen up, though, thinking about everyone

seeing us, because in the end he stopped short. A good four or five inches still stood between us, and now he looked more like he was just leaning in to whisper a secret. "You have to start treating everything in your life like it might be a whole lot more than it seems on the surface," he told me.

"What about you?" I said, dropping my stare, looking down at the pillow of his lips instead of his dark eyes. "Are you more than you seem?"

"You've already found me out," he whispered. "You found me out months ago."

Jarrod had practice after school almost every day, as the team was gearing up for spring scrimmages. So he wasn't waiting at my car anymore like I'd gotten used to. Now we said goodbye after he changed in the locker room and came out wearing a baseball uniform, punching his fist into a glove. I drove home alone later that afternoon, hoping I'd be able to figure out some way to snoop, even though my mom was always around, haunting our hallways like a confused ghost.

Toby, thankfully, had gone back to work and was bringing in money to keep things going. I didn't know what we'd do without him, so I kept up with my before-and-after school chores in the barn, feeding and watering the cows, forking their manure out, distributing hay and clean straw, to help him as much as I could. But it was Toby who started to get the mail and to sort through it; it was Toby who started to pay our bills; it was Toby who was given my dad's old job at the county, rising from road crew to crew supervisor. It all made me feel a little sad and a little guilty, thinking of all the burdens he was taking on for us to keep us going. He was reliving my dad's story. Reliving the story of my dad helping my grandma Bennie after our grandfather shot himself in the same place my father had fallen.

I couldn't let the same thing happen to Toby. I couldn't let it happen to me, either.

When I got home, it would only be my mom I had to contend with. She rarely left the house anymore, and she'd lost weight in the two months since my dad died. Her cheeks had started to sink in a little, and the fine lines in her face had grown like the crack in my bedroom ceiling. My mom was already in her early fifties, but in just a few weeks she'd started to look even older, as if Age, like a harbinger of death, had come to her in the middle of the night and waved his wand over her sleeping body, withering her as she lay there dreaming.

When I came into the kitchen through the mudroom, she wasn't at the table drinking coffee and reading the news on her tablet like she used to. She'd given up most of her old daily rituals by then. I found her in the living room instead, kneeling in front of the fireplace, building a fire. Her new daily ritual. A bucket of ash sat next to her, so she must have spent the afternoon cleaning the hearth.

"Hey," I said as I came into the room and dropped my backpack on the couch. And for a second afterward, I looked at the backpack I'd thrown so casually and wished we could go back to the days when life seemed mostly normal. Back to the days when I came home, threw my backpack on the couch, and thought of nothing but schoolwork and helping out around the house. Back to the days when I'd been blinded, back when I'd been protected from the invisible world. Back when I didn't know a damned thing other than the routines I went through like a trained dog.

"Hey," she said, her voice low and hoarse, as if she found it hard to speak after days of not uttering a syllable. She didn't look away from the fireplace, just kept arranging sticks of wood and twists of newspaper in there, as if she were at a crucial stage in the making of a work of art or a bomb.

"What are you doing?" I asked, as if I didn't already know the answer. It was late March, and even though the temperature had started to rise, melting the snow a little more each day as we moved closer to spring, my mom kept making fires.

"I'm looking," she said. Just that. And I didn't try to keep her talking. I just stood there and watched her light a match against a twist of newspaper, which she used to light the other twists she'd placed along the pile of kindling. I noticed she'd put a bunch of dried flowers on the pile too, which began to emit a strange sweet scent after the petals flared, their edges crisping before blackening in

231

the next instant. My mom sat back on her haunches then, folded her hands on her lap and stared at the flames as they crawled across the wood, popping and sparking.

Since she wasn't talking, I went upstairs, ready to throw myself onto my bed and think about where to snoop. But before I even got to my room, I noticed my mom's door slightly ajar across the hallway. I could see her unmade bed through the sliver of open space, and that was when I realized where I should start my search.

I curled my fingers around the knob and pushed the door open, slowly, trying to avoid the alarm of a squealing hinge. Successfully silent, I stepped inside. But as soon as I crossed the threshold, I stopped, looked over my shoulder, and turned to hear if my mom had broken away from her place by the fire. All I heard was the distant crackle of flames, though, so I went the rest of the way in.

Her blinds were pulled down and her quilts had been cast to the floor at the foot of the bed, as if she'd thrown them off in a nightmare. Otherwise, everything seemed like it always was in there: neat and tidy, as my mother liked things. I felt increasingly stupid as I looked around at her alarm clock, at the framed photo of her and my dad on their wedding day on the stand next to her bed, at her jewelry box on her dresser and the antique wardrobe that once belonged to my grandma. The door of the wardrobe was partially open, revealing the arm of a blazer my father had occassionally worn, dangling in the shadows. My mom kept a few other things in there too: her wedding

dress, a few boxes of old photographs. There was nothing out of the ordinary here, I thought, shaking my head,
pursing my lips like my mother did whenever she was per-
plexed. There were no clues for me to find here.

As I turned to leave, though, I noticed the bookshelf.
It didn't really hold a lot of books but was lined instead
with knickknacks and some of the dolls my mom had collected when she was a little girl. Their eyes were black
buttons and their dresses were made from pale blue linen,
and in my particular circumstances at that moment they
seemed to sit on the shelves and stare at me like eerie
voodoo dolls. I worried that they were spies for her, that
they were already telling her through some kind of tele-
pathic communication that her private abode had been
disturbed.

The only book on the shelf was a photo album with the
name *Seth* written on the spine's label with a black felt-tip
marker. As soon as my eyes settled on that, those letters
flared as if they'd been set on fire, then cooled and blackened.

I reached out to pluck the album off the shelf and stared
at it for a while, examining it like it might be a holy book.
I'd only seen it up close once before, when I was little—
maybe five or six—and I'd come into this room investigat-
ing, like any curious little kid would do. I remember how
the book seemed so big to me, how it felt so heavy I had to
sit on the floor to open it. Back then, I'd only been able to
look at the first couple of pages before my mom had come

in and found me with it. "Aidan!" she'd said, as if I'd been playing with a loaded gun. "Don't touch that!" She took it from me and put it up on a higher shelf, out of my reach, and said that I should never invade someone's privacy. I didn't understand what privacy was, so she explained it. "Privacy is someone else's space. Privacy is where a person can be alone and where they can keep their special things and no one should ever disturb it."

Funny, I thought now, how my mom had invaded the privacy of my own skull, how she'd ransacked my memories with such ease after being so adamant that I keep out of her things when I was just an innocent kid. She was such a hypocrite. The more I thought about everything she'd done and how she'd been since my dad died, the more I felt an incredible disgust for her. And simultaneously felt guilty for feeling that way. *She's your mother*, I kept telling myself, the same way I told Jarrod that his mom just wanted good things for him, even if her actions didn't always seem to show that.

I took the book across the hall to my own room rather than staying in my mother's space this time. I was no longer so innocent. I knew now not to linger.

I opened the album on my bed and started to flip through the pages, hoping that whatever I needed to know would just declare itself to me so I could get this over with. Mostly it was just photographs of Seth as a baby, though. One, two, three years old. Then he was the five-year-old whose portrait still hung on the wall in our living room, looking out at me with the deep green eyes he and my mom and I shared. Those eyes that saw things they shouldn't.

Everything seemed normal—it was just a memory album for a dead child—and I started to feel stupid for thinking the book would somehow hold the answers I needed. But right as I was about to give up, I flipped back to the beginning. There was this one old picture of my mom holding Seth in a light blue blanket in front of a yellow house with crystal wind chimes hanging from the porch ceiling. At first glance, I thought it was our house, because it was almost the same color, and because my mom had had a set of those crystal wind chimes hanging from our porch for as long as I could remember. But something else was off about it, and I felt drawn to look at it harder.

It *wasn't* our house, I realized, despite the wind chimes, despite the similar color. The porch was completely wrong. The porch in the photo had a wraparound railing with decorative spindles lining it. Ours was an open stone porch with just support posts on either side and in the center, no decoration. But the really strange thing—other than the house in the photo not actually being ours—was the perspective of the camera.

My mom and Seth were on the far right of the photo, at its edge, nearly cut off, even though there was a ridiculous amount of empty space ranging from the middle of the photograph over to the left border. It looked like my mom should be standing next to someone, but there was no one there. Why, I wondered, had the photographer taken the photo so off-center?

I pulled the plastic cover away and slipped the photo out of the page, turned it over. On the back, scrawled in my mom's handwriting, were the words *Seth meets Aunt Carolyn, Lily Dale, NY, August 1980.*

"Lily Dale?" I murmured. "New York?" I said a little louder. Why were my mom and dad and Seth in New York when they'd never taken Toby and me beyond Cleveland? And who was Aunt Carolyn? I'd never heard that name before. Not ever.

I turned the photo over again and looked at it even harder, as if I might burn right through it with hyper-focused heat vision, Superman-style. But I only saw the same image of my mom holding Seth off to the right of the photo, with the porch railing taking up the left half. Something was wrong with all this, but I didn't know what.

"The eye is a tricky thing," my mom said suddenly, and I looked up, startled to find her standing in the doorway of my bedroom. "Sometimes," she said, "you have to close your eyes to see what they're missing."

She didn't move from the doorway to take the book away from me like she'd done when I was little. She just stood there, her face sagging with the weight of her collected grief. When she didn't say any more after a while, I looked down at the photo and closed my eyes.

In the dark of my mind's eye, the image floated like a photo in developing chemicals. There was my mother, a young woman in her early twenties, holding her first child in her arms in front of a yellow house with wind chimes hanging from the porch ceiling. But in what had been the empty space beside her, a ghostly figure slowly began to develop, until a dark-haired woman wearing an old-fashioned floral print dress appeared, cupping Seth's chubby hand in hers as she stood next to my mom.

"That's your aunt Carolyn," my mother said as the image of the woman developed. And when I opened my eyes again, there she was in the photo.

"Why haven't I ever met her before?" I asked.

"Because," my mom said, "if I was going to protect you all, she couldn't be a part of the story."

"What's the story you keep mentioning?" I asked.

"It's the story I told," my mother whispered, sounding like she might burst into tears at any moment. "It's the story I hoped would save your father and you boys."

"Are you talking about the curse?" I asked.

My mom's eyebrows rose a little at hearing that. "So," she said, "she finally got to you again?"

"The woman in the tree," I said. "Eva. What do you mean by *again*, though?"

"She first got to you when you were thirteen," my mother said. "Tried stirring things up with you back then. Back when you started seeing things like Old Black Suit. That's when I told the story. I told it to hide you all from her."

"How can we stop her?" I asked. "There has to be a way."

My mom shook her head firmly. She didn't have to say anything for me to know that the subject was off-limits. "You were always a curious child, Aidan," she said. "You were always getting into things you shouldn't. I should have known you'd be everyone's undoing, even after all the trouble I went through to protect you."

"You don't mean that," I said, feeling like she'd just plunged a knife into my chest.

"It's not your fault, baby," she said. "It's just in your nature to want the truth. That's because of me, though. That's my fault. You got your eyes from me, after all."

"What's the truth?" I asked her.

My mother shrugged, defeated. "I've been telling stories for so long, trying to correct things," she said, "I'm not sure if I know any longer."

"Where is this place?" I asked. "This Lily Dale?"

"Lily Dale," my mom said, cupping one cheek in her hand, smiling a far-off smile, as if I'd jogged a memory of a place she'd forgotten or would have liked to forget. "Lily Dale," she said again, shaking her head and grinning like a madwoman, before she turned and left.

THANKS TO
THE INTERNET

Thanks to the Internet, I didn't need my mom to answer my questions. Within a few hours of searching on my laptop, I discovered a few things about Lily Dale, New York, without any trouble at all.

I discovered, for instance, that Lily Dale was a community of spiritualists. Mediums. Psychics. All of those words my mom once said didn't describe her—here they were, glowing on the screen of my laptop. And beside my laptop lay the photo of my mom holding my brother Seth with the words *Lily Dale, 1980* written on the back.

Liar, I thought. How could I believe *anything* she'd ever told me?

Beyond that, I discovered that the house of the Fox sisters—these two girls who cracked their ankles beneath a dinner table in the mid-1800s to convince everyone they were communicating with spirits—had been moved to Lily Dale at the turn of the twentieth century so the house could be appreciated by a community that revered it as the place where spiritualism had first started. *Ankles,* I thought. *Is that all it took to fool people?* When I clicked on a link to the history of the Fox house, I discovered it had burned down in the 1950s, and now the ghosts of the sisters were said to roam the forest surrounding Lily Dale, looking for their front door. I guess that's a suitable punishment for two girls who tricked so many people.

And I discovered that Lily Dale, New York, was only a two-hour drive from Temperance, Ohio. And not a minute after that discovery, I'd downloaded a map telling me how to get from here to there.

I looked again at the photo of my mom holding my brother Seth in front of the yellow house in Lily Dale and could see in the shadows of the porch a house number posted above the front door: a single, solitary four. It was all I had to go on—the name of a small town even weirder than Temperance, and a house number—but it was more than I'd ever had to go on until now. It would lead me somewhere, I was sure. I just hoped it wasn't a dead end.

I called Jarrod to fill him in on everything I'd discovered, and after I finished, the first thing he said was "When do we leave?"

"*We* aren't going anywhere," I said. "You have baseball practice. You can't miss or the coach will throw you off the team."

"I don't care about his stupid rules," said Jarrod. "I care about you. And besides, he'd never do that. The team is total crap. Without me pitching they've got no one, and Coach knows it."

"I care," I said, "even if you don't. You can't come. It might mean a scholarship if scouts don't see you play, and then your mother's dreams will be crushed and it'll be all because of me. So, no, you can't come. End of argument."

Jarrod sighed, but he didn't say anything.

"All right?" I said a few seconds later, hoping he'd relent. "I can do this on my own," I added, trying to make him feel better about it. "I don't always need a protector, though I do appreciate you worrying. I do."

"All right," he said, finally giving up. "But don't do anything dangerous." He insisted that my going there alone be only on this one condition.

"I won't do anything dangerous," I said. "Promise."

"Good," he said. "I didn't get myself kicked out of my dad's house just to come back here and lose you right after finding you again."

"I promise," I said again, trying to etch those words into the ethereal stone of the cell phone wavelengths between us. "I promise I won't do anything dangerous."

But my silent response, the thing I would have never said out loud to him, was: *Jarrod, I don't think there's anything I can do right now that won't be dangerous.*

Because really, in the end?

I was in way over my head.

The next morning I slung my backpack over my shoulder, just like I would any other day as I prepared to leave for school. I didn't want my mom to know my plans. I didn't want some kind of hex being thrown at me to stop me. But even as I followed my normal routine to a tee, my mom appeared on the top step of the stairs between the mudroom and kitchen, calling my name just as I put my hand on the doorknob.

"Don't do this, Aidan," she said, holding one hand against the doorway like she needed its support to ground her, holding the other hand out to me.

I turned toward her but kept my hand on the doorknob. "Don't do what?" I asked.

"Don't go where you're going," she said. "You don't know what you're doing."

"School?" I said, trying to sound normal, hoping I could still fool her.

She smiled down at me, but it was the thin smile she always had for me whenever I disappointed her. "I know where you're going, Aidan," she said. "I've almost always known what you were going to do before you did it. But, honey, you don't have to do this. You don't have to go there. The story I told hasn't completely fallen apart. I can still keep it together. But it will break if you go to Lily Dale, I promise you. It will break if you go, and then I won't be able to do anything to protect you and Toby."

When I heard her say "the story" again, I closed my eyes and pinched my bottom lip between my teeth so I couldn't shout at her in frustration. When I was calm again, I opened my eyes and said, "What *story* is it you keep talking about? If you haven't noticed, it's been a few weeks since you've made any sense."

"The story I told to save you," she said plainly, without shame, without regret, almost as if she couldn't believe I didn't understand where she was coming from. "Some of us—lucky ones, like you and me—we can do that. What about you, Aidan? Can you? Can you tell your own story, or are you being told?"

"I don't know how to tell stories," I said. "Not the kind you're telling. You never taught me how. Or else you did, and then you hid my memories from me, so now I can't remember."

"Don't go to that place, Aidan. Stay with your brother and me. If you go there, I can't protect you."

"You have a funny way of protecting people," I said. "You think that lying somehow protects them."

"Then let me tell you a truth." My mother stood above me like a judge announcing a verdict. "You'll be the one to find me after I've passed out of this world," she said, without tears, without a tremor in her voice. She nodded slowly, holding my gaze with her own, waiting for me to nod in return. And when I finally did nod, she smiled, relieved that I didn't argue with her like I'd been doing for most of that terrible year. It was the fact of what she was saying—that she would die and that I would find her, nothing more—that she wanted me to prepare for. There was nothing I could do but to allow this foretold death of hers to occur.

What can a person say to something like that when they're already halfway out the door?

The only thing I could do, really, was to tell her everything I'd been tamping down for months on end.

"You are completely messed up," I said, spitting out the words like poison I'd sucked from a snakebite. "You're delusional. You're a liar. I don't know how you can even live with yourself after everything you've done to us. To Dad, to Toby, to me. Everything about this family is a sham, and it's because of you and your damned stories. I'm going to do something about it, though. And I hope, if nothing else, you'll eventually realize your lies have only driven people away from you."

"You don't understand, Aidan," she said, holding her hand out even farther, wanting me to take it so she could pull me back into the house and keep me in the world of illusions she'd constructed around our family. "I told that story to hide you from the curse. But there's a price to pay for a story that changes things so much. The price meant you'd have to forget some things, yes, and that people around town would have to forget some things too, if it was all going to work. You have to understand. I know it's hard to believe, but I did this with all of my heart. I did it to save you."

I couldn't. I couldn't understand her. Not then. It was too much to take in, and I'd already decided she was deluded. So finally I turned the knob and pushed out into the open air, breathing deeply, deciding to say no more. If I stayed to argue, she'd get what she wanted. She'd still have me there, in the world she controlled. She'd talk me out of going out into the world to look for answers.

"I'll see you later," I muttered, shaking my head, then closed the door behind me.

When I got into the Blue Bomb a second later, I fired up the engine, then turned the car around in the drive so I could gun it all the way up to the road, spinning gravel beneath the tires like I was some kind of rebel. Before I reached the road, though, I had to slam on the brakes, because there, at the top of the drive, was someone standing in my way.

It was Jarrod, of course. It was Jarrod, standing with his backpack slung over his shoulder, blocking me from an easy exit. I could imagine him getting up early, slinging his pack over his shoulder, hoping to fool his mother into thinking he was going to school instead of what he actually went on to do, which was to walk eight miles in the early hours of the morning to get to my place before I took off for Lily Dale without him.

This guy. He just didn't play fair.

I let the Blue Bomb idle forward, engine sputtering, and stopped when he stood only a few inches away from the bumper. I rolled down the window then, popped my head out, and rolled my eyes before asking, "What do you think you're doing here?"

Jarrod gave me his most winning smile, which honestly was a winning smile, a smile even better than his fastball. I would have never been able to swing a bat fast enough to hit it out of the park. His smile flew straight at me, knocking me senseless. He didn't even have to answer my question, and he knew that he didn't have to.

"Fine," I said a second later, shaking my head, knowing this wouldn't go anywhere but where he wanted. "Get in."

He quickly slid into the seat beside me and slammed the door, then turned to plant a fast kiss on my cheek. "Hit it," he said after he pulled away. Then he slapped the dashboard.

I pushed down on the gas and turned onto the road, hoping the Blue Bomb would get us to our destination without any mishaps. It was a good car, but it had come by its family name honestly.

Then we were off, kicking up dust on the back roads of Temperance as we drove east across the Pennsylvania border.

chapter thirteen

CITY OF LIGHT

We were silent as we drove through the winter-barren fields, where old graying barns sat along the horizon like remnants of a lost civilization. And as the fields began to drop away and the hills of western Pennsylvania grew around us, Jarrod turned to ask a question that must have been sitting inside him since the night before, when I'd told him about the photograph. When I'd told him about my family having some kind of connection to Lily Dale.

"What do you think we'll find there?" he asked.

I shrugged, said, "I don't know. I suppose we'll

find some people like my mom and me there. At least, that's how it seems from what I found online."

"But some of the things you found also said the people up there are just, you know, fakes. Con artists exploiting people who are grieving or unsure of how to get on with their lives."

"Yeah," I said. "So?"

"So what will you do if you don't find what you're looking for? If it all turns out to be just a village full of supernatural hucksters?"

"I'm sure there are a lot of fakes," I said. "But there have to be some who are the real deal, right? Otherwise, why was my mom up there with Seth visiting this Aunt Carolyn? There has to be something there to find. There has to be something that will explain things."

"What do you mean?" Jarrod asked. "What would it explain?"

"My mom, for starters. It would explain how she can do the things she does." And then, with a little reluctance, I looked over and said, "And, you know, maybe it will explain who I am too. What I am, that is. Why I'm this way."

Jarrod reached across the space between us and put his hand on my leg, squeezing gently. "You don't need to be explained, Aidan," he said. "At least, not to me."

I didn't know what to say. I was afraid he'd laugh at any moment after saying that, and then I'd look like a complete idiot if I'd said anything that indicated I believed him. He didn't laugh when I looked over at him, though.

He just met my eyes and kept his hand on my leg for a long time after, squeezing harder.

He was so much more prepared for this thing between us. One night, a few weeks after my dad died, when I'd started to feel weird about us being together, especially after my mom started to imply that my dad wouldn't have liked it, Jarrod said, "If you could remember all the things you told me back when we were kids, when you could see the future clearly, you'd understand there's nothing wrong here. You'd understand this is our destiny."

Now, when I glanced at him in the passenger seat and saw again how much he loved me, all I could do was look down at his hand on my leg and say "Thank you" before turning back to the road and driving us farther toward our destination.

Two hours after leaving, we turned off I-90 into a town called Cassadaga, where the land was soft and gently rolling and the grays of the landscape back in Ohio had turned into browns and greens as spring soaked into the soil. Split-rail fences stood along the border of every field we passed. Grape orchards grew in clusters, just like grapes do, and wineries, it seemed, came into view at every other bend of the winding roads. The sky was bluer than I'd seen in a long while, since before winter, since before what happened with my dad down in Marrow's Ravine. I even rolled down my window for a while. Just to inhale the crisp air, just to breathe something new and clean. It was only a few minutes of driving through that small town, though, before Jarrod pointed out a road sign and said, "Looks like we're headed in the right direction."

I looked to where he pointed. LILY DALE, the sign read. And beyond it, a gravel road snaked off the highway into an old forest, thick with its new leaves starting to unfurl. That was where we had to go, then.

After we'd driven down that road for several minutes, with the tires crunching against gravel the entire way, we came to a large gated arch with the words CITY OF LIGHT etched on it. Beside the arch stood a small shack, where another sign was posted, stating how much it cost to enter for the day, the week, or the month, as if the place were a campground instead of a town you could come to and go from freely. No one was waiting inside that shack. It must still have been the off-season, I figured. So we drove through.

As we rounded a bend in the road, a glint of sunlight on water suddenly flashed through a keyhole opening in the woods, revealing a path down to a lake beyond. Then we passed by an old diner, which from all appearances seemed closed: the doors chained, the row of front windows battened down with peeling shutters. Up ahead, though, through the branches of trees hanging over the road, the roofs of houses finally sprouted into view, and when we passed under those trees, a village appeared before us like a mirage in the distance.

I slowed the car to a stop, the brakes squealing a little right there in the middle of that old gravel road, and said, "This must be it."

But "it" wasn't much more than a small network of streets no more than three or four blocks long, each lined with tiny Victorian houses painted in a variety of pastel colors: pink, yellow, blue, grass green. "It's an Easter egg town," I said as we peered out at it, and Jarrod agreed.

For a while we just sat there, looking at the place as if one of us might suddenly say "Well, that's it, let's go," and then we'd back the car up and head home without really taking a look around. I wanted to do that, actually. I wanted to leave now that I was here, rather than face whatever it was I had to find. Eventually, Jarrod said, "Seems like this place is just nine or ten streets on a grid at most. At least we won't have to look too hard for the house in that photo. Are you ready to do this?"

Was I ready to do this? My knuckles had turned white from my tight grip on the steering wheel, and that was probably an indication that I wasn't ready for anything. But I didn't answer Jarrod. Not at first. I stared out the windshield as the engine occasionally shuddered from all the miles I'd forced the Blue Bomb to take us in one go. Somehow, that ancient heap of a car kept humming while we sat there. If the old wreck had made it this far, I figured I had to do right by it. I had to finish the journey. I had business here. I just wished I knew what to expect from the business.

Was I ready? No, not really. But I made myself nod in answer to Jarrod's question, then pressed down on the gas, allowing the Blue Bomb to crawl forward.

It only took us ten minutes of driving up and down the narrow roads of Lily Dale before we spotted a yellow house with the same kind of spindled front-porch railing I'd seen in the photo from Seth's memory album. Jarrod spotted it first, actually, and then I said there were probably ten other yellow houses around here just like that one, and that we wouldn't find the right one until we came to the very last house. But he was right. As we pulled closer, I took my foot off the gas and let the car idle in the street so I could get a better look. Was there a number posted above the door that sat in the shadows of the porch?

Yes, there was. The number four hung over the front doorway, like a sign from some jerk of a god who was leading me to this place, probably just to hand me some more trouble to deal with, as if I didn't already have enough.

And just being in this place, thinking about a sign from some jerk of a god, so far from home and with Jarrod beside me, made me shiver from this weird feeling that maybe there really were gods all around us—in the trees, in the bushes, in the sky, and in the water of the lake beside us—waiting, watching to see what we would do next, wondering how I would deal with whatever they were about to throw at me.

If that was true, then I hated them. I needed gods who would throw me a miracle for once in this brief life of mine. I'd had enough of dealing with all the trickster types.

At the last moment, I turned the wheel and pulled up the drive of the yellow house. And when I killed the engine, the sounds of that forest-hidden village invaded the vacuum of our silence. Birdsong, the water lapping at the lakeshore, the tinkling of wind chimes that hung from every porch I'd seen as we passed by the old gingerbread cottages that lined these gravel streets. The same kind of wind chimes that hung from my mother's porch back in Temperance. Great, the place was home to a cult, I thought. And my mother was a member. That would explain all of my misfortunes.

I looked over my shoulder again, stalling for time, and also waiting to see if a horse-and-buggy would come trotting around the bend, as if it were still the turn of the twentieth century, when this town was probably a pretty big deal. When no horse and cart appeared, though, I turned back to Jarrod, the vinyl covering of the seat rumpling with my movement, and said, "I guess we have to get out of the car now, don't we?"

Jarrod threw his head back against the seat and laughed, shaking his head, which made me feel a little bit better about having him here with me. To break the tension, to help me laugh instead of getting stuck in my own head.

After he collected himself, he left his head resting against the seat but turned his face in my direction, brushing locks of hair from his brow. "Aidan," he said, "I don't know what's going to happen—not in the next few weeks, not in the next few days, not in the next few hours or even the next few minutes—but whatever does go on, I won't let anything bad happen to you if I can help it. And even if we discover that you're actually a demon or a werewolf or a vampire, or something equally unlikely, I'll still love you. Okay?"

He put his hand out and plucked one of mine from the steering wheel to squeeze. I gave him a halfhearted grin, but even with his words of encouragement, I couldn't help but worry. I didn't say it, but I kept wondering, *What if it's not you I have to worry about after I find what I'm looking for? What if* I'm *the one who can't deal with the truth?*

As I got out of the car, my stomach began to pitch a little, the same way I've always suddenly grown anxious whenever I'm riding a roller coaster, that part where you climb slowly to the top of a high curve, then the rush of wind on your face as the train curls over and sends you plummeting to the bottom with your screams streaming behind you. What would I find when I knocked on that door? Who would answer? And what would they have to tell me? I wasn't sure I even wanted to know any longer.

As we stepped onto the porch a minute later, the front door was already opening to reveal a tall, elderly woman wearing a flowered housecoat and silver-framed glasses, which she adjusted on the bridge of her nose before opening the screen door. She had her hair bound up behind her in a long white braid, as if she were still a young woman.

Or a hippie, I could hear my father saying, if he'd been there with me.

"Well, hello," the old woman said, giving us a warm smile. "What can I do for you boys on this fine day?"

I opened my mouth, but before I could say anything, the woman blinked and took off her glasses, and the smile she'd been offering like Halloween candy disappeared in the blink of an eye. "You're the youngest," she said. Just that. Just at first. Then: "Three boys. Am I right? Three brothers. And you're the youngest of them?"

I turned to Jarrod for a second, a little afraid, but he only shrugged, eyebrows arched in a way that said *This isn't mine to answer.*

"Yeah," I said as I turned back to the old woman. "I'm the youngest. Three boys. But one of us passed away a long time ago."

"I knew that," the woman said, nodding. She shook her head for a moment, pursing her lips, wincing a little, as though she was stifling a cry. When she got herself together again, she said, "Something to see, they are."

"What's that?" I asked her.

She looked at me hard then, and said, "Those eyes. I haven't seen those eyes in years now. Not since your mother cut us off. Not since she told that story."

I looked over at Jarrod again, hoping he'd know how to respond to that enigmatic statement, but his brows were already rising in surprise. *That story.* Of course we'd hear that simple phrase come out of this old woman.

"You're Carolyn," I said, turning back to her. "Right?"

"*Aunt* Carolyn," she corrected me. "But to be completely honest, for you it would be Great-Aunt Carolyn. You can call me whatever feels most comfortable, though. Please. Come inside. We've done enough standing around out here on the porch as if you're the postman. I should have known it was you who was coming here today. I would have prepared better—but these days I don't understand my own inklings like I used to."

I hesitated to follow her inside after I heard her say that. "What do you mean?" I asked. "How would you know I was coming here today? We've never even met."

"Oh, come now," she said. "You know what I'm talking about. You have to understand *some* things, if you found your way here. I dreamed I received mail on a Sunday. Obviously."

"But it's not a Sunday," I said.

"No," she said, "and you're quite unexpected, just like mail on a Sunday. I mean, really. Has your mother taught you nothing at all?"

She turned around after that and went inside, leaving Jarrod and me on the porch to look at each other for a while, before we both shrugged and followed her into the house. Which was this seriously old Victorian place with ornate rugs covering wood floors, and chintz-covered furniture. In each room we passed through, gaudily framed portraits of angels hung on the walls; on every bookcase or lamp stand, statues of winged fairies stood guard. I wanted to laugh, because this was the kind of stuff I'd imagined I'd find in this town, the kind of stuff that would make me think the trip was a waste altogether, but I didn't even let myself share a secret smile with Jarrod. We might crack up laughing if we let ourselves smile, and if I was going to go so far as to surround myself with angel and fairy statues in a crazy old hippie woman's house just to find out what she had to tell me about my family, I was determined I'd at least leave with the answers I'd come for. Even if they weren't the answers I wanted.

Carolyn brought us into her dining room, where Jarrod and I sat at a long cherry table, which, in a moment of trained politeness, I declared one of the finest tables I'd ever seen. And as Great-Aunt Carolyn poured us glasses of iced tea from a crystal pitcher, she said, "It should be. Your father made it for me."

Which was followed by my jaw dropping a little, and the flash of a memory of going down into our basement on those snow-filled nights when my dad would be out in his truck, plowing roads, those nights when I'd wander among the things he made with his woodworking tools, as if they were relics in a museum.

"So," said Carolyn as she sat down at the table. "I suppose the time has come for answers."

I looked back and forth between her and Jarrod, wondering if it was really going to be this easy—in and out, just how I'd hoped, as if maybe a god of haste was on my side after all—and then I dipped my head just once to confirm her suspicion. "Yes," I said. "Answers would be fantastic."

"Well," Carolyn said, "as much as I'd like to help, I'm not sure there's much I can tell you."

"Why not?" I asked.

"Because of the story your mother told. I'm afraid that I'm bound to it as much as anyone she included in it. Though I must say, something has clearly damaged it enough for me to know who you were when I saw you on my porch. Ordinarily, I would never have recognized you. I would have treated you like a stranger."

"The story," I said, sighing, hating that word and wanting to know what she and my mother meant by it all at once. "What is this story? My mom keeps talking about it too. I'm sorry, but I just don't get it."

"The story?" Carolyn repeated. She tilted her head to the side and smiled in this way that announced that she clearly found my lack of knowledge amusing. "Really? Your mother hasn't taught you what you need to know at all, then. Well, I can't tell you *the* story, not the one your mother told to keep you safe, but I can tell you about stories in general."

Jarrod caught my eye from across the table and raised one eyebrow doubtfully.

"A story," Carolyn continued, "is what your mother has woven around you. When you tell a story, you're either changing something or you're changing how people *see* something. In either case, you're bending the world and the minds of others to the will of your story, and you'd best tell it well."

"Sounds like a spell," Jarrod interjected.

Carolyn turned to him now, her own eyebrows rising to match his. "Some of us, young man," she said, "do not approve of such language. Words like that have gotten people killed in the past. But that is a matter of politics, of course, and I have never been one for parties and factions. A spell? Sure. If that makes more sense to you, I suppose it's similar."

A spell, I thought. My mother would have scoffed at that word. But I couldn't help thinking Jarrod was right. Carolyn's description of a story sounded like a spell. And spells do what Eva Jablonski said her story had done to my family. Spells bind people.

"What did you mean by telling it well?" I asked Carolyn.

"You can make mistakes in the telling," she said. "Like the person who finds a genie in a bottle and is granted a wish. How you phrase the wish will shape the final outcome. It works the same way for stories. Telling a story, the sort of story your mother has told, is tricky."

"And my mother's story?" I said.

"Your mother's story," said Carolyn. "Well, I'm afraid that it was told with earnest intentions, and holds up under most people's scrutiny, but not all. That's any storyteller's fear, really."

"What is?"

"That they'll come across people who will see right through their stories."

"There aren't many people like that around Temperance," I said.

"No," said Carolyn. "Which is probably why the story has worked so well for her. There are a few there who could see through her, though. And you're one of them."

"And the story my mother told," I said, "keeps me from seeing the truth."

"And keeps the truth from seeing you," Carolyn added, nodding. "That's the most important part."

"Wait," I said. "I don't understand. You're saying she's still telling this story?"

"She's trying to," said Carolyn. "She's trying her hardest to make you the most normal family in the world, to hide you all."

I thought of my mother sitting at the dining room table for the past two months with her silver pocket watch and her white candle, murmuring words under her breath. I thought she was trying to find my father's spirit in the next world, but maybe she'd been doing something else all along. Maybe she'd been trying to shore up her story.

"But like any complicated story you fabricate, it's gotten away from her," said Carolyn. "There are too many things she didn't account for." She stopped to look at Jarrod for a moment, head tilted to the side like she was studying him. Then she smiled like she understood something. "I wish I could explain it all in more detail, I really do, but it's a struggle to have even this conversation. I hope you'll be patient with me. I'm sure I must sound like a silly old woman. But if you could stay awhile—even just overnight—there may be other ways for you to find what you're looking for here, if you're open to letting others reach across to you."

A shiver ran down my spine then, like fingers running over the keys of a piano. That phrase, the same one Jarrod had used when he'd shown me the memory back in Mill Creek. The same words my mother used to explain how she and I could sync up with the mind and heart of another person. Here it was again, *reaching across*, this phrase I'd thought only a few people knew. Hearing it come from Carolyn, a stranger despite our being related, unnerved me. I looked at Jarrod, who shrugged almost imperceptibly. So he didn't know what we should do either.

In the end I said to him, "We've come this far. I'm game if you are." And when Jarrod nodded, I turned back to Carolyn. "All right, then. We can stay. But just for tonight. My mom probably has the police coming after me already."

After that, Carolyn showed us to our rooms on the second floor, both decorated like the rest of the house with the flashy fineries of angelic communion. Mine had a narrow twin bed and a small bathroom decorated with celestial wallpaper. Jarrod got an identical room across the hall.

Carolyn must not have been able to see that we would rather have shared a room, but I figured it wasn't worth bothering her, since one of us could always sneak across the hall after she'd gone to bed downstairs.

"Thanks," I said after she showed me where I could find everything I might need to clean up, and then she came to stand in the frame of the bedroom doorway, hands clutched together at her waist. When she hesitated, I said, "You have a pretty house, by the way," even though I thought the decor of angels and fairies was incredibly tacky.

"Why, thank you," she said. "I try my best to make the place work as a bed-and-breakfast during the summer." She finally went to leave then, but turned back once more to say, "Really, though, you needn't be so polite. I understand if all of this is a bit much." She waved one hand around to encompass the room with its celestial figures. "Just don't let it distract you from your purpose."

"My purpose?" I said, blinking.

"Yes, your purpose," said Carolyn, not giving an inch. "You're being followed by many who wish you goodwill. Do not waste this opportunity."

Then she turned and crossed the hallway. A second later, I could hear her greeting Jarrod, beginning the grand tour of his room.

Above my bed hung yet another angel painting, the frame almost as wide as the headboard. This angel was a young man with blue eyes and blond hair. He floated in midair, surrounded by wisps of pink cloud and golden light as he pointed down at something outside of the picture, so that it looked like he was pointing at whoever was sleeping in the bed below. I had to put my hand to my mouth to stifle a laugh. And a while later, after I'd heard Carolyn's footsteps going down the staircase, I texted Jarrod to come over in stealth mode.

"Look at that," I said when he peeked around my doorframe a second later. I pointed up at the angel who pointed down at what would eventually be my pillows, all embroidered with small pink and yellow flowers, and we allowed ourselves to laugh quietly for a minute. In the end, though, I stopped laughing before Jarrod did, and slumped down on the bed.

"What's the matter?" Jarrod asked, sitting down next to me, nudging my leg with his knee.

"Before she left, Carolyn told me I was being followed by many who wish me goodwill," I said. I tried to laugh at that, too, to make it into a joke to distract me from everything we were doing—running off on a whim to a village full of psychics in search of whatever my mother was trying to keep from me—but I was having a harder and harder time laughing as I got closer to the truth.

"What's so bad about having support over in the spirit world?" Jarrod asked, snickering a little. "Isn't it a good thing to have someone rooting for you?"

"Well, first of all," I said, "it sounds kind of stalker-y, being followed by spirits or whatever. I'd rather not be so popular with the invisible population, to be honest. But really, I just feel like this is all going to be for nothing. That I'll find out my mother's just crazy, that she comes from a crazy family, and that I'm going to turn out to be crazy too."

"Well, at least you won't be alone in your craziness," Jarrod said. "I'll be crazy with you."

I had a hard time looking at him, knowing what he'd sacrificed to come here with me, even though I'd told him not to. So I turned to look at the angel in the painting above the bed instead.

"He looks like you," Jarrod said a second later.

I looked down to meet his eyes again. They were locked on me, hard, and I felt frozen beneath their gaze. "Who?" I said.

He nodded up at the angel. "You look like that," he said. "You're beautiful like him."

"You love me too much," I said. I couldn't bear to think of someone seeing me in a way that I couldn't. "It scares me sometimes, how sure you are about me."

"There's no such thing as too much love," said Jarrod. He reached out to take my hand from my lap, but I pulled away.

"There *is* such a thing as too much love," I said. "No one should give up everything for another person. I mean, it sounds nice. But what if missing practice to be here with me means you don't play first string this season, and because of that, college scouts don't get to see you play as often? What if all this loving sacrifice means you don't get a scholarship? And all because of my stupid family."

"Who says I want to go to college?" Jarrod said, wrinkling his nose a little. He was trying to play it off like it was no big deal, but I knew different. He'd been trying hard in his classes the past few months, and he'd been working out rigorously to get ready for the season.

"You don't have to say anything for me to know you want to go to college," I told him.

"What," said Jarrod, "are you reading my mind or something?"

I smiled and shook my head. "No," I said. "It's just a logical deduction. I know you're not in love with baseball. You do it because you're good at it, and it's a way to get things you want. Like a scholarship."

"You're right," Jarrod said. "I'm not in love with baseball. I'm in love with you. You're what I want. And baseball, I'm afraid, won't get you for me." He reached out again, and this time I let him take my hand in his.

"But why risk what you need for what you want?"

"Who says you're not what I need?" he said, sounding a little offended. "There are plenty of ways to get by in life other than by playing baseball. I'd rather lose first string and a chance at a scholarship than lose you to whatever's happening here."

"You're happening here," I said. "You're who started all this."

"I wouldn't have it any other way," Jarrod said, pulling me closer, close enough for us to kiss.

Which was what we started doing a second later, softly at first, then harder, more hurried, as if someone might come in and try to stop us at any moment, and if we didn't get those kisses in right then, we never would.

Beneath the painting of the angel, we twisted together, losing ourselves as we explored one another, protected, hidden beneath the canopy of his large white wings.

chapter fourteen

IN PLAIN SIGHT

We spent the rest of that first day talking with Carolyn, who continued to dote on us like you might expect any great-aunt figure to do. I couldn't get her to sit still, really, after Jarrod and I went back downstairs to join her. She made oatmeal cookies and talked to us over one shoulder the entire time, mostly talking about the daily life in Lily Dale, which was quiet as could be at that time of the year, which she preferred. "But the mediums, the young ones, they need the summer season to pay their bills," she added. When I asked if she was a medium too, she scrunched her face up, as if she'd sucked on a lemon. "No, no,

I don't use my gifts that way. I just rent this old house's rooms out and serve tourists their breakfasts."

After the cookies, it was lemonade. And after the lemonade she took a quick nap before making dinner. By the time the day was over, she was exhausted from cooking and baking and talking, and said she would retire to her room, and suggested Jarrod and I go to sleep as well. Which we might have done if Jarrod hadn't appeared in my room moments after we went upstairs, asking if there was any room for him beneath the angel's wings.

The next morning, when we came down for breakfast, Carolyn's first question was "Well? How was last night for you?"

For a second, I thought she'd maybe heard Jarrod and me up in the room, and the red heat of embarrassment swept across my face like a grass fire. "I'm sorry?" I sputtered. I wasn't sure if I said it the way someone says excuse me when they bump into someone in passing, or the way someone says they're truly sorry for a great offense, but I hoped Carolyn would let my and Jarrod's possibly not-so-secret rendezvous go quietly.

"Last night," she said again. "Did you feel it? The energy?"

Jarrod covered his mouth with his hand and pretended to rub a nonexistent goatee, but I kept as straight a face as possible. "I'm not sure," I said. "What kind of energy?"

"The energies of Lily Dale," said Carolyn. "Most people who spend a night in this town say they can feel the place reach out to them. Some say it brings them visions."

"Oh," I said, and almost sighed with relief. "No. I didn't have any visions. I slept like a baby. No dreams, or at least none I can remember. And believe me, after the past six months or so, not dreaming was awesome."

Carolyn nodded, then blinked, seeming a little disappointed by my answer. She tightened her silver topknot and said, "Well, we'll have to try harder, then. Let's go for a walk."

I got up, surprised she was actually hoping for me to have some kind of out-of-body experience, and as I stood, Jarrod said he'd stay behind.

"I need to call my mom," he said, "so she doesn't call the police on us for going missing." I could tell that he really did plan to call his mom, but I also knew he was trying to give me time to be around Carolyn without him. Who knew what she might be holding back just because Jarrod, an unknown factor, was with us? So I agreed to leave him behind in the angel-and-fairy-infested house and went for a stroll with Carolyn down a gravel road that seemed to constantly curve around bends, over and over, encircling the entire place, holding the village inside it.

For ten or fifteen minutes, we ambled along quietly, looking anywhere but at each other, until we came to a break in the tree line beside us, and there Carolyn turned to enter the woods. It wasn't a beaten path she led us down, like I expected, but a cement walkway that went straight up to a white one-story building with cornflower-blue trim around its windows and four pillars holding up an overhanging roof. On either side of the walkway stood rows of pots for flowers, which were just starting to push their way out of the soil. When Carolyn stopped in front of the building, she bowed her head and whispered something, then raised her head again and opened the front door.

From the outside, the place looked a bit like the VFW Hall back in Temperance, and I half expected to find a slew of old-timer veterans inside, sitting on folding chairs around cafeteria tables, arguing about politics and sharing their faded war stories. But what I found instead were rows and rows of blue-cushioned chairs and, at the back of the darkened room, an altar flanked by tall blue-glass lanterns.

"Is this a church?" I whispered, immediately adopting the hushed tone sacred places inspire, and Carolyn turned her wrinkled face toward the ceiling, as if some kind of spiritual force roosted in the rafters. Slowly, she turned in a circle, then looked down at me again and shrugged.

"We call it a temple," she said. "A place for healing. It's where your grandfather did much of his work. Right here within these walls."

"My grandfather?"

Carolyn nodded.

"I don't know much about him," I said. "My mom never talks about him, other than to say she had a falling-out with her family years ago. She doesn't even have any pictures of him around the house. Who was he? What was he like?"

Carolyn frowned at that, and shook her head. Then she pinched her thumb and forefinger together and ran them across her lips like a zipper. I nodded. I understood that whatever story my mother had told—whatever spell she'd cast over so many of us—prevented Carolyn from giving me the answers I wanted. At least direct answers.

Carolyn was taking in the place with a nostalgic gaze now, as if she'd been frozen in a cryogenic chamber for years and had only woken from her deep sleep upon my arrival the day before. I didn't get any of her good feelings about the place, though. The room was strange. Spooky. Even if the grandfather I'd never met had done some kind of work in this place, I wanted to leave instead of lingering in the temple's weird blue shadows.

"I *can* tell you a few things," Carolyn said when she eventually reached the altar. Her back was to me, so her voice was slightly muted. "The cracks in your mother's story continue to widen, allowing me to slip some things through. Things that won't disturb the story's essence."

I bit the corner of my lip, then said, "What kind of things?"

"Some say this is a holy place," Carolyn said, raising her hands, palms up, as if she were about to invoke a god. "Some say that the ties between this world and the one beyond it are stronger here. Your grandfather always said he could feel the energy he needed to heal people more when he came to this place."

"He was a healer?" I asked.

271

"He was," said Carolyn. She sounded proud of this fact, as if he'd been a judge or a police officer, some authority figure out in normal society.

"Could he really heal people?" I asked.

"I saw him do it every summer," said Carolyn, nodding with the firmness of a true believer. "Right here in this room. I hear he sometimes did it in Temperance, too, for people he trusted to keep his secrets. But always here, every summer, people would come to him in the temple and he would heal them."

"How could he do that?" I asked.

"Do you, as I suspect, know what it is to reach across to someone?"

I nodded and said, "I do."

"Well, it's like that," said Carolyn. "The same way you can see the thoughts inside someone if you reach across to them. Just like that, he could see inside people, could see what made them ill. And sometimes he could take their illness out of them."

"But how?"

"I don't know how, really," Carolyn said, turning to face me again. "I was never able to do that, you see. It's far beyond my abilities. But the way it looked, he'd touch them wherever they hurt and would somehow pull the sickness toward his fingertips, like a magnet pulls metal. And when he had all of the illness in his hands, he'd jump back and walk it to the front door over there and he'd scatter the sick on the wind. You could see it all go away. You could see it all fly off like ashes."

"Are you serious?"

Carolyn said, "Serious as a heart attack."

"Could he stop one of those, too?" I asked, thinking of my poor dad clutching his chest in his tree stand a few months earlier.

She shook her head. "Your grandfather always said that those are too quick. One of the things that happen too fast for a healer to catch hold of."

"Too quick," I repeated, grimacing at the bad luck I'd had to be born into a family like this one.

"Too quick," Carolyn repeated. "Too quick for him to save even his own wife when one took her."

"I wish you could tell me more," I said.

"I wish I could too," said Carolyn. "But despite the cracks in your mother's story, it's still a strong one. Come on. There's another place I want to show you."

We left the temple and took up another path nearby. This one led us away from the cottage-lined streets into the thick forest surrounding them, where the trees towered high into the sky. They must have been a hundred years old, at least. You didn't see much old-growth forest like this outside of protected areas any longer, and being inside here, beneath such grand old trees, made me feel small and more like any other human being, which was a comfort.

The path led us deep into the woods, until suddenly we entered a shaded grove where rows of park benches surrounded an old stump. A stump that was so wide and flat on top, it looked like it served as a platform for people to stand on. To speak from.

"What is this place?" I asked.

"Inspiration Stump," said Carolyn, smiling. "When people come to Lily Dale for the summer, these benches will all be full, and the mediums will take turns standing in front of the stump to give messages to the visitors. We used to stand on the stump itself, but over the years it was being damaged by the constant wear, so we put that little ornamental fence around it, see, and now we stand in front of the stump to draw on its energy. It's a sacred place. You can see more clearly from it, you can hear better because of it, you can feel more than usual."

"What do you mean?"

"Go ahead," she said. "Why don't you see for yourself?"

I looked back and forth between Carolyn and the stump, cautiously considering whether I wanted any of those things to happen. I was already too open to the things of the invisible world. They already wandered into my line of sight at random moments, flickering to life like optical illusions, whispering in my ears at night. Why would I want to open myself up even further to their communications?

In the end, though, I knew Carolyn was trying to give me something she couldn't explain in words. So I moved toward the stump slowly and stood in front of the little wrought-iron fence surrounding it. When I looked back,

Carolyn had already taken a seat in one of the empty rows of benches. Sitting with her hands clasped together on her lap, she nodded at me like a teacher might, encouraging me with a smile. "Actually," she said, "I think you should do something we don't do in Lily Dale any longer. I think you should get up on the stump."

"On the stump?" I echoed, raising my eyebrows as I looked at it.

Carolyn nodded vigorously. "Yes," she said. "The stump. No one has to know about it. It'll be between you, me, and the spirits."

"Um," I said, trying to be polite. "Okay. Maybe it'll . . . inspire me." The thing had an aura of magic about it, sure, especially when Carolyn talked about it. But really it was just an old stump in the middle of an old-growth forest.

All the same, I lifted one leg over the fence, then the other, and went up a set of stairs, one, two, three, stopping just before I stepped onto the surface of the stump itself. I stared at it for a moment. A slab of stone had been placed on top of it, smooth and gray. And as I stared down at that slab, a strong wind picked up and blew through the grove, moving the trees back and forth, rattling the new leaves as if spirits rustled through them, urging me to take the last step, urging me to let them help me.

Wincing, worried that I might be electrocuted when my foot finally touched it, I took the last step onto the stump's surface. And when I stood on top of the stone slab, I braced myself for whatever might come next.

At first nothing happened. But after a minute the soles of my feet began to feel warm, as if I were standing on a heated floor. And the longer I stood there, the hotter they grew. Then the heat began to travel up the length of my body, inch by inch, moment by moment, until it reached my ankles, my shins, my knees. Then both of my legs seemed to catch fire. There was no real fire, though, just that faint heat and then sparks flashing, until it looked like my legs were made of fire instead of flesh—two pillars of volcanic light—and I looked down, helpless, frightened.

The fire continued to travel up my torso, my chest and my arms, my neck. Then I was drowning in flames, choking on fire. Light flared behind my eyes, opening up like a series of fireworks, the way it sometimes felt before one of my migraines. I wanted to jump off the stump, to avoid whatever was coming next, but I couldn't move no matter how hard I tried. I tried to scream, but when I finally forced my mouth open, another voice—the voice of the boy whose mother had died in the Living Death Tree back in Temperance—that boy's scream was the one to come out.

Dobry Jablonski screamed. The old woman—his mother's friend Lisbeth—had already managed to pack his meager belongings: a wooden whistle his father had whittled for him, a shirt his mother had made for him. Now Lisbeth was sealing up the shack in which his family had existed together for several years after moving to Temperance, Ohio, where Dobry's father had said they would make a better life. They'd only been there a year before his father had begun to cough up blood, though, and within months Dobry and his mother had buried him. Dobry's mother, too, was now dead. Whether his eyes were open or closed, though, Dobry couldn't help but still see her hanging in the tree where she had died for him. Even now, days after she'd been buried, when he went near the Lockwood orchard, he could see his mother's ghost in the tree.

"You must stop this, right now," Lisbeth said as she shook him by his narrow shoulders. The boy had begun to scream when she removed a portrait of his parents from the wall. "You have already said something terrible, done something terrible. Something that you cannot take back. If you cannot control yourself, you will do so again without thinking. How many people do you want to hurt?"

Dobry didn't know what she was talking about, though. "To name a thing," Lisbeth told him, "brings the thing into your possession, under your control. But a great responsibility is undertaken when you do this. To be a master of something, or someone," she added in a dark tone, "means you are bound to them as much as they are bound to you. You did not think of this when you made your curse, did you?"

Lisbeth shook her head, disgusted, and left him standing there as she moved to bar the windows with planks of wood. "No," she muttered as she put a sense of order to the shack Dobry's father had built, wiping the last crumbs from the table so that vermin did not invade. "No, how could you think of this? You do not know better. Your mother did not teach you this part. Your mother, she is shaking her head in heaven right now, regretting what she did not tell you. Now, though, you will learn from Lisbeth. And from others like us." Lisbeth stopped to look around the room one last time, and to tuck a few strands of sweaty gray hair back under her babushka.

"My mother is not in heaven!" Dobry shouted. She was still here on earth, still caught in the tangled branches of the apple tree where she had died for him.

Lisbeth folded her hands in front of her stomach and said, "This too is because of you, now, isn't it?"

And Dobry began to scream louder and louder, as if his voice could shatter every word she'd said.

Lisbeth is a red-faced hag, Dobry thought as the old woman loaded him into a car she had borrowed to complete her final duties to Dobry's mother. I followed them, claiming the backseat quietly, hoping the boy and the woman wouldn't notice my presence inserted into their lives from the future, a watcher brought there by way of an ancient tree stump in Lily Dale, New York. They were seers too, after all.

When Lisbeth climbed into the driver's seat, she turned the ignition over and over, but the engine whinnied as if it would never start. And then, finally, it roared to life, making the vehicle shudder.

Dobry watched the woman from the corner of his eye

as she looked ahead at the rutted roads, driving them toward Warren, the city where Lockwood had promised to put Dobry in jail for stealing apples. Her face looked like melted wax. It dripped with age, the skin pooling in various places: under her eyes, beneath her jawline. Lisbeth had been his mother's best and first friend in Temperance. She had appeared on their doorstep only days after their arrival in that little scratch-in-the-earth place, bearing gifts of thread and yarn for his mother and a basket of food that would last them several days. Dobry could remember how his mother hadn't acted surprised by Lisbeth's sudden appearance, could remember how Lisbeth had told his mother, "Welcome, fellow traveler," and how his mother had smiled and said she'd worried there wouldn't be others like her where they were going. Dobry thought his mother had meant she'd feared there would be no Poles in Temperance, but while Lisbeth did share the kinship of their homeland, it was something else his mother had referred to. He could see that now. Too late, as always.

At ten years old, Dobry learned what his mother had been talking about. This was when his father, after dying, began to come to him in his dreams, and sometimes even in Dobry's waking hours, when his eyes were wide open. His mother had told him the truth then, when it was clear that he was like her. "You are a lucky one," she'd said.

And Dobry had said, "What's a lucky one?"

"Someone who sees," she told him.

"Everyone but the blind can see," Dobry countered.

His mother had shaken her head slowly, her gaze steady. She put a finger to the side of his face, near his left eye, tapped it gently on the thin bone of his temple. "No," she said. "I am not speaking of sight. I am speaking of visions. Not everyone sees what you see. Not everyone sees what you will come to see in your lifetime, child."

In Warren, Lisbeth took Dobry to the train station, and they boarded the line to Erie, Pennsylvania, where an hour later they transferred to go on to Jamestown, New York. Dobry felt anxiety flutter within his stomach like a caged bird after they stepped down to the platform there, in a much bigger city than he'd ever been to. He looked around at the bustling station and asked, "Where are we going? Where are you taking me?"

Lisbeth held one hand over his head, as if she might lower it to affectionately stroke his hair. After a moment, though, she thought better and took the hand away. "You will see," she said. "Be patient."

Later that afternoon, she hired a driver to take them out of Jamestown, a city full of smoke and the noise of factories and the clamor of cars and trains. It was more than Dobry could take in all at once. The fields of Temperance were what he'd become accustomed to. But the streets of Jamestown soon fell away from the car windows, and after a while Dobry looked back to find the city buildings jutting up like the peaks of lean black mountains in the distance.

He didn't see me there, behind him, looking over his shoulder. He pinched his lower lip between his teeth for just an instant, then looked back at the road in front of him.

Ahead, the road wound and dipped as the car traced the outline of a lake. Surrounded by trees, Dobry couldn't see anything but a flurry of leaves float past, and the clouds of dust that formed in the road behind the car, sparkling like molten gold whenever a beam of sunlight passed through them.

Later, after falling asleep against Lisbeth's side, Dobry blinked awake as the car pulled into a gravel drive that curved around the front of a three-story hotel: an inn with its shutters still open, the eyes of the house staring as they approached.

The hotel had a wide front porch held up by white pillars, and in all of the windows the shades were half drawn. The land around the building looked like it belonged in a park, manicured to perfection. And the tall trees cast the perfect shade against the inn's white walls. People sat along the wide wraparound porch at small tables, drinking glasses of iced tea, wearing formal clothes, boaters and bow ties, the newest fashions. A man standing on the front porch took a watch from his jacket pocket to examine the hour. He twisted his mustache, clicked the lid shut, and slipped the watch back into his pocket. It reminded Dobry of the silver pocket watch Lockwood had given him. Out of guilt, Dobry assumed, for destroying his family. It sat in his pocket like an anchor now, mooring him to the day his mother had been killed.

"Where are we?" Dobry asked.

"You are in Lily Dale," Lisbeth told him. "You will be at home here. And now your mother—maybe she will come out of that tree and rest peacefully."

Lisbeth took Dobry into the hotel, where a room had been prepared for him. She instructed him to clean up while she attended to making a situation for him. He didn't understand what she meant by *making a situation,* but he did as he was told. The only alternative was to run away, and since his mother had trusted Lisbeth, Dobry decided he should trust her too, no matter what he thought of her melted face and oily gray hair.

So he washed his face and behind his ears, as his mother had taught him to do. He changed the shirt he'd been wearing while they traveled for the only other one he had: the one his mother had made for him. He dusted his pants off, combed his hair with his fingers. It was curly and dark, and with a little water he could get it to look like a sea of black waves.

When he looked in the mirror over the washbasin, he blinked. Beneath those dark waves, his eyes were green flecked with gold. They were his mother's eyes. She had always said so. Other than the shirt she'd made for him, the one he'd changed into, those eyes were all he had left of her.

Later, after Lisbeth returned and praised him for making himself ready, she led him from the hotel to a yellow house a few streets away. And as they walked down the dirt road to the house, Lisbeth said, "This is where you will live now. The people here are good. If you are good to them, they will take care of you. Can you be good?"

Dobry looked up into Lisbeth's face, which was shadowed by her babushka. He nodded like a duty-bound soldier.

There were introductions all around as Dobry met his new family. The father, Elias; the mother, May; the oldest daughter, Margaret, a girl with fiery red hair who was around Dobry's age. And then Carolyn, a small child who waved her hand and smiled when Lisbeth introduced Dobry. The first thing this spritely creature said to Dobry, before anyone else had a chance to greet him, was "You're going to marry my sister, did you know that?"

Everyone laughed at her announcement; everyone except Margaret, the little girl's older sister, who blushed and turned her cheek into her lace-covered shoulder. Little Carolyn continued to chatter. "And one day," she said, "we will be best friends, and I will help care for your children and your grandchildren."

Dobry narrowed his eyes at the little girl, her blond coils and blue eyes, so like a doll he would find on the shelves of a store. She managed to make the entire room shift from cheerful to uncomfortable as she went on and on, divulging a future neither Dobry nor Margaret, apparently, had ever thought of, until the adults began to shush her.

"Carolyn," her mother said, "it's rude to give messages when they haven't been asked for. Please contain yourself or go to your room."

Carolyn bounced up and down on her heels. "I *can't* contain myself," she said. "I don't want to." She ran, then, up the staircase. A moment later, footsteps thudded in a straight line overhead as she ran down a hallway on the floor above. Dobry looked up, then back down at his new family, who were still smiling at him, still trying to make him feel welcome.

Later Lisbeth helped Dobry settle into his new room, where he sat on the corner of his new bed, looking at his hands in his lap, afraid to move. "You will be fine," Lisbeth said. "You will learn who you are here. They will teach you since your mother is now unable. Do you understand my words?"

Dobry nodded, even though he didn't understand. I could see that in his eyes: two deep, frightened wells of insecurity. Lisbeth tried to smile fondly at him, and finally allowed her hand to rest on his head, to stroke his fine dark curls. She didn't say goodbye, but the next morning, when Dobry came down for breakfast, she was gone, and no one mentioned her except to say that Lisbeth would be back soon to visit.

A sunburst filled my eyes then, sending out shards of light, shattering the vision, leaving me momentarily in a great, empty white space. Then the vision began to reshape itself, to become a different time.

Dobry was now a few years older, sixteen or seventeen, with a dusting of hair on his chest and the face of a young man. He was staring into the mirror over his dresser, whispering at his own image. "Who are you? Who are you?" But the answer he received was always the same.

Silence.

In the silence, his worries and regrets were nourished. I watched as they grew in his mind like weeds overtaking a garden. He was always getting caught in them, entangled, as in dreams. Getting caught in his worries and regrets always began with this question he posed in the mirror, then the hated silence. And in the silence, all of the memories that composed him would begin to shimmer and coalesce.

The baskets of apples he used to hide at the edge of the orchard, where he'd retrieve them on his walk home from work.

Mrs. Lockwood holding her little boy's hand, asking after Dobry's mother.

Lockwood himself, that murderer. In Dobry's memory, the man holds a thick hand over his brow to shield his eyes from the sun as Dobry's mother reaches out her hand, stretching to grasp the last apple from the orchard. She twists the stem and it drops into her open palm.

There were other memories Dobry had made since then—with his new family, who were kind and good to him, as Lisbeth said they would be—but the memories that anchored him, the memories that became his idea of himself, were the ones that had occurred down in the orchard, on the spot of land people in Temperance had started to call Sorrow Acre since his mother's passing.

He had said words that day, had hurled a curse at Lockwood without realizing it. The words had burst through his throat and found their way into the world, changing reality even as they entered it. At the time, Dobry hadn't realized what he was doing. How could he have understood the power he'd drawn on when his mother hadn't taught him that lesson?

And would his mother have known how to teach him anyway? Was it something she was even able to do? His new parents, the Foresters, had roots in spiritualism—that was how they explained the source of Dobry's abilities, both to themselves and to Dobry—but even Mr. Forester once told Dobry, "You are capable of more than I can understand. To be honest, I am quite in awe of you."

Lily Dale was full of people with minor talents. The occasional spirit would whisper into their ears or lift the veil from their eyes to let them gaze at the world beyond for an instant. Dobry, though, was known for manifesting miracles. When he held a finger out, birds came to perch there. When he closed his eyes to reach across to someone, he could see what ailed a person, in mind or in body, and if he drew his fingertips over a person's skin, his fingers would twitch as they passed over the illness. And if he held his fingers over the illness for long enough, the tips would begin to jump, as if he were playing a piano, until sour-smelling beads of black sweat rose to the surface of the person's body, collecting on Dobry's fingers, eventually sagging from his hands like strings of dark sap. He'd take the sickness outside and throw it into the air then, where it would turn to ash and float away on the wind.

He could go into another place, too. Another space, really. The back side of here and now, was how he thought of it. The place where everyone in this world was sleepwalking. Everyone, that is, but him. He could do things there, could suggest things, could change things. When people awoke from their dreams in the morning, they tended to see things his way.

"Who am I?" he asked himself in the mirror.

The boy who had watched his mother die for him, that boy was gone.

He was sixteen, then eighteen, then twenty, married to his adopted sister Margaret, slipping a ring on her finger, kissing her in the center of the woods near Inspiration Stump, its energies thrumming around them, her coils of red hair lifting in the wind like flames. "A piece of good luck," Margaret's mother had told them. "Marry near the stump if you want your marriage to be a blessed one."

He and Margaret had lived in close proximity for years already, and had slipped into loving one another with a certainty that eluded most young people, because they had been friends for so long. Only one thing seemed to escape them: Margaret couldn't carry a child. Each attempt ended in disappointment. So they lived alone, their hands intertwined before they fell asleep each night, thinking they would die this way, just the two of them, with no one to go on after them, with no one to carry their stories into the future.

One night, though, Dobry remembered the way the words felt in his mouth when he was twelve years old and so angry that reality began to waver as his words re-shaped it. By now the curse he'd made that long-ago day had killed his enemy, he was sure. Although Dobry didn't know where or how it had happened, he knew that Lock-wood was dead. He'd felt the string that attached them, that braided coil of sorrow and rage made on the day he'd cursed the man, snap when Lockwood drowned in his own reflection during the war in Europe. Lockwood's son would be next, according to the law Dobry had brought into being that day. And so on, and so on, and so on, the next and the next and the next, until they were all gone. The Lockwood family erased from existence. He could do that again, he thought now; he could bend the world to his will if he wanted the thing badly enough. But this time his wish would be made from the materials of disappoint-ment instead of vengeance.

He whispered words that night: "A child will come to us. A child will come through." And he doled the wish out little by little, encouraging it, nurturing it, giving it more and more power as he repeated it like a ritual every night thereafter, until eight and a half months had passed and

Margaret was holding her hands over her ever-growing stomach, shouting with glee because her water had broken. The child was coming. The child Dobry had wished for every night for months and months was finally coming through to them.

"Right now, Dobry!" she called from their bedroom, and Dobry rushed up the stairs to help her. At the top of the landing, though, he stopped, shocked, when he saw the blood staining her nightdress, the blood streaming down her legs. The way it kept coming.

When the baby finally made its way into this world, Dobry set it aside and began to run his fingers across his wife's body, looking for the place inside her that bled so badly. But even as his fingers twitched upon locating the problem, Margaret's chest heaved violently, and then her body stopped moving altogether.

Her heart had seized up. The beat had gone out of her. It flew from the room faster than Dobry could move to catch it. And even as the heartbeat disappeared like smoke on the wind, the child Dobry had wished into the world opened her mouth to send up a fierce howl.

Too fast to catch, Carolyn had told me. One thing a healer can't mend: a heartbeat that's flown away from a person.

The child, though, lived and grew. Her red infant face widened into the shape of a heart, like her mother's, and her hair grew in auburn. She was toddling, falling over, crying, picking up toys after she'd been scolded—a doll her aunt Carolyn gave her for her birthday, a book of stories about fairies who live under the floorboards of children's rooms—then she was striding across a field of clover, arms pumping as she found her pace, a smile blooming on her face. Now she sat at a school desk practicing her cursive, which was the best, the most finely modeled hand in class, her teacher told her. "Very good, Sophia," her teacher said, and the girl looked up, beaming with pride. "My aunt Carolyn practices with me at home," she said. "That's why."

Aunt Carolyn. There she was, bringing the girl, Sophia, my mother, a cup of warm milk in bed. "It'll help you sleep," she told my mother. "Don't worry. Your father will be back before you know it."

"Where did he go?" Sophia asked. She was ten, her face still round with childhood, her hair just a little darker.

"He's gone back to the place where his own parents once lived."

"Where is that?" Sophia asked. She sipped the warm milk, scissoring her legs back and forth under the covers.

"Temperance," Carolyn said, running her hand across the coverlet, smoothing it down again.

"Where's Temperance?"

"In Ohio," Carolyn answered.

"What's he doing there?" Sophia asked. Her words had started to come slowly with the onset of drowsiness.

"He's reclaiming your past," Carolyn told her. "He's making you a home there."

"I don't want to live in Ohio," Sophia murmured. "I want to stay here with you." She blinked, trying to stay asleep, but eventually her eyes closed and her protests ended.

"It's not so different there," Carolyn replied. "Don't worry about it. You'll still spend your summers here with me, my love."

"I love you, Aunt Carolyn," Sophia murmured. The words barely escaped her lips before she drifted off to sleep.

Carolyn tucked the comforter under my mother's chin, then went to the doorway, where she rested her hand on the light switch for a moment, looking over her shoulder at the sleeping child once more. Then, for just a moment, she turned toward the corner of the room where I stood in the shadows, invisible to them, I believed, like Scrooge being taken into his past, present, and future, watching in silence as everything transpired.

"Love you too," Carolyn said, her eyes meeting mine for longer than a moment, it seemed, before she turned out the lights.

When I opened my eyes, the fire that had consumed me was gone, but the wind still streamed through the trees, shifting the leaves against one another, whispering.

"What did you see?" a voice called out, and I blinked, disoriented. The day had passed from late morning to early evening already, and somehow I'd stood there, dreaming, for hours.

Carolyn stood from her bench in the grove, and I

started to remember myself again, to remember where we were, to remember what Carolyn had brought me here for.

"He was my grandfather," I said. "My mother's father. Wasn't he? The boy who cursed us?"

Carolyn's long white hair had fallen out of its knot and now flowed over her shoulders like spilled milk. She nodded, frowning a little, sad to admit it. "He told me that eventually someone would see the truth and understand him," she said. "He didn't mean for it all to happen as it has."

"My mother?"

Carolyn shook her head. "How could your mother understand him? They did nothing but argue. She couldn't forgive her father for that. Not when she loved your father more than anything."

"I don't know what you mean," I said.

"Keep looking," Carolyn said, nodding at the stump beneath my feet. "Keep seeing. She has told you things without telling you what they mean. She has hidden things from you in plain sight."

So there, on that old stump in the woods, I closed my eyes once more, to see the pieces of my family's puzzle, the pieces my mother had hidden from me.

chapter fifteen

UNRAVELING

W hen the vision took me this time, I found myself floating over a bed in a room that reminded me of the one I'd slept in the night before at Carolyn's house. Angels flew across the wallpaper. Fairy statues stood guard on bedside stands and windowsills. It was, in fact, Carolyn's house, but the person in the bed was my mother, who was stretched out on the comforter, staring up at the painting of the angel who pointed down. She was maybe twenty years old. Her hair spread across the pillow in long auburn curls like licks of flame rolling off her. She wore a summer dress, grass green, decorated with a bright print of sunflowers. One arm lay across her forehead, the other on her stomach, and her skin shone with sweat as she thought about the boy she'd left behind in Temperance. The boy she loved.

I could see everything inside her—her thoughts, her memories, her feelings—bubbling and stirring. The boy who took up all of her thoughts and feelings, that boy was my father, John Lockwood, a handsome young man who, in her memory, seemed carved out of stone: face chiseled, arms thick and ropy with muscle. The salt of the earth, she'd always called him. He was far away from her at the moment, back in Temperance, where she'd left him, and she wasn't sure what to do about him. She wasn't sure what to do about anything right then, really.

In the next room over, a salt-and-pepper-haired man sat at a desk writing in a leather-bound journal. His hand scrolled across the page, leaving wispy black ink in the wake of his pen. He wore a short beard, neatly trimmed, black with one stripe of gray down the center. Green eyes like his mother's. Green eyes like my mother's. Green eyes like mine.

Suddenly he set his pen down on the page and scraped his chair back to stand. Leaving the journal open on the desk, the pen collecting ink in a tiny bubble at its tip, he buttoned the top of his shirt as if he were going to a formal occasion, then left the room to cross the hallway, where he briefly hesitated before knocking on my mother's door.

Knock, knock, knock.

"Who is it?" she asked softly.

"It's me," he said. "Will you please open the door, Sophia?"

My mom got up but only opened the door a sliver, enough to see a fraction of his face. "Daddy," she said, "we've been through all this already. There's nothing left to say." She didn't look up into his eyes. Instead she focused on a number of other items: the white button he had just slipped through its hole at the top of his shirt, the black hairs on the backs of his hands, the light-switch panel beside the doorframe. She flicked it on, then off, then on again, like a restless spirit.

"There must be more to say," her father said. "I don't like it when there's bad blood between us. You know that. Your mother wouldn't have liked it either."

So, I thought after hearing that, *my mom learned how to guilt me from a professional.*

"Momma's dead, Daddy," my mother said.

"That doesn't matter. She wouldn't have liked it all the same."

"I don't like it either," my mother replied. But she still didn't look up at her father. She rubbed her forefinger and thumb together at her side, a gesture I'd seen her make all my life whenever she was anxious.

"Do you understand why I can't approve of this?" her father asked through the sliver of space she'd opened for him.

She nodded once, but she still wouldn't look at him.

"I don't think you do," he said. "I've told you the story, but you don't understand it."

"I understand," my mother said, her voice flat and heavy. "I saw what you did to his family."

He nodded and said, "Yes, but I'm not sure you understand why."

"I know what it means," my mom said, and finally she turned her face up to his. "I know what it means, and it's nothing to do with me and him. What happened years ago between you and that man isn't our problem."

"But it is," her father said. "And it's irrevocable."

"I don't see why you can't change it," my mother said, almost spitting the words at him. "If you made the curse, why can't you unmake it?"

"She won't let it go," her father said. "I told you, darling. She won't let go of it."

My mother's face turned red in an instant. "I'll make her let go," she said. "I promise I'll make her give up on it."

Her father shook his head, though. "There's no way to do that, Sophia. The only way to destroy it would be to make her leave."

"And to make her leave, someone has to leave with her," my mother mumbled. "I know. You've told me a thousand times."

"Don't be like this," her father pleaded, his voice falling to a whisper.

"Don't tell me how to talk," my mother snapped at him.

Her voice rose as his fell, and she cringed because she could hear how she sounded like a child and she couldn't stop herself from going even further. "I'll talk how I talk, just like I walk how I walk. You can change so many things, Daddy, but you can't change that. You can't change that I love him."

"You have important work to do," her father said. "There are things I still need to teach you."

My mom looked over her shoulder into the shadows of her room, as if she knew I was in there with her, watching her, judging her. Then she turned back to her father, her face devoid of feeling. "I don't think I want to learn any more," she said, quietly now. "I think I've learned enough from you, Daddy."

"Sweetheart," her father said, but my mother closed her eyes and shook her head.

"I'm done with all this," she said. "I just want to be left alone for a while. I just want to be normal."

"Some of us aren't meant for that," her father said. From his vest pocket, then, he fished out a silver watch. The silver pocket watch my mother kept in her bedroom. The pocket watch I'd seen her hold when she entered the world's shadow and when she sat at the dining room table with a lit candle, looking for my father's spirit or else making changes to the story she'd bound us all up in. That pocket watch, silver and gleaming, was taken from my granddad's vest pocket and held out toward my mother. "You're going to leave me," he said. "I can tell it."

"You don't know everything," my mother said sullenly.

"I know," he said. "I know more than you might understand. Here." He held out the pocket watch farther, the same watch his mother's murderer had given him, and forced it into her grasp. "Be smarter than I've been," he warned her. "Save some time up for yourself and the ones you love. I didn't know I could do that myself. I learned too late. If I'd known, I might have been able to save your mother. I might have been able to undo all the mistakes I've made."

"Daddy," my mom said, shaking her head, one tear slipping out of one eye.

"There will be three to come, if you do this," her father said, gesturing toward her stomach. "Three that you won't be able to protect no matter how hard you try. They'll be like any of the others from that family. It won't matter that your blood is in them, because his will be there too. They'll all die early."

My mother didn't move: not to nod, not to shake her head, not to speak. She was completely still in that moment.

"I can help," her father said then, "if you'd only let me. I could help relieve you of your burden."

"Do you mean the burden I saw in my dream," my mother said, "about what happened over in that orchard when you were a boy? Or do you mean the burden I carry?"

She looked up to meet his eyes then. They flickered

down toward her stomach, accusing. That was his answer: that look. Her bottom lip trembled. "That would not be a relief," she replied firmly. "No, sir, that would not be a relief to me." Then she shut the door on him and locked it.

She went over to her bed again, taking up the same position she'd been in before her father disturbed her. One arm flung over her forehead, one hand on the slight curve of her stomach. "There will be three to come," she whispered to the angel in the portrait hanging above her. She caressed her stomach, ran her fingers in circles over its growing roundness. "So be it."

Later she stood and went to the dormer window, slid it up so that the night air drifted in and lifted her hair. She looked up at a star that seemed larger and brighter than any other in the sky, and recited the rhyme that she would teach me when I was little.

"This is my home and I know it. Even if I go away, it'll still be here. If I lose my way, it's your job to show it."

Then she reached out three times, as if to press the star with the tip of her finger, and it glimmered three times in return.

A sliver of light no bigger than a blade of grass appeared before her. It was so small and narrow, she had to push the tips of her fingers inside to begin pulling at it, stretching it, making it bigger, until the outline of a doorway had taken shape in front of her, with bright white light pouring from it, filling up the room.

She looked back at the door to her room once more,

thinking about her father across the hall, what he'd said she should and shouldn't do. She thought about what she'd be giving up if she followed his plans for her. She thought about how the boy she'd left behind two months earlier had said he didn't care about what came before them, he didn't care what their families thought about who they should be or who they should be with. He'd said he didn't care about consequences. He loved her. That was all that mattered. Then he had leaned down and kissed her like it was the first time they'd ever kissed, two years earlier, right before they'd graduated from high school and were still trying to hold on to some part of themselves by holding on to each other.

My mother turned back to the door of light in front of her, clutched the pocket watch her father had given her, and took a deep breath, then stepped through.

And arrived on the other side, on a dusty back road lined with towering maples, where a yellow clapboard farmhouse stood behind the shade of those old silver branches, glowing beneath the moon.

To the side of the house, across the creek, was an orchard with only a handful of apple trees still standing in it. The wind blew through them and their apples shook loose, landing and rolling down the slope toward the glistening water of Sugar Creek.

A young man, my father, stood on the stone porch of the house in his blue jeans and a thin white T-shirt. He was smoking a cigarette, something I'd never seen him do in my entire life. Startled by my mother's appearance in the middle of the road, he flicked the cigarette into a planter on the porch and raised his hand to wave at her.

"Sophia?" he said. "Where'd you come from? I thought you'd be in New York until August."

"It's not important," my mom said, not mentioning the way she'd gotten there. He knew she could do it, touch a star and it would open a doorway. But it made him uncomfortable these days, the older they grew. And he disliked the way people in Temperance sometimes talked about her and her father knowing things other people didn't or couldn't possibly know. He was uncomfortable too, she knew, because all of it reminded him of the thread of magic that ran through his own family, the way that thread bound them all together. He'd told her once, soon after they started dating a few years earlier, that he'd found his father's body back in Marrow's Ravine, where the man had shot himself when my dad was just sixteen. He'd called out for my mother to come to him then. Made a wish and hoped she heard it all the way in Lily Dale, where she did hear it, and later came to him when he needed her comfort.

"It's not important," my mother had said when he asked where she'd come from, though, not wanting to remind him. "I'm here," she said now. "Here is where I am."

My dad beamed. She'd gone away that summer with their fate clasped within her hands. Said she needed time to think about the two of them, what they were doing together, whether they should stay that way forever. He'd argued, he'd railed against her. But she'd left anyway, secretly carrying their child within her, not wanting him to know until she was sure of what she wanted.

Here she was now, telling him. Telling him she wanted him.

He stepped down from the porch to go to her then, and my mom moved toward him. When they came to stand on the front lawn beneath the shadows of the maples, they took each other's hands. My dad leaned down to kiss her, but my mother stopped him, put a hand to his lips.

"Wait," she said. "There are things I need to tell you." And because she'd told him bits and pieces of the future that had come true in the past, because my dad trusted her to know things he couldn't ever know of, he stopped and waited for her to continue.

"There will be three," she said. She took her hands from his and put them on her stomach, then looked up into his eyes again, hoping he would understand. "There will be three children, and we won't be able to protect any of them."

"No one can do that anyway," my dad said, bold and foolish. "No one can protect their children from everything."

I stood apart from them, watching in the dark, trying to understand them, trying to understand myself through them somehow. If ever I'd had the chance to unravel my own life, to give it back like an unwanted gift, this was the moment to do it. I could change things, if I wanted. I could do what I'd seen my mother's father do. I could say the words to bend reality, to make myself grow backward, to become younger and younger and younger, until I disappeared inside my mother and reduced myself to the atoms that I'd begun as, and then reduced myself to nothing, winking out of existence, as if I had never been.

Or I could make myself visible to them, interrupt this moment. I could reveal their future to them, the whole thing, the big picture, our future as a family. I could warn them. I could say, *Don't do this. Her father is right. You will do and say terrible things to each other, you will involve your children in the messes your parents and grandparents and great-grandparents made. You will bury your first child when he's five years old and you'll die too young yourselves. It's not worth it. I'm not worth it. Please. Don't do this.* If I slipped out of the shadows of time and space to reveal myself and tell them all the things that would happen when they trusted their hearts to lead them forward, I could take up this knot in our shared history and undo it. I could unmake the curse by unmaking our lives together.

But I didn't move. I waited for another moment, and then another. And then I closed my mouth, put my hand over it, shaking, frightened that I'd almost said something I could never take back, the way my mother's father had done in the orchard. Even with the burden of our history, I wanted this life, I realized. This one. Not someone else's. I wanted mine.

My father leaned down to kiss my mother beneath the moonlight then, and that was when it happened. They began to bring us, my brothers and me, out of the ether of possibility and into the world.

⁂

When I opened my eyes back in Lily Dale, I found a vault of stars spiraling overhead. Night had fallen around me. And when I looked for the star my mother had said would lead me home if I was ever lost, the one she'd used to take her back to my father in Temperance, it was still there. Up in the sky. Still blinking.

The Probable Stone.

From the surrounding leafy shadows, Carolyn stepped forward, and the blue light of the moon washed over her face, making her look like a ghost in the forest. "So?" she said. "Did you find the answers you were looking for?"

"I found something," I said, nodding. "But I missed my chance to save everyone."

"Well," Carolyn said, "*you* may not have to be the one to save everyone."

"What do you mean?"

"Now that you've seen the truth," she said, "the truth can see you. The story your mother told can no longer be believed. Now that you know the truth, now that you see everything, the curse . . . the curse can now see you. It can find you. And it can find your brother."

"Why did you let me see it, then?" I said, raising my

304

voice a little. I hadn't understood everything, exactly, that unraveling my mother's story would mean. "I thought you were trying to help me!"

"I *am* helping you," Carolyn said. "You've undone your mother's story, and now you—and everyone she bound to it—can see things clearly. Remember. Your grandfather could see the future clearer than anyone. Clearer than your mother. Clearer, even, than you. He saw all of this coming to pass beyond a time he'd be able to do anything to fix it. He saw your mother's story unraveling because her son would fall in love with a young man who didn't fit into her story, a young man who knew it wasn't the truth because she'd forgotten to write him into it, the way she wrote the entire town into it. And he saw how that would be her story's undoing. He knew something would have to be done to save you, and he prepared me to help you see the truth, even though it would endanger you."

"But why?"

"So that your mother would do what must be done now," Carolyn said. "What she promised she would do a long time ago, if she couldn't figure out another way. The only thing that can undo the curse he made."

I didn't like what I was hearing, and wasn't sure I wanted to know anything more than what I'd already discovered, but I asked the question anyway: "What? What does she have to do now?"

Carolyn had stopped smiling as she explained things, and before she answered my question, she frowned. "Your mother must walk Eva out of this world and into the next one," she said. "She must take the curse with her. Your mother can't keep telling this story forever, trying to make you invisible to the eye of the curse. If she dies without walking Eva and the curse out of the world, her story will die with her, and the curse *will* eventually find you."

"If that's the solution," I said, "then why hasn't she already done it?"

"Because," Carolyn said, raising her silvery-white brows in shock that I didn't yet fully understand. "In order to walk Eva out of this world and into the next one, your mother must give up her own life."

Blackness then. Blackness and a painful howl of rage and desperation filled me. I'm not sure how long it consumed me, but when I returned to myself, I was running through the front door of Carolyn's house, running through the rooms, out of breath, shaking, until I found Jarrod. He was in my room, waiting for me under the angel painting, asleep, one arm thrown over his forehead. "What's wrong?" he asked when I burst in, startling him awake.

"It's my mom," I said, breathless. "She's going to do something terrible."

"What?" Jarrod asked.

I melted into his arms as he stood to hold me and kept me standing. When I could, I pulled away and told him what I'd seen in the woods. "She's going to give herself up for my brother and me," I said.

Jarrod's face twisted with confusion. "How?" he asked. "When?"

Before I could say anything, though, Carolyn answered.

Behind me, she said, "If everything your grandfather told me years ago is still true, then she has already done it."

She looked at the clock on the desk in my room. It was five in the morning and I hadn't even realized it. I'd been out in the woods for half a day and an entire night, traveling through the world's shadow to find the truth of my family, and here it was: my family would soon be just me and Toby.

Unless I did something. Unless I found another way to change things.

"Are you telling your own story," Carolyn asked when she saw the idea in my eyes, "or are you being told?"

They were my mother's words, the trick she'd taught me years ago to outwit Death, after I'd witnessed a red-bearded man come into my seventh-grade classroom in his black suit and wide-brimmed black hat to look my teacher up and down like he was a cow going to slaughter.

One day Death will pay you a visit, my mother had said, *but if you can tell the story of your life before Death tells its version—if you can tell it true—you can maybe keep on living.*

Mr. Marsdale didn't tell Death his story? I'd asked.

He might not have known that he could, my mother answered. *He might not have known how to. Most people don't know that trick anymore.* She had looked at me then, and it seemed as if a breath she'd been holding was suddenly released, filling the room with the scent of peppermint and coffee. *Now you know,* she said, *and you can use that trick one day if you want to. But the thing is, you have to tell your story true, and not everyone can do that.*

Why not? I'd asked.

Because, my mother said, *telling the truth is the hardest thing a person can do.*

"The teller shapes the story," Carolyn said from the doorway. "If you don't tell it, the story shapes you."

I turned to Jarrod. "We have to go right now," I said. "I have to help her."

"But it'll take at least two hours to get back to Temperance."

"No," I said. "There's another way. Do you trust me?"

And Jarrod said, "You know it."

Outside the sky was beginning to pale, but the stars still winked weakly. There were only a few minutes left, I figured, before I'd see a red line grow on the horizon, and then the stars and the moon would disappear. So I stepped off the porch, pulling Jarrod behind me, and ran out into the middle of the road, where all of the tiny cottages of Lily Dale blinked their eyes in the sleepy hours of early morning, and there I reached a hand up to touch the place where my mother had pinned a spell to the sky.

As I raised a finger to the star, I found that I could feel it, warm and soft, thrumming with life and energy. Energy my mother had made, shaped into this form. Energy she had placed in the sky for safekeeping.

"This is my home and I know it," I said, reciting the rhyme my mother taught me when I was little. "Even if I go away, it'll still be here. If I lose my way, it's your job to show it."

I pressed my finger against the star a second time, a third, and then the air around us began to shimmer. The Probable Stone glowed brighter, then grew larger, and finally it began to lower itself from the sky until it stood in front of me, changing its shape so that it looked like an open door filled with white light.

I looked back at Carolyn, who was already raising her hand to wave goodbye. I nodded at her, and when I looked back at Jarrod, I said, "Are you ready?"

"Always," he said, "if it's with you."

So we stepped on through.

chapter sixteen

HOMECOMING

And came out on the other side, at the end of
the long gravel drive of my house back in
Temperance, where Jarrod had met me two days
before, blocking me from going to Lily Dale without him.

All of the windows were still dark as the last
smudge of night began to disappear from the horizon, and a red glow from the rising sun hung over
the back tree line. After Jarrod and I came closer
to the house, we found light escaping around the
edges of the blinds in the kitchen windows. Ordinarily no light would be turned on until my mom
woke up and started fixing breakfast, but when I

let us in the front door and we searched the first floor, she was nowhere in sight. And when I raced upstairs to her room, taking two steps at a time, I discovered that her bed had already been made. Or else it had never been slept in.

Across the hall, Toby was still asleep. His chest rose and fell peacefully. If nothing had disturbed him the night before, I thought maybe my mom had figured out some other way to walk Eva out of the world. Or else Carolyn had been wrong and maybe Jarrod and I could have driven back home after all. Maybe I didn't need to talk my mom out of doing anything.

"Toby," I said, trying to wake him. He'd know where she went, I figured. And if he didn't know, he could help us look for her.

But Toby didn't wake when I called his name. Not the first time, not the second. And when I went farther into his room and stood directly over him, when I shook him by his shoulders and called his name over and over, he still didn't wake up.

That was when I knew that she'd done it after all.

"What's wrong with him?" Jarrod asked from the doorway.

I looked over my shoulder at him. "He's been put to sleep, I think."

"What do you mean?"

"My mom did something to him."

It was clear to me then too that she didn't want anyone to get in the way of her plans.

I went to Toby's window to look out at our property, sweeping from orchard to stream to pasture to cornfield to the woods at the back of the place, hoping to see her moving through the landscape somewhere. But the view offered me no answers. Our farm remained silent, asleep and dreaming.

There would be no answers forthcoming, I knew then. Clearly she'd foreseen my coming back here, foreseen that I'd try to stop her. *I've always known what you were going to do before you did it,* she'd told me before I left home. And it was true. She'd always seen our futures laid out like a map in front of her. There were gaps in her vision, of course, but she'd seen enough. More than I ever realized.

None of that mattered now, though. I had to find her. Her trail would most likely be invisible, but I knew how to see invisible things, thanks to the eyes I'd been born with, the eyes my mother had given me. Now that her blindfold had been lifted, I could recall what it had felt like to interact with the invisible world when I was little, when it wasn't unnatural for me to see a spirit cross the railroad tracks on its way to wherever it was going, or to see a white stag slip between the trees down in Marrow's Ravine. And if my mother had tried to cover her trail so that I couldn't find her, I'd just have to go back to the moment she left here. I'd have to look for her in the world's shadow.

I'd seen her do this—return to the past by counting

backward to the hour she wished to revisit—and by now I knew how to do that trick without even thinking my way through the steps. So I sat down on my bed, preparing to dream, like my brother was doing in the next room, but with a purpose. Jarrod pulled the chair from my desk and put it beside my bed, straddling it, his arms folded on top of the back, his head resting on his folded arms. "If you see me struggling with something," I told him, "don't wake me."

"But what if you're in danger?"

"If I need you to wake me, I'll squeeze your hand. Here," I said, and slipped my palm into his. It was warm and only slightly rough-skinned from all of the training he'd been doing, but it felt solid because of that, and someone solid was what I needed.

Then I lay down and began to count back through the minutes and back through the hours. Back and back and back I traveled. And as I counted, the events of the hours that had passed before my return whirred by like ghostly visitors: my mother putting the fire out in the downstairs fireplace, advising Toby to go to bed, reminding him that he had work in the morning; Toby going into his room to sleep later; my mother going in a while afterward, putting two fingertips on top of his eyelids to conjure some kind of deep sleep within him. And as the right moment arrived—when my mother walked down the staircase from her own room, pulling her arms into an old denim jacket she wore each springtime—I passed out of this world to join her in that last hour of that morning, right as she left the house and, under the remains of the moonlight, crossed over the railroad-tie bridge into the orchard.

When I opened my eyes again, I was in the orchard with her. The wind blew through the trees, making the few scraggly leaves that had opened up for spring whisper against one another. In the distance, the chimes on our front porch were ringing. And in front of me, my mother stood beneath the Living Death Tree.

With her back to me, she placed one hand on the trunk of the old tree and curled the other around the knotty rim of the hole at the top, where the tree began to branch outward. She was talking to the woman who lived in there. Eva. Eva Jablonski. Her grandmother. My great-grandmother. The woman who held her son's curse in the folds of her dress and wouldn't let go of it. I couldn't make out what my mother was saying, though, so quietly I moved forward.

"There's no reason for it," my mother was saying. "My sons have nothing to do with it. It's time to end this, Eva. Let it go. Please. Release it."

When no answer came from the tree, my mother changed her tone. "I've tried talking sense and I've tried being patient. I've tried for years now. But these are my children. I've already lost one, and you've taken my husband from me too. I won't let the others come to harm.

If you force me to, I'll burn this tree down to its hateful roots."

With the threat in the air, Eva stepped from around back of the tree, as if she'd only been hiding on the other side of it. She wore the same clothes I'd seen her wearing in the vision she'd shown me: a ragged dress with a babushka wrapped around her ruddy face. I knew she had probably been no more than in her early thirties when she died, but she looked more like an old woman. Her bare feet were covered with mud and bloody scratches from climbing through the Living Death Tree's branches. But even in that wretched condition, she smiled briefly before she said, "You cannot make me leave here, child." And then she turned to pat the trunk of the tree like a sturdy horse. "If you burn this tree, I will simply move into your house with you."

"You can't," my mother said, and there was no tone of family feeling in her voice. "You can't go beyond the creek without my permission. That land is mine by marriage, as this tree belongs to you by blood."

Eva narrowed her eyes and wrung her hands in the folds of her dress a little, fingering what must have been the curse she clasped within it. "Do you really think you can drive me away with fire?" she asked my mother. "I cannot burn, girl. And if this tree burns, it does not matter. I will find another. Will you burn them all down?"

My mother nodded, just once, firmly. "Yes," she answered. "You've twisted these trees beyond their lives anyway. Their fruits spoil even as they grow. Eva, we must end this. Now."

"I can stay without them," Eva said, frowning, pouting as though she thought my mother hadn't made her plans very carefully. She seemed to almost feel bad for her. "I do not need the things of this world to stay within it, my sweet one. One thing and one thing only keeps me here, and it will not let me go until it is finished." She clutched the folds of her dress tighter then, clutched the place where she'd put her son's words and shook it like a purse full of coins. "These trees?" she continued, looking around at them, shaking her head, closing her eyes sadly. "They do not matter."

"Old Black Suit is coming," my mother said fiercely, and Eva's eyes snapped open. "I saw him the other day, in fact. It's time again, you know, for you to deal with him. Or have you forgotten?"

"Why are you doing this?" Eva said, wincing. A note of fear had crept into her voice. My mother was threatening her with something, and she seemed to actually feel threatened by it, but I didn't understand what my mom was using against her.

"I'm doing this to free you," my mother said. "I'm doing this to free all of us."

They looked at each other for a while after that, silent and serious. Finally Eva said, "It is not so easy, leaving after having stayed for so long. Do you know how it is?" She shook the folds of her dress again, rattling the words inside, and this time she looked down at her skirt as though it were a chain locked around her body. When she looked up again, she said, "I'm not sure I know the way to leave any longer."

My mom held her hand out to Eva then. "I will take you where you need to go," she told her. "I know the way. It's not as far as you might think."

Eva stared at my mother's outstretched hand, hesitating, but in the end she said, "If you are willing to take me, then I must go with you. I know that rule, even though I forget so many others." Then she reached across the space between them and took hold of my mother's hand.

For a while they stared into each other's eyes, searching each other's face for the shared spirit between them—an old woman wearing a babushka who had saved her son's life only for him to unwittingly curse the lives of her great-grandchildren, and a middle-aged woman in a pair of jeans and a jean jacket that had belonged to her dead husband—and when they found what they were looking for, a glint of recognition behind both of their green eyes, they turned together and began to walk into the field behind the orchard, taking the lane beside Sugar Creek back to the woods.

"She's in the ravine," I said, gasping for breath back in my bedroom as I swam up and out of the world's shadow.

I said the words before I even had a chance to open my eyes.

"The ravine?" Jarrod said. He was still sitting there beside me, holding my hand.

"She's going to walk Eva out of this world," I told him, "and she paid their way across with her life, to take Eva and the curse with her."

I sat on my bed and shook my head, recalling what my mom had told me. *You'll be the one to find me,* she'd said, *after I've passed out of this world.*

She knew this would happen. She'd been preparing me for this moment more than for any other in my life, even when I hadn't realized it, but she was leaving the choice to do something about it up to me. High school graduation would be just another day on a calendar, but this day? In her estimation, this day would be my first as an adult.

I got up from my bed and left Jarrod behind me. "What are you doing?" he said as he stood to follow.

At the door I turned and said, "Please stay here and look after my brother until I come back."

"But what are you going to do? Where are you going?"

"I'm going back there," I said. "To Marrow's Ravine. I'm going to find her."

It was a long walk. Longer than the walk I'd taken down to Marrow's Ravine to find my father's body that winter,

318

it seemed. Each step was an effort. Each breath I took was a rusty blade cutting me open. The earth was soft beneath my feet, and I left a trail behind me, like the trail of my father's blood in the snow, the trail that had led me to the Living Death Tree in the winter. Eva had somehow been behind his fall. Probably because my mother's story had begun to unravel after Jarrod came home, picked up a loose thread of it, and started pulling. Pulling on me, pulling on my memories. I kept thinking that there was a chance to change things, that she'd be down there when I arrived, still alive, climbing up the side of the ravine, having found a way to return Eva without giving herself up in exchange. But when I made it to the edge of the ravine and looked down the slope to its bottom, all of those thoughts were ruined in an instant.

My mother's body was down there, resting in a bed of early buttercups and daisies, in the same place my father's body had fallen.

And I saw something—or someone—standing near her, casting a large shadow across her outstretched body. The wide brim of his black hat rose before I saw anything else. And when I did see his face, it was the red strings of his scraggly beard I noticed first, and then his eyes, dark as coal, lined with veins of fire.

He smiled when his eyes locked on mine, then put one hand on top of his hat and nodded, like he'd done when I was in the seventh grade, when he'd noticed I could see him.

My heart started to beat faster, and a cold sweat broke out in beads across my skin, making me shiver in the chill morning air. I wanted to run back the way I'd come, back through the woods, beating branches aside, back through the lane and through the pasture, until I was home and could slip inside, where I'd be safe. Or felt I could be safe, though there was nowhere truly safe anymore, and I knew it.

There was no wish I could make that was strong enough to break the reality in front of me. There was no way I could get out of this without regretting it later. This was my only chance.

You can't outrun Death. But sometimes you can make him take off his hat to stay a while and listen.

So I took a big breath and started to pick my way down the slope, to go to him, to meet him where he waited for me.

I went slowly, hesitant to actually see my mom this way, up close, not breathing, her heartbeat flown away from her, and hesitant to be so near to the creature that had come into my classroom on the day he would take my teacher's life. Eventually, though, after stepping into the notches that the Lockwood men's feet had made in the side of Marrow's Ravine over the decades, I reached bottom. And there, in that place that held so much death in its embrace, I finally paused to return Old Black Suit's nod.

I didn't smile, though. I didn't think I needed to be nice to him, just civil.

We didn't say anything at first, and I decided to go to my mother's body, to attend to it however I could. Kneeling next to her, I saw that she was holding the silver pocket watch she'd had when she went into the world's shadow to end a blizzard. The watch her father had given her. The watch Lockwood had given Dobry after his mother had died for him. That watch was in my mother's hand, held against her chest, right where her heart should have been beating. Dawn light filtered through the canopy of trees above me, and when it fell onto the filigree around the watch, the silver gleamed.

Tears sprang to my eyes as I uncurled my mom's fingers to take it from her. I wanted to hold it for just a moment, to feel the last heat of her touch on its surface. And when I slipped it away from her clenched fingers and opened the lid, the first thing I saw was the photo she'd put inside it, a picture of her and my dad on their wedding day—both of them standing beneath an arbor grown over with roses— and under the glass of the watch itself, there was time, still being kept, still ticking and ticking.

But there was something else in there too. Something I hadn't expected. *We had time left*, I remembered her saying when we found my dad down here a few months earlier. *I was saving it up. I had heaps and heaps of time saved for us.* I saw something more in there, not just the gears of a watch moving. A golden flicker of light moved under the watch hands, like a goldfish swimming counterclockwise in a bowl of water. To others it might have seemed an illusion, but I knew it was True time, a way of saving up the seconds to stretch out a person's life by hours or days or years. It was no more than an extra hour, from the looks of it, but I knew my mother had kept this one hour back for me, had hidden it in there like a stash of money.

There wasn't much left. Most likely, she'd been using whatever time she'd saved sitting in front of the fireplace or her candle, trying to find my dad, using it to go back to the moment he died, trying to understand the true nature of his death, trying to see what had been invisible to her: the trail of my father's blood that had led me to the Living Death Tree in Sorrow Acre. This was what was left of the time she'd been using to bring him back to her: one solitary hour.

It might be just enough, I thought, to turn back the clock and let her heartbeat return for a moment. If I wasn't too late.

I wiped away a tear and looked up at the man in the black suit. He was looking down at me where I knelt beside my mother's body with a face full of infinite patience. He had time, after all. He had all the time in the world.

"Well," he said, and his voice was low. He didn't sound particularly thrilled or excited by his task, as I'd imagined he would be when I was a kid. "The child who saw me."

"I knew you saw me that day," I whispered. "I knew it."

"I see those who see me," he said, spreading his hands.

"Most often, it's the dying. But sometimes it's a little boy who can't help it. You have your mother's eyes, you know."

"She gave them to me," I said proudly.

"A great burden," Death's agent said, shaking his head as though he sympathized with me.

"Or a blessing," I said. "It can also be a blessing, depending on your view of things."

"Your brother once told me the same thing."

"Seth?" I said, and the man in the black suit nodded.

"Yes," he said. "He was a sage child, that one. He saw far too much for his own good."

"Like what?" I said, chilled by his words. They were the same ones my mother had said whenever she talked about Seth.

"He saw Eva," Old Black Suit said. "He heard her voice, like you did. This was before your mother truly understood that her father was right. That Eva would never let go of the curse. This was before your mother decided to tell a story so that Eva couldn't reach you, so that the curse couldn't find you."

"The curse," I said, and Old Black Suit nodded once more. Then he waved one of his arms to the side like a showman, and from behind him a small child came to stand beside him.

It was the boy in the photo in my living room. It was Seth. It was my older brother. The brother who had died before I was even born.

He was quiet as he stood there, looking up at me with

innocent eyes, wearing what was most likely the little suit he'd been buried in. I blinked and blinked again, and my breathing quickened as Seth reached up with his tiny hand to grasp hold of Old Black Suit's outstretched fingers.

"Go ahead," Old Black Suit told the boy. "You can show him."

Seth looked back at me then, his green eyes seeming to glow a little, and a vision appeared between us.

It was a vision of Seth, waking up in the early hours of the morning, after hearing a voice call his name. The voice from the Living Death Tree. The voice of Eva Jablonski.

Seth, she called to him. *Seth Lockwood.*

And Seth had risen from his bed to follow the trail of her voice, until he came to the old tree in the orchard, where she showed him what his great-grandfather had done to her. She showed him the day that she'd picked the orchard clean to save her son. She showed him the day she died in the very tree Seth stood under.

And then she had stepped from behind the tree itself, curling her finger for Seth to come to her. "I have something else to show you," she told him. The same thing she'd said to me once, before my mother interrupted her.

And Seth, curious, innocent, went to her.

It was then that she crouched beside his small frame and undid the knot in her dress, where the curse throbbed in its folds, hot and white and blinding in its ferocity. Eva spread her dress so that she could show the child the curse, reveal his fate to him. Show him the truth that would consume his life in an instant. It was blindingly bright once placed before him. So bright. So bright. Bursting and popping with hate.

It was then, looking down at it, that Seth fell backward and began to shake, to convulse, to turn blue, to stop breathing.

My parents discovered him an hour later, his face lifeless, after they'd woken and found his room empty and begun to search for him.

The vision faded then, but Seth still stood before me, clutching the hand of Old Black Suit.

"You can go if you want, child," Old Black Suit said, and Seth nodded. Looking at me for a moment, he waved his small hand in a polite fashion, then retreated to his place behind Old Black Suit's coat and was gone from sight again.

I felt tears, hot and burning, well up in my eyes as Seth retreated from me. A moment later, one rolled down my cheek, and quickly I raised the back of my hand to my eyes to wipe away any others before Old Black Suit could see what he'd done to me by showing me my brother.

"It isn't fair," I said after he'd left us.

"Life," said Death's agent, "isn't very fair to anyone, now, is it?"

"No," I said. "It's not life that's unfair. It's Death. Death is unfair."

"You are quite mistaken," the man in the black suit said,

looking almost insulted. "I give many chances, over and over, to people whom I could easily take in a moment."

"You haven't been fair to my family," I said. "You might have turned away those people I love, those people Eva brought you."

"Why don't you tell me about all of this?" Old Black Suit replied, as if he knew nothing of what I was speaking about. He looked around and, finding an old fallen tree nearby, sat down with his big hands draped over his knees. "I like a good story," he said, "and your mother's family have always been good storytellers. Why, your great-grandmother Eva kept herself alive for many years by telling me stories. Your father's family, though? Not so good at this, I'm afraid. How far, I wonder, has the apple fallen, and from which tree?"

"Everything," I said, before I could think about what I was doing. "I'll tell all of it. Even the things my mother said others wouldn't understand. Like the Living Death Tree of Sorrow Acre, and how I came to discover I'd been cursed or blessed with visions even my mother couldn't keep from me. I'll tell you about how the white stag haunts my father's family, the way you haunt my mother's. I'll tell you all of these things and more. I'll tell you the secrets of my heart, the things that are invisible to even you, if you'll make a deal with me."

The man in the black suit raised his red eyebrows, and a corner of his mouth twitched just a little, barely enough for a person to see he was grinning.

"If you think I'm here to carry you out of the world, you needn't worry," he said, waving my proposition away like a fly. "It's for your mother and great-grandmother that I came today. Your mother also made a bargain with me. This bargain, actually." He looked at her as if the evidence of her body explained everything. "A bargain to pay the way across for the two of them, and to take away the burden Eva carried."

"I'm prepared to make a different bargain," I said, and he raised his brows even higher, doubting my words. "My story for my mother's life. There's an hour left in this watch before she is yours to take. And if you'll agree to bring her back, I'll tell you everything."

Old Black Suit threw his head back and laughed at me. But when I didn't join him, when he noticed my straight face, he quieted down and looked at me with narrowed eyes. Scratching his stringy red beard, he took some time to consider my offer. And finally he said, "If you tell me your story now, you will not be able to tell it again later, when it's you I've come for."

"I understand that," I said.

Then, after adjusting the tilt of his hat, he nodded.

"Go on, then," Old Black Suit said, settling in to listen.

And I began telling stories.

chapter seventeen

PAPER PEOPLE

Here's the thing: we're all as thin as paper. Like those paper people you used to find in children's magazines, inhabiting a two-page spread with other paper people, all of them hanging out somewhere together—at the park, at church, at school, at the mall, in the family room—until some kid took a pair of scissors to the dotted lines surrounding them and cut them out of their paper world. That's us, that's anyone. That was me. A cut-out paper person removed from the world I once belonged to.

Until someone called my name, and I turned toward him, leaving my life in paper behind me.

That was how my story began. That was how *I* began, really. Before that moment when Jarrod called and I turned to find him, it was like my life was this object that had been packed away in Bubble Wrap. And even though it was a safe enough life, it was no life at all, really. I moved through the world like a ghost, invisible to the people around me. I wasn't an athlete like my brother or father, and I wasn't charming, witty, or artistic, though I did have a talent for making my mom laugh at things. I was a decent student, even though I did tend to daydream during classes. But basically, yeah, there was nothing to me.

Or so it seemed.

There are more things in Heaven and Earth, Horatio, than are dreamt of in your philosophy.

There was more to me, actually, than I'd ever dreamed.

What happened down in Marrow's Ravine that day in early spring is the story I'm telling. It's about this young guy, seventeen years old, who falls in love with the best friend he's forgotten. It's about this son whose mother has made him forget parts of his own life in order to protect him. It's about a family and their secrets. It's about curses, and how a story can change the world depending on how you tell it. It's about a mother who sacrificed herself for her son, and a son who told his story to save his mother.

Which I managed to do, though just barely. Old Black Suit, after all, is a finicky listener, having been around so long and having seen as much as he has. I have no illusions; I realize that some of the things I told Old Black Suit that day were probably pretty mundane for someone like him. Old Black Suit doesn't have any interest in seeing or hearing about high school or marriage or babies, or any of the memories we've all been told to retain. Old Black Suit is interested in our invisible moments. The unnoticed gestures and forgotten conversations, the unlikely incidents and the dying light of abandoned places, the conflicts that evaporate from memory once they're resolved, the people we have no idea are important and no way of understanding why until it's all over, the last page turned, the story finished.

Then it all goes away.

Everything.

Except for my mother, who returned.

He brought her back to me after I finished my story, after I'd spent the last flicker of a golden hour my mom had saved. Right there, in the bed of buttercups and daisies, my mother's eyes fluttered open, and she gasped a breath that sounded like it was the first she'd ever taken. And when she'd gotten her bearings and was able to sit up and see me waiting there next to her, holding her hand, the first thing she did was shake her head as if she was amazed by everything her eyes were seeing.

"You are so brave, Aidan Lockwood," she told me, after she'd had a chance to look around, to accept the reality of her return. "You are so brave, my son."

I didn't think I was as brave as she was. I mean, it wasn't like I'd gone to Death and back, like she had. But I got what she was saying, and I appreciated the fact that she could look at me and see me and tell me that. It kind of made me embarrassed, actually, to be called brave, when for most of my life—or at least, most of the life I'd been able to recall for a long time—I'd been nothing. Just this kid who went to school and roamed the hallways, took his classes, got good grades, and had nothing, nothing, nothing of any importance to say to anyone.

I had to start getting used to being me again, now that I was returning to myself, my real self, whoever that was. And maybe, I guess, brave was one of the things I was, or it was one of the things I could be.

"Come on," I said, and held out my hand to help my mother stand.

She hugged me for a while afterward, rocking me in her arms like I was still the little boy she'd taken outside one summer to show the constellations only she could see. And after she hugged me, after she pulled away, wiping the tears from her eyes, we quietly climbed out of Marrow's Ravine.

We made our way back through the woods, back through the lane, back through the pasture, taking our time, because in all honesty we were both exhausted. And when we found ourselves at the back door of our house, my mom stopped to look up at it and to say, "I used to see the Lockwood house from the bus on my way to and from school every day when I was just a girl. I was drawn here. Sometimes I think I fell in love with this place before I fell in love with your father."

I didn't say anything to that. I just looked up at our house with her, seeing it—I mean, really seeing it—almost for the first time. Admiring it a little, even, like my mom was doing. There was history in those rooms and hallways. My history. And I'd never understood that before.

After we went in, the first thing I did was to go upstairs to look for Jarrod. I found him still sitting in a chair next to my brother, who was just then waking up from the heavy sleep my mother had weighed him down with.

"It was all a bad dream," I said before Toby could shake the cobwebs from his head and ask where I'd gone and why Jarrod was sitting in his room with him. Then I grabbed Jarrod's hand and pulled him out of there and into my own room, where we stretched out on my bed and fell asleep together, even though my door was open and anyone who passed by could see us in there, holding on to each other like it was the most ordinary thing in the world.

It was a long sleep, and much needed, for me, at least. When I woke, Jarrod was gone, leaving me curled around the empty space where he'd slept beside me. It was light out, and I could hear voices coming up from the kitchen through the vents. Above me, the crack in the ceiling that threatened to split my room apart was still there, but I didn't pay it any attention. Instead I rolled out of bed and went downstairs to find my mom and Jarrod sitting at the kitchen table, talking. When I came into the room, they stopped and looked at me.

"There you are," my mother said, as if this were any other morning, even though when I looked at the clock on the wall, I saw it was already two in the afternoon. Not morning at all, and not an ordinary hour for me to be waking.

"Where's Toby?" I asked.

"At work," my mom answered. I blinked, speechless, because going to work seemed like something too normal to do on a day like this one. But Toby had slept through everything because of my mom, so for him it must have felt like the exactly right thing to do, like today was, in fact, just like any other.

After I sat down to join in on the coffee, my mother caught me up on her and Jarrod's conversation. She said that a whole lot had happened, and none of it easy to explain, and that she thought we should probably keep it a secret between just the three of us. "To spare Toby," she said. "We've had a lot to deal with, and there's too much he doesn't know about. Where would we even begin?"

"I don't think we should do that," I said, and my mom tilted her head and asked why not. "I'm tired of secrets," I told her. "My whole life feels like it's been one big secret for too long already. I don't want to live that way anymore.

I don't want to do that to Toby. I don't want to do that to me and Jarrod, either." I looked over at Jarrod after I said that, and reached across the table with my hand palm up, and right there in front of my mom, he took hold of it, squeezing back gently.

My mother's cheeks flushed a little, and she looked down into her cup of coffee. I could tell that I'd embarrassed her by reminding her of how she'd done that very same thing to me. Made me forget things. Left me clueless. *And look where it got you,* I wanted to say. I didn't, though. Jarrod was there, and being corrected by your youngest son in front of another person can't feel good. So I just said, "I don't know where we'll begin either, but we should tell him. Somehow. We'll figure out a way to do it if we try."

My mom straightened her head, her lips pursed resolutely, and nodded. "You're right," she said. "We'll figure out how to tell him the truth. Didn't I always say it was the hardest thing for a person to do?"

Jarrod and I took a bus to Lily Dale a few days later to retrieve the Blue Bomb. Without it, we were both stuck taking the school bus, which was incredibly lame, especially for seniors who were graduating in a month. On the way up, Jarrod held my hand, and for a while I felt a little afraid, like someone might see us, and I was just then getting used to our being together that way in front of my family. But then, when some people on the bus obviously did see us and didn't do or say anything, didn't even make a face like I expected, I let myself sink down in my seat with his hand in my lap, and looked out the window at the passing scenery.

There were these brittle pine trees, greening under the sunlight.

And this almost crayon-yellow sun above.

And the sky was so blue—watercolor blue—with white, scarf-like clouds soaring through it.

Everything about us was entirely normal, really. We were as ordinary as anything we might come across in this world.

Maybe Jarrod's father wouldn't see things that way, and sure, there were probably a lot of other people who would see things the way his father might. But what other people saw wasn't necessarily the truth. And in the end it was the one truly and totally not-normal thing about me— the kind of sight I'd been born with—that helped me to understand and forgive the people who couldn't look at Jarrod and me and see us for who we were: just two people in love.

When I looked at other people now, I could see how so many of them were wearing blindfolds like the one my mom had put on me. I could see how so many of them had damaged vision. How they couldn't see things clearly. How they saw only the stories other people had told them. And understanding how all of that worked now, I started to even feel bad for them a little.

Carolyn was happy to see us again, and we stayed overnight in the angel-and-fairy-infested house once more, to tell her about what had happened after we left her. I promised her that I'd bring my mother up for a visit soon, now that my mom, too, was released from the constraints of her own story. "Please do that," Carolyn said. She told me to remember to tell my mom something else: that time, however much of it exists in the universe, does eventually run out for everyone.

There was only one month of school left, and even though I thought it was way too late to become the kind of guy who suddenly makes friends with everyone at the end of the movie, I decided I also wasn't going to go back to being invisible. So when I saw Jarrod in the hallways at school, I'd meet him with an open smile, or I'd make fun of his hair being too long, because he was constantly having to brush it out of his eyes. He was the starting pitcher—the coach, as he'd expected, wasn't willing to let someone with Jarrod's talent go just because he'd missed a couple of practices—and he was earning his keep, with two no-hitters already on his scorecard for the season.

Sometimes, during breaks between classes, Jarrod would lean against the locker next to mine as I put books away or got out new ones, and he'd reach over to hold my door open, wanting to be near me. Before, I probably would have flinched, worried that he'd give us away. But now I'd just close my locker and lean back against it with him, our shoulders touching, watching everyone going by like a parade that didn't know it was a parade.

I was keeping hold of all of the details as I experienced them. I was committing them all to memory. I was going to store up everything I could. I was going to savor all of the moments as I saved them for the future.

Because here's the thing: Death does come for everything. But Death can also be bargained with, if you know how to strike a deal. Death likes to hear true stories, and I traded my own to save my mother's life. Old Black Suit had warned me that if I did so, I wouldn't be able to tell him my story when he eventually came to claim me. I'd nodded, acknowledging that I understood, and handed my story over to him anyway.

But there was something in our deal that the man in the black suit hadn't considered: the fact that all of us lead more than one life in our lifetimes. The fact that, in the years to come, I would become someone different from the seventeen-year-old who had struck a bargain with him at the bottom of a ravine to save the life of his mother.

I'd have other life stories to tell him later. And when he realized that, if that bothered him—if he was insulted by being manipulated—I'd sympathize with him, of course. Because no one likes being manipulated. But maybe he'd also enjoy the fact that I'd had enough foresight to think of it in the first place.

After school sometimes, Jarrod and I would go to Mosquito Lake, the first place I'd taken him when he came back to Temperance, when he came back to help me remember myself, and we'd look out at the small gray waves, rocking and rocking. Beneath those waves was an old coal-mining village, with a schoolhouse and a church, and the tiny houses of the workers who used to live there. You'd never imagine all of that was down there if you didn't already know about it. The past is like that, really. If you don't know it, it's hard to imagine what's come before you.

The future, I'd started to think, was kind of like that too. Hard to imagine, because we don't know it. And even though I could know the future if I wanted to, just by closing my eyes and willing it, I'd made a decision not to look into mine too often. I wanted to be just here, in this life of mine, to live it just like anyone.

We'd sit on the railing or on one of the flat rocks down near the water, looking out at the rocking waves, talking about our past, talking about our future, our hands linked together. Between us, we had the present, and we were not surprised at all to be happy with that, to be happy with now, to be happy with nothing more than now.

Acknowledgments

This book owes a lot to the people who have shaped my life from the beginning. It's for my grandparents—John and Sophia Leeper, Donald and Bernice Barzak—and it's for my parents, Donald and Joyce Barzak. It's for my brothers, Donald and Stephen, and my sister-in-law, Darlene. And it's for my nieces and nephew, Justin, Valerie, and Jenna. My family has always been an incredibly important part of my life, reaching backward and forward, providing me with a story to live within, and this is just one of the stories I've made out of the many stories I've been told by them, and out of the ones that we are still telling.

I would also like to thank Richard Bowes, who read far too many drafts of this book before I was finished with it, and my agent, Barry Goldblatt, whose encouragement kept me working on it through even more drafts. Carter Smith unknowingly revived my faith in this material while he was turning my first novel, *One for Sorrow,* into the film *Jamie Marks Is Dead,* which shares the same setting. I could not have brought the novel to its final form without the perspicacious vision of my editor, Melanie Cecka, and there might have been a great many mistakes within without the wonderful team of copy editors at Knopf, who spent so much time going through these pages with me. Thank you also to my instructors and classmates at Chatham University, where I worked on this book in one of its earliest incarnations, and to Mary Rickert, who never fails to give me the right perspective on things.

And finally, thank you to Tony Romandetti, who believes in me even when I've lost hope.